"Didn't you enjoy your engagement ball?"

Wesmorlen questioned, his tone deceptively calm.

"My engagement ball? Of course," Regana said, forcing a false note of gaiety into her voice. "I found it very *revealing*, if you will."

Wesmorlen's eyes widened at this strange pronouncement, scarcely able to believe that the cold, distant woman in front of him was the same laughing girl he had held in his arms only hours before.

"Regana, I'm beginning to lose patience with you. You're not making any sense. If you have something to say, then say it. This...roundaboutation is not at all like you."

"Isn't it, my lord? Then perhaps you don't know me as well as you think," she flung at him harshly, "or as well as you'd like to think. Because, unfortunately, I find that I do not know you. Not at all!"

BITTERSWEET REVENGE

GAIL WHITIKER

Harlequin Books

TORONTO • NEW YORK • LONDON
AMSTERDAM • PARIS • SYDNEY • HAMBURG
STOCKHOLM • ATHENS • TOKYO • MILAN
MADRID • WARSAW • BUDAPEST • AUCKLAND

To Margaret and Ken,
for their love and encouragement

Published July 1992

ISBN 0-373-31178-8

BITTERSWEET REVENGE

CHAPTER ONE

THE EARL OF WESMORLEN relished the quiet comfort of his Town carriage as it made its way over the greasy, rain spattered cobbles towards Hanover Square. Darkness had begun to fall, and though the gas lamps had been lit, their cold, yellowish light did little to irradiate the gloom already gathering in the shadowy back streets and alleys.

Despite the dreary weather, however, the earl was in an unusually expansive mood. Having enjoyed an early dinner at his club followed by a brief but most gratifying visit to the Contessa Gisella de Robichard at her cosy house in Kensington, Lord Wesmorlen settled back against the squabs, aware that for the first time in months he actually felt in charity with himself and with the world. So much so, that he was able to view the fact that tomorrow marked the six month anniversary of his younger brother's injury in the duel against Lord Botheringham with a good deal more tolerance than he might otherwise have felt.

It was hard to believe that six months had already passed since the night of the duel. At the time, Wesmorlen had thought to remember it until his dying day, just as he remembered the night at Lord Montrose's house when Botheringham had originally accused his brother of cheating at cards and when Peter, with all the dauntless exuberance of youth, had called the man out, blissfully unaware of the fact that he was challenging one of the deadliest pistols in London.

Wesmorlen glanced out of the carriage window, considering his brother's youthful naïvety with a sigh of resignation. God, had he himself ever been that young and foolish, he wondered, suddenly feeling every one of his five-and-thirty years.

In spite of his best efforts, the duel had taken place. And, as expected, Peter had received the worst of the injuries. The bullet which had entered his leg just below the knee had shattered the bone, and it had been weeks before the doctors had been able to say with any conviction that Peter would not lose his leg altogether. Lord Botheringham had retired to the country the victor, and to the best of Wesmorlen's knowledge, had not been heard from since.

"Will you be needing them any more tonight, m'lord?" the groom asked as he drew the high-stepping blacks to a halt in front of the earl's elegant Town house. Wesmorlen looked out at the steady downpour of rain, and shook his head. "I think not, Roberts. Give them to their beds. The rest of the night is yours."

The earl missed the young man's surprised but grateful nod as he quickly climbed the front steps and went inside.

"Ah, good evening, my lord," Hawkins said, coming to take his master's wet outer garments. "I trust you had a good evening?"

"Tolerable, Hawkins. Quite tolerable," Lord Wesmorlen replied. "Is my brother at home this evening?"

It was a rhetorical question. No one knew better than the earl that since the duel, Peter had almost stopped going out altogether, especially to functions held in the evening. He still tired easily, and Lord knew only the heartiest could withstand the veritable crushes which were deemed to be the most successful of parties for more than a few hours.

"He's in the library I believe, my lord," Hawkins informed him. "Shall I fetch a tray?"

"Not for my benefit," Wesmorlen said with a grin. "The effects of my last brandy are still very much upon me."

Hawkins nodded and withdrew, his suspicions confirmed that the highly eligible earl's evening had been much more than just tolerable.

In the library, Wesmorlen found his younger brother comfortably ensconced in a high-backed chair in front of the fire, a decanter of Wesmorlen's best port on the table, his attention rivetted on the weighty tome in his lap.

"Humph! I might have known I'd find you in here," the earl greeted him wryly, settling his tall frame into a chair opposite. "You're turning into a bookworm, my boy."

Peter glanced up in surprise, the book immediately forgotten. "By Jove, Richard, you're home early. I hadn't expected to see you for hours yet. What happened? Did the lovely Gisella turn you out?"

The dark eyebrows rose a fraction, and in spite of himself, Wesmorlen emitted a low throaty chuckle. "Turn me out? 'Pon my word, stripling, you do have a low opinion of my charms. Turn me out, indeed," he mused, not a little surprised by the extent of his brother's knowledge. "And what do *you* know of the lovely Gisella?"

"Oh, come, Richard, I'm not as green as all that," Peter said, grinning. "You stormed out of here this afternoon with a face as black as a poker and twice as long, only to return hours later with a disposition that could charm birds out of the trees. Now if that isn't a woman's doing, I don't know what is."

Wesmorlen had the decency to laugh. He sometimes forgot that even though he was ten years older than his sibling, at twenty-five, Peter was no youngling any longer and was well versed in the ways of the world.

"I had no idea my doings were so ardently followed, nor that my moods were so transparent," the earl remarked astringently.

"Don't worry, you're far from transparent," Peter assured him, removing the stopper from the crystal decanter and pouring himself a small glass of port. "But you forget I'm your brother. I know you better than most."

Wesmorlen acknowledged the point, and continued to study the face in front of him with growing satisfaction. Yes, the doctor was right. Peter was beginning to look better. The deep hollows in his cheeks were filling out, and the dark purplish circles under his eyes which had given him a gaunt, hunted look were finally fading away. With the addition of a few more pounds, he would be back to his normal, buoyant self. Or almost, the earl amended, his glance resting briefly on the cane beside the chair.

"Peter, I thought we might go down to Blackoaks for a while," the earl announced, coming straight to the point. "It's about time I started taking a more active interest in the old relic. Goodness knows the countess has been tireless in her efforts to make me aware of that. Furthermore, I spoke with Dr. Wickham and he's very pleased with your progress. He feels that your leg is healing remarkably well and that it's exercise you need now. And I can't think of a better place for you to get it than at Blackoaks. What do you say?"

To Wesmorlen's surprise, Peter did not answer immediately, his hesitation causing the earl a moment's unrest. Had he been wrong in suggesting they go down to the country? The plan had been on his mind for some time, and Wesmorlen was convinced it was exactly what Peter needed. His only concern had been in exposing Peter to the denizens of local Society and the vagaries to which they laid claim. That, he admitted, would be enough to discourage anyone from re-entering Society. Still, the earl acknowledged philosophically, Peter would have to do it sooner or later. Might as well be sooner, as later.

Peter, who had briefly turned his attention to the study of a particularly fine Gainsborough over the mantel, looked back towards his brother, his expression carefully veiled. "When were you thinking of going?"

The earl shrugged. "Nothing is definite, of course, but I thought Friday, if that gives you enough time."

"I see," Peter commented. "And Dr. Wickham said there would be no trouble with my travelling?"

Wesmorlen shook his head again. "None at all. He felt the change in scenery would be good for you, in mind and body. Besides, you didn't have any trouble coming down from Scotland, did you?"

When Peter still didn't answer, the earl sighed. Obviously, he had been mistaken. "It was, of course, only a suggestion. If you don't feel up to it—"

"Not up to it!" Peter interrupted, the slow smile which spread across his face transforming his features. "I should say I'm up to it. Do you know how long I've been waiting for you to make this suggestion?"

"The devil!" Wesmorlen replied, glancing at him in surprise. "Why didn't you tell me before? And why the hesitation just now?"

"Because, dear brother, I know how much *you* dislike the country."

"Me? When did I say that?" the earl said huffily.

"When didn't you say it!" Peter exclaimed with a laugh. "You've always insisted it's not to your liking, Richard. Something about being too rural, and too rusticated. Not to mention the fact that every mama with a marriageable daughter encamps on our doorstep the minute they hear you're in residence."

The earl threw back his head and laughed. "Good Lord, did I really say all those things?"

"And more," Peter affirmed. "I omit some of the more intemperate things."

"Yes, well, perhaps you should," the earl mumbled, sobering slightly. "I'm sure I had my reasons for saying them at the time. However, the ladies are the least of my concerns, since this year I shall be sharing the distinction of being the district's most eligible bachelor."

"Oh?" Peter replied warily. "How so?"

"Because you, dear brother, are just as eligible as I, and it's about time you gave some thought to looking for a wife and settling down."

The smile faded from Peter's face, and a decidedly obstinate frown took its place.

"Richard, we've discussed this matter already. You know my feelings on the subject."

"Yes, I do, and you'd best start changing that attitude, my boy," Richard remonstrated firmly. "There's no reason why you shouldn't marry and have a family like everyone else."

"There's a very good reason, and you know it," Peter retorted mumpishly. "What young woman of good family is going to want me for a husband? I can't ride, I can't hunt, I can't even walk without the aid of this blasted cane. What am I to say to a pretty young lady at a dance: 'Sorry, I'm not dancing—for the rest of my life', or 'Would you care to join me for a limp through the gardens'?"

"Peter, you're talking nonsense," the earl interrupted, impatient with his brother's mule-headedness. "Dr. Wickham says there's no reason you shouldn't be able to do all the things you used to do again, including riding. You'll just have to ease into them slowly."

"Fine," Peter muttered. "I'll do all my courting from a gig!"

"He also said the limp will become less noticeable and that eventually you'll have no need of the cane."

"Eventually?" Peter echoed in exasperation. "How long is eventually? Damn it, Richard, it's already been six months! Perhaps I should look to Lord Cheddarbrook's example and wait until I'm fifty before I take a wife. By then everything will be working again."

He paused, his smile twisted as he gazed up at his brother. "At least, I hope everything will be working by then. With my luck, some things may have *stopped* working."

Richard's lips twitched, and the devastating smile which had set the hearts of so many young ladies fluttering in their breasts warmed his features. "Everything shall be working long before then, *and* long after. And you *shall* find a wife—the most fetching young chit in the county—even if I have to see to it myself."

"You? Find me a wife? I say," Peter declared, diverted by the very idea of his brother's suggesting such a thing, "that's rather a change of occupation for you, isn't it?"

"Such is the lot of the eldest brother, I suppose," Wesmorlen replied sardonically. "No doubt Mama would approve."

"Sink me if she wouldn't," Peter laughed. "But tell me, dear brother," he continued irrepressibly, "if you secure the loveliest young lady for me, where does that leave you? Who will the Unmarriageable Earl choose?"

"The Unmarriageable Earl?" Wesmorlen gave a bark of laughter. "Good Lord, where on earth did that bit of nonsense come from?"

"No doubt from all the anxious mamas who've been trying to marry you off to their daughters for the past God knows how long," Peter chortled. "But never mind that— you still haven't answered my question." He grinned. "Which comely young miss are you going to favour with your charms? Unless of course, you mean to pursue the winsome widow."

"I take it you mean Lady Chadwick," Wesmorlen retorted drily.

Peter nodded, his smile broadening. "Well, she's hardly likely to be amongst the ladies I'll be making my choice from," Peter replied, clearly amused. "She's made it quite clear any number of times that it's the Earl of Wesmorlen she's interested in, and not some lowly second son."

The earl waved his hand dismissively. "Amanda Chadwick is not the sort of lady I'd envisaged you with, widowed or not. She needs a somewhat heavier hand, I think."

"Yours?" Peter asked with interest.

Wesmorlen shrugged with studied indifference. "I wouldn't advise you to wager money on it one way or another." He grinned, giving his brother a knowing look. "But enough of Lady Chadwick and all the other tempting young ladies awaiting us. And no more questions," he said, quickly raising his hand as he saw Peter about to continue. "We have plans to make. In three days' time, we set off. Will you be ready?"

Peter chuckled, looking for a moment remarkably like the Peter of old. "Three days? I'll be ready tomorrow!"

"But Regana, I am telling you the truth!" Miss Jane Harding said, her golden curls bouncing as if to lend emphasis to her words. "Lady Ross informed me of it herself."

The young lady being served with this irrefutable evidence smiled, seemingly unaffected by its import, and continued pouring a cup of tea. "That's all well and good, Jane, but how would Lady Ross know? Lord Botheringham doesn't strike me as the sort of gentleman who would be likely to tell all and sundry who he's intending to propose to."

"I shouldn't think many gentlemen are," Regana's younger sister, Clarisse, observed thoughtfully. "Especially Lord Botheringham. He doesn't seem the sort to give away very much about himself at all."

"He isn't," Jane admitted, then added triumphantly, "but his sister-in-law, Lady Loring, is."

"Lady Loring!" Hearing the name of one of the foremost gossipmongers in the area, Regana shook her head and laughed. "Really, Jane, I am surprised at you. You know very well what a meddler Lady Loring is. When she hasn't any bonafide gossip to spread, she simply makes some up. Isn't that true, Clarisse?''

Not presupposing to think otherwise, Clarisse quickly nodded. Jane, however, was not so easily put off. "Think what you may, Regana, but I have it on good authority that Lady Loring told Lady Ross that Lord Botheringham expressed a definite interest in you, and that it's only a matter of time before he declares himself.'' She lowered her voice conspiratorially. "Apparently Lord Botheringham confides things of even the most personal nature to his sister-in-law. And not all of what she says is idle gossip. Remember last year when she announced that Lord Chester was going to marry Penelope Brooks? You didn't believe her, did you?''

"Good heavens, Jane, nobody believed her," Regana pointed out reasonably. "Rodney and Penelope fought like cats and dogs.''

Jane grudgingly acknowledged the point. "They still do. But the fact remains he did propose. And not that long after Lady Loring put it about, as I recall. Goodness,'' Jane reflected, accepting the proffered tea, "do you know it's already been a year since all that transpired? I remember as if it were yesterday how shocked everyone was when the official announcement appeared in the *Times*. I hear there was quite a to-do made about it down at White's.''

Yes, there certainly was, Regana reflected, idly stirring cream into her cup. No one, including herself, had believed the rumours Lady Loring had been circulating about Rodney Chester and Penelope Brooks. But in the end, Penelope and Rodney had married, and were still living happily, albeit argumentatively, on the Chester estate somewhere in the north of Scotland.

Some of what she was thinking must have appeared on her face, for Jane sat back and said with obvious satisfaction, "There, you do remember. Lady Loring was right.

And I declare, she certainly can't be that far wrong about you and Lord Botheringham."

Regana raised a well-shaped eyebrow in amusement. "And just what do you mean by that, cousin dear?"

"Tosh. Regana, you know very well what I mean," Jane replied tartly. "Lord Botheringham has been dangling after you since last Season. You only have to see the way he acts in your presence to know that he's interested."

Clarisse glanced up from her needlework and giggled. "And you have only to see the way Regana responds to know that *she's* most definitely *not* interested!"

Regana's lips twitched irrepressibly, while Jane, fixing Clarisse with a decidedly speak-only-when-you're-spoken-to look, ignored the remark and rounded on her elder cousin again. "Think what you like, Regana. The point is Lord Botheringham is very interested in you and that *you* might do well to consider his suit. I vow he'll not court you forever!"

The fact that Regana could not deny what her cousin was saying did little to alleviate her growing sense of unease. Of all the gentlemen to whom she had been introduced, Lord Botheringham had been the most persistent in his attentions, despite the fact that she gave him precious little encouragement. He constantly sought her out at routs and assemblies, proclaiming his dislike of dancing, then proceeding to sign her card for as many dances as were socially allowable. He always seemed to be on hand to take her in to dinner, or to procure whatever manner of refreshment she desired. His overtures to her were polite, never effusive and never overdone. Perhaps that was a good description of the man himself, Regana thought absently: polite, never effusive and always...predictable.

"Well, I still say it isn't likely to happen, Jane," Regana replied with as much confidence as she could muster. "Just because Lord Botheringham seems interested in me doesn't mean he has serious intentions. Many men are infatuated with females they have no intention of marrying."

"True, but *that* kind of female usually ends up a mistress, so why— Oh, I'm sorry, Clarisse, did I embarrass you?" Jane asked innocently.

Clarisse bent to retrieve her dropped embroidery hoop, her cheeks rosy.

"Shame on you, Jane," Regana scolded, only just able to hide her own mirth. "You've quite discomfited my sister. You're not supposed to know about such things."

"I don't let on that I do," Jane whispered, "but I know them just the same. But we're not talking of me, we're talking of you—and in particular, you and Lord Botheringham."

"And I tell you," Regana repeated patiently, "that no matter what Lady Loring predicts, Lord Botheringham has never made any mention of his intentions towards me, nor do I have reason to suspect he has any. Besides," she added as an afterthought, "as I recall, Lady Loring has been wrong in a few of her predictions. Didn't she predict that Diana Drewbrook and Edward Thompson were going to marry this year?"

Jane seemed suddenly intent upon the study of her gold bracelet. "I suppose I did hear something to that effect," she mumbled evasively.

"Fiddlesticks! You remember very well hearing something to that effect, Jane Harding. In which case you'll also know that they are nowhere near to marrying."

"You are quite right," Clarisse chimed in innocently. Jane sent her a quelling glance.

"You'd agree if your sister said black was white and white was black!" Jane muttered. "Goodness, it's no wonder your poor aunt suffers with megrims." She observed the two laughing faces in front of her and shook her head. "Really, Regana, you truly cast one into despair! Clarisse's obtuseness I can allow, given her age and relative inexperience," she said, directing a condescending look at her younger cousin, "but *you* should know better. It's really no wonder you're getting a reputation amongst the ton, and you know how damaging that can—"

As soon as she detected the glint in her cousin's eye, Jane broke off, aware of having committed a grave error. "Well, not a reputation, exactly—"

"No, do go on, Jane," Regana interrupted, glancing at her cousin in surprise. "You were about to tell me what kind of reputation I'm acquiring, weren't you?"

"Of course I wasn't," Jane retorted quickly. "I was going to do nothing of the kind. As if I'd be one to listen to such nonsense, anyway. It's just more of the ton's silliness," Jane babbled uncomfortably. "You know how they go on."

"Yes, I do." Regana laughed. "Now, what were you going to tell me, Jane?"

"Regana, I'd tell you if it were important, but it's really noth—"

"*Jane?*"

The tone brooked no argument, and notwithstanding the fact that she was two years older and supposedly two years more worldly-wise, Jane was no match for her cousin when it came to a confrontation. Clearly discomfitted, she huffed, "Well, all right, if you must know, they're calling you the Ice Maiden."

A startled silence greeted her words. "The Ice Maiden!" Clarisse breathed in dismay. "But that's not true! Why would they say such a thing?"

"Because, pea-goose, your sister won't respond to any of the gentlemen who are constantly trying to win her affection," Jane explained patiently. "She holds them all at arm's length, no matter what they do. Hence, the sobriquet. There, you see, I told you it was just silliness," Jane said mumpishly. "And don't look at me like that, Clarisse

Kently," Jane added defensively. "I told you I didn't want to tell her."

"Then why did you speak of it in the first place?" Clarisse asked reproachfully.

"Oh, Lord, out of the mouths of babes," Jane muttered. "Regana, *say* something."

Regana sat back in her chair, the twinkle in her clear blue eyes becoming even more pronounced. "The Ice Maiden," she repeated, not even attempting to suppress the amusement with which she viewed the epithet. A trifle disparaging, she supposed, though probably not that far off the mark. After all, she was hardly a blushing young debutante any longer, having completed one full Season without accepting an offer. And here they were already well into a second and she still hadn't seen fit to favour any of the gentlemen with her hand. It wasn't that she hadn't had offers, Regana thought complacently. But no one had ever made her feel the way she'd always thought she should when contemplating marriage. None of the gentlemen she'd met had set her pulses racing, or caused her heart to beat faster at his approach, or left her dreaming of what it would be like to feel the touch of his lips against hers. Indeed, no one had even left her wondering about it. Was she perhaps expecting too much of love in general, and marriage in particular?

Regana refilled her cousin's teacup and passed her the tray filled with Mrs. Burton's delicious homemade pastries. "I suppose it's really not surprising they've given me such an epithet," she admitted, "though to be honest I wasn't aware of being so extreme about it."

"You weren't!" Clarisse said, always ready to spring to the defence of her sister, even if she was the elder of the two. "The silly ton are just being spiteful because you won't choose one of their ranks. Isn't that right, Jane?"

"I suppose," the older girl remarked, contentedly munching on a cream-filled brandy curl. "Though why she won't is quite beyond me. You're not getting any younger, Regana, and if you continue refusing offers, soon there won't be any."

"Dear me, I suppose I'll just have to take my chances then, won't I?" Regana replied, trying to fix a suitably concerned expression on her features. "There are worse fates than being a spinster, Jane."

"Bless me if I can think of one," Jane remarked drily.

"Maybe Regana doesn't want to marry," Clarisse suggested. "She doesn't have to, you know."

"Not want to marry? Fustian!" their cousin replied tartly. "Every girl wants to marry and have a family of her own. Don't you?"

"Well, I don't know," Clarisse replied uncertainly. "I haven't really given it much thought. I would like to have children, of course...."

Jane rolled her eyes expressively. "Then a husband is a definite requirement, my dear. Unless you intend to reverse the order and cast yourself and our family into unending shame."

"Cousin Jane!" Clarisse gasped, clearly mortified beyond measure. "How could you even suggest such a thing!" Her cheeks flamed red, while her grey eyes flashed with unexpected fire. "I would never dream ...! Regana, you know I wouldn't...."

"Of course you wouldn't, dearest," Regana said, quickly coming to her younger sister's defence. "She was only teasing, weren't you, Jane?" Regana added, sending a reproachful look towards her cousin.

"Of course I was, silly goose." Jane laughed, seemingly not in the least abashed. "Never mind, you still haven't told me why you keep turning down offers, Regana. And don't tell me you haven't been receiving any," she said shrewdly, "because I know you have."

Regana rose gracefully and crossed the room to the antique armoire, her lips curved in a smile. Though not the typical blue-eyed, blond-haired Society beauty, Regana was, nevertheless, a stunning girl. Her hair, of a colour not unlike that of fine brandy, was drawn smoothly up into a knot on top of her head, a few wispy tendrils escaping to frame a delicate oval face of porcelain smooth complexion. Eyes an unusual mixture of blue-green, the shade of which tended to change with her mood, were set above a delicately retroussé nose and a mouth which was moved frequently to laughter. This, combined with a notably merry nature and a figure which was rounded softly in all the right places, had caused more than one young buck to lose his heart.

"Yes, I admit to having received a few offers," Regana said, returning to her chair, "but to be honest, I really couldn't see myself entertaining any of them."

"But why not, for goodness' sake?" Jake asked, clearly at a loss to understand her cousin's reluctance. "Surely you're not looking for a ... a perfect man?"

"Of course not," Regana said, clearing amused. "I don't think there is such a creature. But I *am* looking for honesty. And *that* I've found in shockingly short supply. In fact, most of the gentlemen I've been introduced to have struck me as being quite laughable, the way they prance about like peacocks on the strut. And such a fuss they make ensuring that their cravats are folded just so, as though they feared a confrontation with the great Mr. Brummell himself. I'm wont to believe that most of them spend more time in front of the mirror than we ever do."

"No doubt you are right," Jane acknowledged drily.

"And the way they go on, paying a girl empty compliments at every opportunity and then expecting her to fall willingly into their arms. Praising the colour of her hair and the smoothness of her skin. Comparing the sparkle in her eyes to the stars twinkling in the night sky. Really, it's all too ridiculous."

"Of course it is," Jane said flatly, surprised that her cousin should find this at all remarkable. "No one expects the gentlemen of the ton to be honest."

"Well, I do," Regana replied simply. "I don't expect to be flattered and fêted, then left to my own devices once I'm married. I want to be courted and loved every day of my life, and by only one man. I want to know that what my husband says he says to me alone, and that he means it. If he can't, then I'd rather not hear it at all."

"Regana, I vow you're as naive as Clarisse," Jane retorted, setting her cup down and rising to leave. "Mayhaps more. I only hope you find this paragon before you're too old and grey to enjoy him."

"I shall," Regana pointed out sagely. "You did."

Drawn to the recollection of her own recent engagement, Jane had the decency to blush. "Yes, well, I suppose I did. But I was very lucky to find someone like Mr. Baselstoke. There aren't many like him about."

"I know, but I'm not looking for many," Regana said, her eyes twinkling once again. "Only one."

Jane laughed, and kissed her cousin's cheek affectionately. "Why is it that every time I see you, I come away feeling as though you're the older, wiser one and I'm still the gawky, inexperienced girl?"

"I suppose age can't count for everything, cousin Jane," Clarisse said sweetly, her eyes never lifting from her embroidery. Jane stared at the girl for a moment, opening her mouth and then closing it again, as if not quite sure what to say. In the end, she merely shook her head, muttering something about "out of the mouths of babes" again, and took her leave in a swish of lavender and silk, leaving the girls to smile secretly behind her.

"Dear Jane," Regana mused affectionately. "I think she despairs of me and my ideas. But then, I suppose it's only natural. If we had been raised by Aunt Melphonse rather than Aunt Mary, I don't doubt our ideas should be vastly different from what they are.''

Clarisse smiled, knowing full well what Regana was alluding to. ''Perhaps, though I don't know that your beliefs would have been all that different, Reggie. I think your strength of character would have rebelled against such restrictive teachings.''

''Oh, do you?'' Regana teased, her eyes twinkling. ''And how do you think Aunt Melphonse would have dealt with my strength of character when I challenged her strongly held principles?''

''I shouldn't like to think—'' Clarisse laughed ''—though I wonder if you wouldn't have accepted the first offer of marriage you received just to escape her strictures.''

''Clarisse Kently! I do believe you think me a rebel!''

''Oh, never that,'' Clarisse responded, her soft grey eyes brimming with laughter. ''*Rebel* is far too strong a word.''

''Is it? Then what would you call me? You know me better than any. Perhaps another sobriquet like the one awarded to me by the ton?'' Regana murmured, her own smile rueful.

''No, I think not.'' Clarisse smiled, putting aside her embroidery. ''It's not in the least appropriate. Nor do I believe that the gentlemen are just paying you empty compliments, as you seem to think. Your hair *is* a glorious colour, and your skin *is* smooth and white. And upon occasion I've even seen your eyes sparkle and dance. Especially when you laugh. So you see, it's not that the gentlemen make up things to flatter you,'' Clarisse explained. ''It's that you are all those things they say.'' She paused for a moment, then added, ''I only wish they would say such things of me.''

Regana shook her head and laughed. ''No you don't, dearest. You'd soon tire of it.''

''Would I?'' Clarisse demanded. ''Perhaps. Though I rather don't imagine so. For now, however, I'll be happy to settle for a half-full dance card at Arabella Dalmeny's ball," she replied with a laugh. "And to that end, I think I shall begin to look for a less attractive companion than you with whom to attend these functions. Maybe I'll ask Hortense Chapman if I may accompany her to the ball. Next to poor Hortense, even I look rather appealing."

"Clarisse!" Regana reprimanded, before bursting into her own fit of giggles as an image of Hortense Chapman's rather plain and horsey countenance appeared in her mind.

Later, as she prepared for bed, Regana considered their conversation again. In truth, Society was not kind to those not blessed with an enviable beauty or a suitable portion. While it was true that Clarisse's looks would hardly set the ton on its ear, it was also true that she possessed a far more valuable gift: a good and caring nature. She deserved an equally good and loving husband, one who would appreciate her worth and cherish her all the more because of it.

But where did one find such a man—a paragon, as Jane had put it—in a milieu which placed such high value on a woman's physical appearance and where honesty was so often sacrificed in the pursuit of a suitable mate? Indeed, was there such a man to be found?

CHAPTER TWO

AWAKENING THE NEXT morning with the sun shining brightly through her bedroom window, Regana felt her spirits rise, and put her less than charitable feelings towards the gentlemen of the ton aside. After all, just because her expectations of love and honesty hadn't been met certainly didn't mean that they never would be. Nor did it mean that Clarisse would suffer the same fate. It might take time, but no doubt the right man would come along.

Cheered by the thought, Regana quickly finished her cup of hot chocolate, and rose, donning the riding habit Marie had set out. The enforced confinement brought about by four days of rain had caused Regana endless annoyance, but now that the weather seemed to have taken a turn for the better, she intended to linger indoors no longer!

"Good morning, Miss Regana," Robbins, the head groom, greeted her as she came in view of the stables a short time later. "I thought I might be seeing yer down this morning, the sun being out and all, so I took the liberty of getting Duchess ready. I'll bring her right out."

Regana grinned, amazed at the wiry Welshman's perceptiveness. "Robbins, I think you must have been reading my mind."

"Wouldn't be the first time, miss," the groom returned with a laugh, his musical voice rolling like waves on the ocean. "Up you go, then," he said, gently assisting her to mount.

Regana settled her skirts about her, and after saluting him with her crop, gathered up the reins and set off at a gentle trot. She preferred to ride alone in the mornings, and the staff, knowing her penchant for solitude, turned a blind eye to this slight flouting of convention. Miss Regana was far too sensible a young lady to get herself into any kind of trouble.

Once clear of the paddock, Regana set off down Lundy's Lane and out towards the rolling fields behind Grantly Hall. The early morning air brought the colour back into her pale cheeks, and under her breath, she hummed a little tune. At moments like this, she could forget all about Lord Botheringham and his tiresome courtship. Somehow, on a day like this, with a clear blue sky above her and the sweet country breeze tugging at the wispy tendrils of hair escaping from under her hat, obligations and annoyances seemed a long way away.

"All right, my love," Regana whispered, feeling her mare tugging impatiently at the bit, "let's have a gallop and blow the cobwebs away, shall we?"

At the lightest touch of her mistress's heels, Duchess sprang into a canter, her smooth, easy gait carrying them over the lush green fields of the uplands, and easily clearing the low hedges which divided one field from another. Regana was completely at home in the saddle. Her father had taught her to ride as a child, and she was ever thankful that he had shown her more than just how to trot sedately in the park. Nothing lifted her spirits more than a good gallop across open terrain. Now, as Regana listened to the soft thud of Duchess's hooves on the turf, her body moving smoothly to the mare's gait, she felt her anxieties melt away like the early morning mist on a summer's day.

Regana had ridden this path many times and never seen a soul; that was one of the reasons she chose it. But when she detected the sound of a horse approaching from behind, and at considerable speed, she quickly slowed Duchess to a trot and eased her closer to the nearby hedge, assuming the oncoming rider would slow his own pace as he passed. It seemed that he was, but it didn't take long for Regana to realize that he was not going to ride by. The hooves were coming to a stop, and turning, Regana wondered who the horseman might be.

When she first caught sight of the magnificent black stallion, Regana caught her breath, her eyes widening in silent admiration. Big and black as the night, with a snowy white blaze running down his nose, the stallion was as beautiful an animal as she had ever seen. His jet black coat glistened as if wet, and Regana could see the proud arch of his neck and the way his nostrils flared as his rider began to check his speed.

Not that halting him was an easy task, she realized, watching the masterful way in which the man controlled the stallion, the muscles in his arms and broad chest straining. Even when they came to a halt beside her, the horse continued to prance. A fine animal with a touch of the devil, Robbins would have fondly dubbed him.

"Good morning," the man said, his deep baritone rich and clear. "Pray forgive my intrusion, but I seldom see a lady galloping with such abandon. I was afraid your horse had taken its head."

Regana coloured slightly at the less than flattering description of her riding, but returned his gaze levelly. "Thank you for your concern, sir, but as you can see, I am quite in control of my mare."

There was an unintentional note of defiance in Regana's voice, and hearing it, the man smiled. "Forgive me, I did not mean to sound patronizing. Indeed, I would compliment you on your ability. Not many ladies of my acquaintance could stay in the saddle beyond a sedate trot."

Cognizant of the tribute, Regana's lips curved in a reluctant smile. "My father taught me to ride," she admitted. "Perhaps my mother should have done so."

"On the contrary," the man said quickly. "I find it most refreshing."

Regana hastily lowered her eyes, but not before acknowledging that the stranger was handsome, disturbingly so. He towered over her, an imposing figure in a dark riding jacket over buckskin breeches and highly polished top boots. Piercing black eyes regarded her from a decidedly aristocratic face, while the straight aquiline nose, decisive chin and firm mouth lent distinction to a face already browned by the sun. His head was uncovered, and his hair, tousled now by the wind and curling just to the top of his collar, was so dark as to appear almost black. A strong face, Regana decided, and one not easily forgotten.

"Do you mind if we walk on?" the stranger asked abruptly. "Midnight becomes restless when he stands too long."

And indeed the stallion was. He pranced and pulled as though treading on hot coals, and out of concern for her own mare, Regana carefully edged away from the dancing hooves.

"He's not dangerous," the man was quick to point out, noting her action. "Just highly strung."

"He's a stallion," Regana acknowledged, her glance admiring. "I doubt he could behave any other way."

The stranger looked at her with renewed interest. "My compliments," he said, bowing his head. "It would appear your knowledge of horses extends far beyond merely knowing how to ride them."

Aware of the warmth which crept into her cheeks, Regana smiled and shook her head. "You flatter me unduly, sir. My knowledge of horses merely stems from my love of them, and my father was wont to say it was hard to have one without the other." She glanced at the stallion again. "He's a magnificent animal. Have you had him long?"

The man nodded briefly. "From the time he was a foal," he informed her, running a hand along the horse's glossy neck. "I wanted him from the moment I saw him at his mother's side." His laugh reflected a rueful impatience. "I had to wait a few years, and I almost lost him once, but he's mine now." His eyes assumed a darkly possessive glint. "I seldom lose what I really want."

The words were spoken softly, but there was no mistaking the conviction behind them. Glancing up at that darkly handsome face, Regana experienced a momentary stab of alarm, and wondered at the wisdom of continuing her ride. She was unaccompanied and a fair way from home, and though Robbins knew in which direction she had set out, he would hardly come looking for her all the way up here. Nor would he even think of doing so for a while yet, knowing that she normally rode for a good two or three hours.

Glancing covertly at the strong, commanding face, Regana felt sure this man was capable of anything. Yet, on the other hand, his speech was that of a gentleman and his clothes, for all their countrified appearance, bespoke London tailoring. The smooth buckskin breeches and perfectly fitted jacket were as fine as any to be found on a Town Corinthian. And his tassled boots had certainly enjoyed the attention of a personal valet, Regana noted, their gloss so high as to enable one to see one's reflection in the leather. Perhaps she was being overly suspicious.

Nevertheless, when they reached the point of land which overlooked Hanton-on-Grange a few minutes later, Regana reluctantly pulled Duchess to a halt. "I think I had best start my journey back," she said with an apologetic smile. "I don't normally ride this far..." She hesitated, and glanced at him uncertainly.

"Unaccompanied?" he supplied for her. Seeing her discomfiture, the stranger smiled. "I'm sure you don't. Allow me at least to accompany you part of the way back. That way I know you'll arrive home safely."

The muscle just below the corner of Regana's mouth twitched irrepressibly. "Do you refer to my riding ability, sir, or to the fact that I may be approached by other, less well-intentioned, gentlemen?''

Lord Wesmorlen, appearing to consider this, was in fact trying to ignore his growing fascination with this bewitching creature. When he had set out from Blackoaks that morning, he'd had no expectation of encountering such a startling beauty in the wilds of the country.

There was no doubt in Wesmorlen's mind that the lady was gently bred. Her clear, precise manner of speaking and the refined way in which she conducted herself provided ample proof of it. He was drawn against his will to that beautiful face with its obvious intellect and the sense of humour he saw lurking behind those lively and indisputably blue eyes—to say nothing of the perfect figure outlined so becomingly by the well-cut Georgian cloth of her riding attire. But an attachment was something Lord Wesmorlen neither welcomed nor invited at present. He had come down to the country, ostensibly to learn more about the running of the vast estate he'd inherited, though more truthfully to help Peter further his recovery. Little help he'd be indeed, if he spent all his time chasing after this enchanting creature.

Nor did he harbour any delusions that she would compromise herself by a dalliance. She was clearly destined to marry well, if not the local curate, then perhaps some London aristocrat. Better to keep his distance than risk losing his head over an unknown, albeit enticing, young lady.

"I think it safer if I decline to say," the earl replied briefly, sounding more curt than he'd intended. "I'll accompany you back, none the less."

Regana blinked, a mixture of hurt and surprise banishing her smile. What had happened to cause him to speak to her so abruptly? Had she said something to which he'd taken offence? Or had he mistaken her reasons for riding unchaperoned, assuming her to be something she was not and thinking merely to indulge in a dalliance with her? Perhaps by suggesting that they turn back, she had made him aware that she was, in fact, a proper young lady and as such, not open to any but the most honourable of attentions. Realizing that the latter seemed the only plausible explanation, Regana felt her cheeks glow crimson. How could she have compromised herself so, if only inadvertently? Perhaps Aunt Melphonse was right, Regana reflected unhappily. Her upbringing should have been more strict; then perhaps her actions wouldn't be open to misinterpretation by every gentleman who happened along.

Wesmorlen, misunderstanding the reason for her suddenly downcast eyes, cursed himself for his lack of sensibility. There was no call for him to have spoken to her so sharply. How was the girl to know that it was impatience with himself which had made him react so, rather than anything she had said or done? If he hadn't been drawn to her so strongly in the first place, he wouldn't have had to reprimand himself so firmly in the second.

Thus, with each enmeshed in private thoughts, they rode back to Grantly Hall in near total silence. Regana felt little compunction to talk and rode slightly ahead of him, painfully aware of the fact that, on top of everything else, the man hadn't even bothered to enquire as to her name, another point which signified, in her mind at least, that he'd mistaken her for something she was not. A gentleman would always ask a lady her name.

Well, he'd hardly do so now. Nor had she any intention of trying to discern his. Better to leave things as they were, Regana thought wretchedly: brief, humiliating and anonymous.

When at last they came down Lundy's Lane and Regana spied the familiar towers of Grantly Hall in the distance, she breathed a heartfelt sigh of relief. Never had a ride seemed so long, or a silence so uncomfortable. Anxious that Robbins not see her in the company of a stranger, Regana reined Duchess to a halt and turned to face him, her chin lifting proudly. "Thank you for your company, sir, but you need accompany me no farther. I shall be able to manage the rest of the way on my own."

Regana felt the dark eyes on her and quickly averted her face, unaware of how lovely she looked, even in profile. The ride had brought a renewed sparkle to her eyes, while her cheeks were flushed a delicate pink.

"My pleasure," Wesmorlen answered smoothly. "Perhaps we shall cross paths again, my lady."

"Perhaps," she replied, knowing she would take pains that they should not. Regana gazed at him a moment longer, then turned Duchess towards home, not once looking back.

Watching her ride away, her back straight, her bearing as proud as any duchess's, Wesmorlen felt the strangest pounding in his veins. Who was she, this mystery woman who spoke like a lady but gazed at him with such fire in her eyes? And why had he never seen her at Court? Could it be that she was not yet out? No, that hardly seemed likely, Wesmorlen decided, recalling with pleasure the curves so charmingly outlined in the deep blue habit. She had to be at least nineteen or twenty. Yet she was possessed of far more presence than he would have thought possible in a girl that age.

Amongst all the things Wesmorlen was not sure of, there was certainly one thing that he was. No woman had ever intrigued him so quickly nor so thoroughly as had this unknown lady, and despite his resolve not to pursue her, he was damned if he was going to remain uninformed as to her identity.

Turning his horse in the direction of Blackoaks, Wesmorlen nodded to himself. "Oh, yes, we shall cross paths again, my lady. I don't know when, or where, but we shall meet again. I intend to make certain of it!"

IN SPITE OF her threatened plans to the contrary, Clarisse did accompany Regana to the Dalmenys' ball the following week.

The girls had spent considerable time over their preparations for the evening and were both well pleased with the results, though for entirely different reasons. Regarding Clarisse as they stood in the front hall waiting for Aunt Mary, who unfortunately had never quite mastered the art of arriving anywhere on time, Regana felt sure no gentleman would overlook her sister tonight. In a gown of deep rose, the overskirt caught up with bunches of tiny, pink roses to expose a filmy underdress of an even paler shade, Clarisse looked radiant. The colour set off her soft golden hair, while the pink sweetheart roses skilfully arranged amongst the curls complemented her dewy complexion.

For her own part, Clarisse felt sure that none would dare to call Regana the Ice Maiden tonight. In a gown of shimmering gold silk, she looked the very antithesis of cold. The bodice was low-cut and close-fitting, while the material fell from a high waist in soft folds to the floor, touching on each and every delectable curve as it did so. To add to the effect, Marie had dressed her hair in a flattering new style, weaving a strand of golden pearls amongst the rich waves. Her only other adornment was a dainty gold-and-diamond necklace which had belonged to their mother.

A week had passed since Regana's fateful meeting with the stranger, and although she had been tempted, she had not ventured out upon that path again. She had tried to convince herself that she truly did not want to see the man again, recalling the embarrassment which he had inflicted upon her at their first meeting. But in her heart, Regana knew she was not being truthful. The stranger had intrigued her in a way no other man ever had, and she found herself wanting to know more about him: in particular, who he was, and why she hadn't seen him in Hanton-on-Grange before. She even admitted to feeling a twinge of remorse for

her hasty assessment of his character. Perhaps she had
misjudged him, she thought guiltily. Perhaps he had not
drawn the conclusion she'd assumed he had, and there was
another explanation for his sudden coolness. But what
could it have been, Regana asked herself, trying hard to
find a logical explanation. What had she said or done to
make him change so swiftly?

Reluctantly accepting that a satisfactory answer was unlikely to be forthcoming, Regana had resolved to put the
meeting from her mind. She hadn't even told Clarisse of it,
deciding it was wiser to avoid the inevitable questions.

Hence, arriving at Lord and Lady Dalmeny's impressive Georgian house, Regana fixed a smile on her face, and
went inside, aware of a frisson of excitement as she glanced
about the crowded hall. It seemed an age since she had been
to a gala ball, and she had little doubt that Arabella Dalmeny's would prove to be rather spectacular. Besides, Regana loved to dance, and though she was admittedly
reluctant to encourage attentions of a lasting nature from
those gentlemen already known to her, she was quite happy
to allow them to prattle on while they partnered her on the
dance floor.

After dutifully acknowledging Lord and Lady Dalmeny
and their daughter, Arabella, the ladies proceeded into the
main ballroom where, under the light of countless glittering chandeliers, the cream of local society were already
mingling. The dowagers had taken their seats along the
walls from whence they could gossip amongst themselves
while still overseeing the goings-on on the floor. It was to
this group that Aunt Mary removed herself quite happily,
assuring her nieces that she would see them throughout the
evening and adjuring them to have a good time.

Directed thus, Regana and Clarisse crossed the crowded
floor and made for some seating by a clump of potted
plants. Settling themselves on the gold-and-white striped

satin, they glanced excitedly round the room, enjoying the chance to view the other guests, male and female alike.

"Oh, look, Regana," Clarissa said, placing a light hand on her sister's arm. "Isn't that Charles Wickworth trailing at Arabella's heels?"

Following her sister's gaze, Regana nodded. "Yes, I believe it is," she said, then added with a smile, "Poor Charles. It's obvious he's hopelessly smitten. Unfortunately, I don't think Lady Dalmeny considers him a suitable match for her dear Arabella. I hear she's holding out for a title."

Regana watched the progress of the young beauty across the floor, feeling a swift stab of compassion for the lovelorn young man following closely in her wake. "But surely Arabella's feelings have some bearing on the situation," Clarisse objected, her sense of fair play aroused.

"Not a lot, I fear," Regana said realistically. "Lady Dalmeny has made no secret of her wishes and, knowing Arabella, she will probably be quite happy to go along with them. Somehow I can't see Arabella contesting her mother over someone like Charles."

It was a fair assessment. Though not possessed of unlimited intelligence, Arabella was clever enough to know what to say, and to whom to say it. Consequently, Regana felt certain she would make a good marriage, though how high up the social ladder she would rise, only time, and Lady Dalmeny, would tell. Both girls watched, therefore, as after what looked like considerable pleading, Arabella finally allowed Charles to sign her dance card, leaving the triumphant young man with a somewhat dazed expression on his face.

Turning to address a remark to Clarisse, Regana noticed the arrival of another Incomparable, one whose renowned beauty cast even the lovely Arabella into the shade. Resplendent in a gown of dark emerald green silk cut daringly low, Amanda, the widowed Marchioness of

Chadwick, paused on the threshold of the room, her dark, almost black hair glowing in the light of a thousand candles. Her lips curved ever so slightly, as if withholding some tantalizing secret, while her beautiful green eyes, their colour almost as deep as her gown, surveyed all before her with just the slightest hint of condescension.

It was an impressive entrance, and one calculated to make the most of her outstanding beauty. But then, Lady Chadwick had always known how to create a stir, Regana thought wryly. And she was certainly doing it now. A veritable ripple had run round the room at her unexpected appearance, prompting even their aunt to come bustling forward.

"What's she doing here?" Aunt Mary bristled, her face registering disapproval. "Surely she's not out of mourning yet. It can't be a year since Lord Chadwick was killed in France."

Regana smiled blandly, watching with amusement the crowd of ardent young gentlemen already forming round the young widow. "It isn't quite a year, Aunt. I understand she . . . shortened the required period somewhat."

"Shortened it? Did she indeed!" Aunt Mary huffed. "Where did you hear this?"

"Cousin Jane told us," Clarisse supplied. "She and Mr. Baselstoke saw Lady Chadwick riding in the park last week."

"Unescorted?" Aunt Mary ventured.

"I believe so."

Aunt Mary shook her head disparagingly. "She's always been a little too full of herself for my liking. I thought she and Anthony deserved each other. Goodness knows *he* considered himself a nonpareil, too."

Regana turned away to hide her smile, taking care not to meet her sister's eye. Aunt Mary had never been one to withhold an opinion, especially about someone or something she didn't particularly like. And she clearly did not like the widowed Marchioness of Chadwick.

"She is beautiful, though, isn't she, Regana," Clarisse commented, watching the widow's progress, and careful to wait until Aunt Mary had returned to her seat with the dowagers before voicing it.

"Very," Regana agreed. "I can't imagine any man remaining immune to her for long."

"No, I don't suppose so. Oh, dear, speaking of immune, look who else has just arrived," Clarisse noted reluctantly, her eyes on the door. "And who, if I'm not mistaken, is quite anxiously looking for you."

Regana had no need to look to know to whom Clarisse was referring. Resolutely, she glanced towards the door and felt her heart plummet as she saw Bertrand, Lord Botheringham beat a slow but determined path to her side.

CHAPTER THREE

To say that Lord Botheringham was corpulent would have been somewhat unkind. Although it was true that the buttons on his yellow silk waistcoat did strain somewhat, one could not truly claim that it was solely owing to the wearer's girth. No doubt it had something to do with the poor cut of his clothes in general, and to the apparent negligence with which he wore them.

Of medium height, Lord Botheringham had dark brown hair, seen to be thinning rapidly, and was of indistinguishable age, though Regana had heard it placed somewhere between fifty and sixty. His watery blue eyes held a look of continual boredom, and his singular lack of interest in almost everything was neither affected nor assumed, as was the case with so many of the younger dandies.

"Ah, Miss Kently, so glad to have found you," the baron greeted her now, his slightly protruberant eyes lingering on the smooth expanse of skin above her low-cut neckline.

"And the younger Miss Kently," he added, turning to address Clarisse. "Delighted."

"Lord Botheringham," the girls said as one.

"May I say you are both looking in fine form this evening."

"My lord is too kind," Regana said quietly.

Lord Botheringham's eyes made a leisurely perusal of the crowded room before coming to rest once more on Regana's face. "I hope I may have the honour of escorting you in to supper this evening, Miss Kently," he said smoothly. "And to have several dances with you. Including a waltz, if I may be so bold."

Regana felt the colour rise to her cheeks, and was thankful she had thought to bring her fan. The waltz was still creating a good deal of excitement, being the only dance which actually required a gentleman to hold his partner in his arms, and while many members of the beaumonde still viewed it as quite immoral, it had nevetheless been declared respectable by the loftier matrons of the ton. Regana had, in fact, received her nod from Lady Jersey at Almack's, allowing her to officially participate in the waltz, and she had done so a number of times while in London. It was the dance's required intimacy, however, which now inspired Regana's reluctance. "You may have your dances, my lord, though I cannot promise you a waltz. That depends on the order of my partners and the choice of the orchestra."

Lord Botheringham took her card and filled in his name, a knowing smile curving his lips. "Rest assured, Miss Kently, we shall have our waltz. I am not above resorting to gentle persuasion," he observed with a smugness Regana found distasteful. "A word here, a request there and *voilà!* we shall have our waltz."

Regana fixed a smile on her lips, knowing that it was expected. At the same time, she happened to glance across the room and spied Lady Loring eyeing them with interest.

Botheration! Regana thought, snapping her fan shut with unwarranted force. The last thing she wanted was to give that nosy woman more reason for gossip. But how was she to escape her scrutiny? Unless...

"Oh, dear, I wonder how that could have happened," Regana said, apparently finding something amiss in the folds of her gown. She rose smoothly, one hand clutching the fabric of her skirt. "Clarisse, would you be so kind as to accompany me upstairs? Your skill with a needle is so much better than mine."

"Oh, yes, of course," her sister said quickly, reaching for her reticule.

"Lord Botheringham, pray excuse us," Regana said, turning back to him, "but I have only just noticed a small tear in my gown. I must attend to it before it becomes larger. You understand."

If the baron was surprised by the haste of her departure, he gave no sign. He merely inclined his head, and replied, "Of course, Miss Kently. I anxiously await your return."

With one hand holding the offending garment, Regana led the way back across the floor, trying not to appear as though she was fleeing.

"Is there really a tear in your gown, Regana?" Clarisse whispered as they ascended the wide, curving staircase to the ladies' withdrawing room upstairs.

"Did I sound distressed enough to make you think there was?" Regana asked, nodding at an acquaintance as they passed on the stairway.

"Well, yes, of course you did."

"Then let us leave it at that. Have you a needle in your reticule?"

When Clarisse nodded, Regana smiled in relief. "Good. If anyone enters, it shall appear that you are diligently mending the rent in my gown. And indeed, so fine shall be the job you do that upon close inspection, even I shall be hard-pressed to locate the original damage."

Aware now that there was no tear, Clarisse lowered her eyes and giggled. "Regana Kently, you are quite the one. I only hope if I ever have need of an escape, I can manage it half as convincingly as you."

Regana smiled, her lively sense of the ridiculous bringing a mischievous sparkle to her eyes. "Needs must when the devil drives, dearest. But even I know it will do little more than stall Lord Botheringham. I'm afraid that if I told him I had to retire until a whole new gown could be delivered, he would still be downstairs waiting for me."

It was true enough and both girls knew it. Consequently, they took as much time as they dared. Finally, when they felt they could stall no longer, Regana rose and shook out the folds of the silk. At that very moment, the door burst open and Arabella Dalmeny rushed in, her pretty cheeks flushed with excitement.

"Oh, pardon me for startling you," Arabella said, noting Regana's hasty step back. "But Mama told me to remove myself until my colour settled." She glanced at herself in the mirror. "Am I really that flushed?"

"Your colour is quite high," Clarisse confirmed, "but not unattractively so."

"Do you think not?" the lady replied, studying her reflection. "Oh, I hope so. Only I never thought he'd accept Mama's invitation to come. But he did! And now he's here. Oh, dear, I hope he didn't see me."

"Hope *who* didn't see you, Arabella?" Clarisse asked. Suddenly, her eyes opened wide. "Oh, my goodness, is the Prince Regent here?"

"The Prince Regent? Oh, dear me, no," Arabella trilled. "Much better than that." She paused, as if savouring the moment. "The Earl of Wesmorlen has just arrived. Imagine, right here at my ball. The Unmarriageable Earl. Oh, didn't you know?" She giggled, catching sight of Regana's look of surprise. "That's what they call him because he's managed to elude every trap that's ever been set."

The girl was clearly euphoric, and Regana couldn't prevent a smile at her obvious infatuation. She'd heard about the dashing earl, of course. It was virtually impossible not to. Surprisingly though, she had never seen him.

"Oh, no, it's not surprising at all," Arabella explained when Regana gave voice to the question. "He's been in London the past few years, only returning home once for a brief period when he ascended to the title. Apparently he's back now to start taking over the management of the estate, which Mama thinks means he's going to set up a household of his own. Which also means he'll be looking for a wife."

Arabella's face assumed a rather perturbed expression. "He hasn't attended many functions, though, and Mama says he's going to have to change his ways if he wants to attract the proper kind of wife. She said he probably knows that every mother with a marriageable daughter is hoping to attach his interest. I knew Mama had invited him, but I had no reason to think he'd come. La, what a wonderful night," she breathed, her eyes shining. "Do you think he might dance with me?"

"I see no reason why not," Regana said kindly. "You are, after all, his host's daughter."

"Yes, yes I am, aren't I!" Arabella nodded. But then, her pretty mouth drooped. "But Lady Chadwick is here, too."

"Well, what does that matter?" Regana asked brightly. "There are many lovely girls here this evening for the earl to dance with."

"Oh, I know that, but I've heard tell that Lord Wesmorlen and Lady Chadwick were close friends before she married. They even say that they might have married, but that she turned Wesmorlen down for the marquess. But I fear now that she is widowed, she'll favour him again. Oh, I do hope not," Arabella said, glancing quickly in the mirror again. "I should so love to be the Countess of Wesmorlen. There, my colour is a little better. Do you think I should go down now?"

"By all means." Regana nodded. "I'm sure the earl will be rendered quite speechless when he sees you."

With a nervous giggle, and rather unladylike haste, Arabella started for the door. She checked herself before opening it, however, and began her descent in a manner more befitting her station. Once she had gone, Clarisse looked at Regana in amazement. "Goodness, I've never seen Arabella in such a fidge. She was positively beside herself.''

"Yes, and no doubt her mother will be atop of the house, too,'' Regana concurred as they quit the chamber. "I hardly think Lady Dalmeny would turn down an earldom for her beloved daughter.''

As soon as Regana stepped out, she became aware of a new excitement in the air. It was as though someone had lit even more candles so that everything seemed brighter, and more glittering. Descending the staircase, she noticed a number of girls tittering together, their eyes sparkling as they cast covert glances at someone beyond Regana's view, obviously the newly arrived guest. Even the servants seemed to be moving with increased alacrity. Whoever this Lord Wesmorlen was, Regana acknowledged, he certainly had the ability to stir up a gathering.

"Ah, Miss Kently, I quite despaired of seeing you again,'' Lord Botheringham said as soon as they reentered the ballroom. "I feared perhaps you had deserted me and gone home to change, after all.''

Regana heard a distinct note of censure in his voice, and unconsciously bristled. "I am flattered by your concern, my lord, but as you can see, I did not.''

The baron effected a quick survey of her gown before smiling blandly. "I take it your gown is suitably repaired?''

"It is.''

"It must have been considerably damaged to take so long to repair.''

Regana's smile remained fixed. "My sister is very adroit with her needle, Lord Botheringham, but mending a tear in a gown such as this is a time-consuming process, and one not to be undertaken with haste. However, she has done an excellent job. So good, in fact, that I am hard pressed to find the damage at all.''

"Indeed," he drawled. His eyes suspiciously searched Clarisse's carefully averted face. Then, deciding there was little to be gained by belabouring the point, effectively dismissed it. "Miss Kently," Lord Botheringham said to Regana as the music began, "I believe this is our dance."

The baron extended his hand, and aware there was nothing she could do to delay any longer, Regana allowed herself to be led on to the floor, casting one last despairing glance towards Clarisse as she went.

Unbeknownst to Regana, however, Clarisse was not the only one to watch her removal to the floor, or to intercept that glance. Standing amidst a group of friends, the Earl of Wesmorlen had noted Botheringham's presence the moment he'd arrived, and had watched the older man's movements ever since.

Six months, the earl marvelled to himself. Six months since the night of the duel, yet his animosity towards Botheringham had not lessened one particle, nor was it softened by the knowledge that Peter was finally improving. Wesmorlen had sworn revenge against the baron the night he'd shot his brother and he fully intended to get it, by whatever means necessary. It was probably just as well Peter hadn't been feeling up to attending tonight, Wesmorlen allowed, accepting a glass of champagne from a passing servant. The sight of the pompous, overbearing Botheringham attending a ball right here in Hanton-on-Grange might have dissuaded Peter from ever reentering local Society, something which Lord Wesmorlen was at great pains to avoid. The only way Peter was going to get on with his life was to marry and start afresh. And Wesmorlen was damned if he was going to let Botheringham stand in the way of that again.

Observing the baron earlier, it had soon become apparent to Wesmorlen that Botheringham was waiting for someone. Not unnaturally assuming it to be a woman, the earl continued to watch, wondering what sort of woman would capture Botheringham's interest. In turn, he wondered what manner of woman would tolerate the attentions of a corpulent, balding peer, whose only saving grace was his reputedly vast wealth. Although that, he acknowledged sardonically, would be enough for some women.

In the end, his patience had been rewarded when two young women had entered the room. Though their features were difficult to discern as their faces were averted, there was no mistaking the predatory, almost possessive gleam in Botheringham's eye as he approached the pair.

The baron seemed to be addressing himself to the darker-haired girl in the golden gown. Wesmorlen noted that during the course of the conversation, her companion pointedly looked away. The first young lady seemed to tense, and then lifted her head, gazing proudly back at Botheringham, her eyes flashing fire.

Wesmorlen started, not prepared for the shock which coursed through his body. He knew that face, those flashing eyes and bewitching mouth. It was a face which had haunted his thoughts since that morning he'd met her out riding in the field. And the very one he had tried, though without success, to see again.

Stepping slightly behind one of the others in his group so that she might not detect his presence, Wesmorlen continued to observe her. He could hardly believe that this enchanting creature was truly the object of Botheringham's pursuit. Why would she sully herself with such a sad excuse for a man, when Wesmorlen felt certain she could have had any man in the room?

"I say, Winchester," the earl said, turning to address one of his cronies. "Who is that lady dancing with Botheringham? The one in the gold."

Alfred, Lord Winchester, who claimed a close friendship with Wesmorlen as a result of their brief time together in France, transferred his attention to the dance floor and soon espied the lady in question. "Ah, I see your taste in ladies hasn't changed, old man," he said with a chuckle. "But I'm afraid you'll have to admire that one from afar. The lady's name is Regana Kently, and she's had more offers than Prinny's had routs. Turned every one of them down flat. Beautiful, isn't she?"

"Quite the most exquisite woman here," the earl agreed.

"I say, Wesmorlen, I wouldn't care to let Amanda hear that coming from your lips," taunted Claude Prestwick, another member of the party. He glanced in the direction of the Incomparable, who was still surrounded by doting swains. "She's had her eye on you from the moment you arrived."

"Has she?" the earl replied in a lazy drawl. "I hadn't noticed." He turned back to Winchester. "What do you know of Miss Kently? And what is a diamond like that doing with Botheringham?"

"Yes, what *is* she doing with Bertrand?" Claude Prestwick echoed, raising his quizzing glass to better observe the pair. "I thought she'd given him the cut direct."

"It certainly seemed that way," Winchester agreed, "though of late there seems to be some speculation that she might be entertaining his suit again."

"The devil you say! What on earth for?"

"Nothing definite, though the rumours are that the aunt, the one over there in the puce silk, is not well and that it's costing them dearly to keep her in medicine. In which case a wealthy husband would be a rather propitious find at the moment, wouldn't you agree, Wesmorlen?"

The earl, who had purposely adopted a casual air, shrugged eloquently. "I've heard worse reasons for marriages to take place. At least the girl has someone's interest other than her own at heart." He continued to study her, feigning an indifference he was far from feeling. "What about these previous offers? Why did she turn them down? Is she holding out for a title?"

"It don't seem that way," Winchester replied. "The Duke of Asply made an offer for her last year, and that would have made her a duchess."

"A widow more like. Asply's old enough to be her grandfather," Claude muttered disparagingly.

"And Botheringham ain't?" Winchester retorted. "Granted, he's a little younger, but not by so much."

"No, but he's as rich as Croesus and everyone knows it. Still, all that money and he doesn't spend a farthing of it on his clothes," Claude sniffed, smoothing down his own virulently lime-green waistcoat banded with purple stripes. "Only look at the shocking cut on that coat. I'd as lief be caught naked as be seen in that."

As Mr. Prestwick's singular preoccupation with fashion was well known, Winchester didn't bother to reply. "Well, all I can say is, if she *is* planning to marry him, I wish her the best of luck. Miss Kently is a diamond of the first water, and she don't deserve the likes of him. Especially considering his reputation."

"Sink me, Alfred, but you're doing it up a bit brown," Claude mocked, drawing forth a pinch of snuff from an elaborately gilded box. "Don't tell me you're one of the poor saps she turned down."

"Don't be such a chucklehead, Claude!" the viscount snapped. "Beyond being courteous, she's never given me the slightest indication that she'd entertain my suit. I only wish she had."

The four men continued to study the object of their discussion. The earl, watching the proud, beautiful face, was suddenly struck by something his companion had said. "What did you mean when you mentioned Botheringham's reputation?" he asked Winchester. "What kind of reputation were you referring to?"

For a moment, the other man actually looked uncomfortable, and the conversation was picked up by Sir Gerald

Bancroft, another member of the party and one of Wesmorlen's closest friends.

"It may only be hearsay, Richard, but there was some talk a while back of Botheringham's being involved with a local girl, and of his rather questionable behaviour towards her. Though to my knowledge, nothing was ever proven."

"Nor is anything ever likely to be," Claude intervened, affecting the drawl so popular with the dandies of London fashion. "You don't even know those rumours were true. It happened a long time ago, and I doubt the sources quoted were the most reliable. After all, are you really going to believe the word of an innkeeper's daughter, who was, as I recall, in the family way at the time?"

"She was," Bancroft acknowledged, "though I don't see that as any reason not to believe her. She had the bruises to prove it. Besides, the girl was not your common run-of-the-mill trollop."

"Of course she wasn't," Claude scoffed. "She was with child because of her good and virtuous nature. And no doubt the bruises were placed there by her loving father!"

"Say what you will," Bancroft said, ignoring the other man's sarcasm. "The point I'm making is that the poor girl had nothing to gain by speaking ill of Botheringham. I firmly believe she didn't even know who he was, or what position he held in Society. If the rumours were true, he dressed plainly and concealed his identity. No," he said, shaking his head, "I really don't think she was telling tales. To my way of thinking, she was merely passing along what she'd had the misfortune to discover."

Wesmorlen ruminated on this information, when a disturbing new thought occurred to him. "Where did all this take place, Gerald? And when?"

The baronet looked thoughtful for a moment. "Two years ago, if my memory serves."

"Yes, that would be about right," Winchester concurred. "As to where, Botheringham was spending a good deal of time just outside London. Near Oxford, if I'm not mistaken."

Wesmorlen nodded, aware that he might have stumbled across something very significant. Peter had been at Oxford two years ago. Could that be where he and Botheringham had met? Further, could Botheringham's shadowy past have had something to do with his obvious hatred of Peter? Had Peter stumbled, knowingly or otherwise, onto the affair Bancroft had just referred to?

The more Wesmorlen thought about it, the more sense it seemed to make. It would certainly explain a lot of things. The problem was, how did he go about proving it? Peter had remained stubbornly closed-mouthed about the whole episode, refusing to answer any of Richard's questions. Would Peter admit the truth, even if Wesmorlen served him with it?

Wesmorlen knew that unless he discovered the truth of the matter for himself, he might never know exactly what had happened. Perhaps a trip to Oxford was warranted. If by spending a few days there he was somehow able to discover what he needed to know, it would certainly be well worth the effort.

Moving away from his circle of friends, the earl leaned against the wall, thoughtfully watching Miss Regana Kently. There was no doubt in his mind that Botheringham was courting her, or that she was worth winning. The dignity with which she conducted herself, the way she moved all bespoke a gentle and careful upbringing. But there was spirit there, too, as evidenced by their meeting on horseback the other morning. That was no simpering miss galloping at full tilt along the meadow.

But why would such a diamond settle for a man like Botheringham, when according to Winchester, she could have her pick of the crop? Was it simply his wealth which attracted her, albeit for a good cause? And if that was her motivation, would he himself not serve equally well?

Wesmorlen blinked, amazed at his own dull-wittedness. *Serve equally well?* But of course he would! How stupid he had been not to think of it sooner. Ever since the night of the duel when he'd sworn revenge on Botheringham, Wesmorlen had been waiting for an opportunity to exact that revenge. Was he not now viewing that very opportunity in the form of the beautiful and highly desirable Miss Regana Kently?

As Wesmorlen watched the pair move through their dance, the plan took hold in his mind. Yes, it was perfect! Botheringham wanted her, of that Wesmorlen was convinced. As, too, were most of the occupants of this room. What better blow to strike against the baron, than to whisk the very woman he was quite openly and most ardently courting right out from under his nose?

The more Wesmorlen thought about it, the more he liked it. Not only did it give him the perfect chance to exact revenge against Botheringham on a most personal level, it also afforded Wesmorlen the opportunity of getting to know the delightful Miss Kently better—something he had been wanting to do since that morning he'd first seen her. Now, all he needed was a legitimate introduction and the game could begin!

At that precise moment, as though aware someone was watching her, Regana lifted her head, wondering what had compelled her to look up. She did not particularly believe in Fate, but when her blue eyes meshed with the dark eyes which were watching her so intently from across the floor, Regana gasped, aware of a tremor that ran the entire length of her body. But for the firmness of Lord Botheringham's hold, Regana knew she would have fallen, because the last person Regana had expected to see tonight was the dark, compelling stranger she'd met out riding!

IF REGANA WAS STRUCK by the impact of that glance, the earl was no less moved. Something in those unusual turquoise eyes pierced right through him, startling him afresh. He watched her move across the floor, aware of the heightened colour in her cheeks, aware, too, that he had never seen a more beautiful woman in his life.

Regana, her own mind spinning, was having trouble concentrating on her steps. The dark stranger was here, and staring at her in a most shockingly bold manner, as if she were the only young lady on the floor. She knew she was breathing quickly and that it had little to do with the dance. She realized, too, that Lord Botheringham was impatiently trying to regain her attention.

"Forgive me...my lord," she stammered, tearing her eyes away from the stranger's. "I was...lost in thought."

"Lost in thought," Botheringham snorted. "Looked more to me as if you'd seen a ghost. What were you staring at?"

"Nothing, my lord. I simply remembered something I had previously forgotten," she said, hoping it sounded a plausible excuse.

Lord Botheringham sniffed again in a most ungallant manner. "It must have been something quite extraordinary to make you trip over your own feet. You're not usually so clumsy."

Regana felt her face flush and stiffened at the insult. Immediately, Botheringham realized his mistake. "Still, as you say, Miss Kently, I'm sure your thoughts were elsewhere for but a moment. It happens to all of us, does it not?"

Try as he might, Botheringham could not pacify her with his chatter, and when he finally returned Regana to her seat at the conclusion of the dance, she dismissed him with the briefest of nods. Clarisse waited until he was well out of earshot before she leaned across and asked in evident concern, "Are you all right, Regana? You seemed rather upset when Lord Botheringham brought you back."

Regana shook her head and forced a smile to her lips. "It's nothing, Clarisse," she assured her. "Nothing worth speaking of, anyway."

Unbidden, Regana's eyes returned to the spot where she had first seen her stranger. Had she really seen him, or had she simply been dreaming? Perhaps in desperation she had merely imposed his face on that of another.

"Are you looking for someone, Regana?" Clarisse asked quietly, aware that her sister was anxiously scanning the faces in the crowd.

"No, not really," Regana said, her eyes continuing to search. "I just thought I saw someone I knew while I was dancing. But I must have been mistaken. I don't see him now."

"Him?" Clarisse repeated, her interest caught. "Which 'him' in particular are you referring to? Perhaps if you tell me what he looked like, I could help you locate him."

But such was not to be the case. The stranger was nowhere to be seen, leaving Regana to wonder if he might have already left. To further complicate the situation, Regana spied the imperious figure of Lady Loring bearing down upon her. "Oh, drat, if it's not one thing..." she murmured, glancing about for an escape.

It came to her in a most unexpected and delightful manner. Emily, Lady St. Hyde, an old and very dear friend from school, was beckoning anxiously to her from across the room and, pretending not to see Lady Loring, Regana fled.

"Regana, my dear, how wonderful to see you again," Emily said, her lovely face lighting up in genuine pleasure as Regana approached. "It's been an age since I've seen you."

"Far too long," Regana agreed affectionately, grasping the hands which were extended towards her. "Goodness,

I've missed you, Emily. It simply hasn't been the same since you left. You've no idea how much I missed the good times we used to have together.''

Regana studied her friend's face and thought how happy she looked. Inseparable at school, the two girls had continued to see each other right up to the time of Emily's brilliant marriage to Lord St. Hyde the previous year. Briefly, they'd lost touch when the St. Hydes had removed to Paris. Then, a letter had come informing Regana of their imminent return due to Emily being close to her lying-in time. A few weeks after their arrival, Emily had given birth to a beautiful girl, and had only recently returned to the whirl of events which marked the social Season.

"Emily, you look absolutely wonderful!" Regana complimented her friend now. "Motherhood certainly agrees with you. How is little Elizabeth?"

"Beautiful. And tireless," Emily laughed. "She's wound St. Hyde round her little finger. I never thought to see him so besotted by something so tiny."

Regana saw the pride in her friend's face, and experienced a momentary pang of envy. Would she ever know that kind of happiness, she wondered.

Emily cut into her thoughts. "But what about you? Why aren't you married? I hear you had a wonderful Season last year."

Regana laughed ruefully. "And how did you come by that information?" she asked. "You weren't even in England!"

"Ah, I have my ways," Emily replied knowingly. "My spies keep me very well informed. I hear any number of young gentlemen were falling all over themselves to impress you."

Regana smiled wanly, and nodded. Emily, seeing the momentary dullness in her friend's eyes, decided not to ask the question she'd been about to and said instead, "And Clarisse, how is she?"

"Clarisse is extremely well," Regana replied warmly. "She's here tonight, actually. I was speaking with her when I saw you wave."

"Good heavens! That was Clarisse? The pretty girl in the rose gown?" Emma asked. "I hardly recognized her now that she's quite the young lady. She made her come-out this year, I believe."

Regana couldn't prevent a silvery tinkle of laughter at the statement. "Emily, you never cease to amaze me. I shouldn't be surprised to hear that you know what the Prince Regent is doing even before he does."

"La, what a diverting idea," Emily said with a laugh. "Just think how sought-after I'd be for parties then. And speaking of being sought-after at parties," she said, her glance going beyond Regana, "I see another infrequent guest is gracing the gathering tonight. Dear Richard," she said, her voice softening. "How good to see him again. I must speak with him," she said, and lifted her hand to beckon to someone.

"Richard?" Regana repeated blankly, gazing out at the crush of people.

"Yes, Lord Wesmorlen," Emily explained, her surprise evident. "Oh, my dear girl, don't tell me you haven't been introduced to the most eligible bachelor in London."

"Actually, no, I haven't." Regana shook her head. "From what I've heard, though, he attends very few functions. But I wasn't aware you knew him."

"Dear me, yes. He used to visit us in Paris quite often. He's a very good friend of St. Hyde's, actually. I believe they were at Eton together."

"His arrival had Arabella Dalmeny in quite a fidge earlier," Regana remarked. "I fancy she's another one of the many hoping to catch his interest."

Emily glanced at her friend shrewdly, her sharp eyes seeing beyond the smiling exterior. "Why haven't *you* married, Regana?'' she asked softly. ''I know it couldn't be because of a lack of offers. You're far too lovely for that.''

From anyone else, the question would have been impertinent. From Emily, it was anything but. ''I don't know that I'm so terribly anxious to marry, Emily,'' Regana replied lightly. ''I've yet to find anyone who inspires that kind of emotion in me. None of them make me glow the way you do, for example, when you speak of Cecil. And until I find someone who does, I'd as lief remain single.''

Emily looked troubled at her friend's declaration. There was a sadness on Regana's lovely features she had never noticed before. Still, the girl was far from stupid, Emily thought practically. If she chose to remain single until the right man came along, so be it. After all, had she herself not done more or less the same?

At that thought, Emily broke into a smile. ''Well, we're just going to have to find someone who does make you glow. But for the moment, Regana, I think I have taken up quite enough of your time, and I perceive a gentleman here who wishes to make your acquaintance.''

Regana glanced at her friend, then in answer to her nod, fixed a smile upon her face.

''Regana, may I introduce Lord Wesmorlen? Lord Wesmorlen, Miss Regana Kently.''

As she'd long been taught to do, Regana gracefully rose and turned in the direction of the gentleman, extending her hand to accept the introduction. The words which had formed on her lips, however, were never uttered. For as her outstretched hand was grasped and raised, Regana could do little other than stare into the handsome face of Lord Wesmorlen—her tall, dark stranger!

CHAPTER FOUR

"MY PLEASURE, Miss Kently." The earl smiled down into her eyes. "And how delightful to be introduced by Lady Emily. I wasn't aware the two of you were acquainted."

"Dear man, we're far more than just acquaintances." Emily laughed affectionately. "Regana and I were at Mrs. Langdon's School for Young Ladies together. We are, in fact, the very best of friends. We haven't seen each other for a little while, so we were just having a pleasant little coze to catch up. But do tell, Richard, why is Peter not here? I understood he came down to Blackoaks with you."

"He did, but unfortunately my brother was not feeling quite up to snuff this evening," Wesmorlen replied perfunctorily. "However, I did exact a promise from him to visit you at the very first opportunity."

"And so he'd better." Emily beamed. "I miss the dear boy. And you, too, for that matter. But, goodness, here I am, prattling on, with Regana standing by ignored. I think I've monopolized you quite long enough, my dear." Emily smiled at her friend. "You should be dancing. I have no doubt your dance card is positively overflowing with partners."

Regana blushed prettily and made some demur, unable to meet the earl's eyes. Somehow, knowing that her stranger was the much sought after Earl of Wesmorlen, Regana felt uncommonly shy. Nor could she forget the abruptness with which they'd parted company on the oc-

casion of their first meeting. The earl, however, seemed
intent upon changing that impression.

"I wonder, Miss Kently, if there is one dance left on your
card which I might claim?"

Regana looked up, her surprise evident. "I'm afraid
there is not, my lord. I have just spent my last free dance
chatting with Lady St. Hyde."

"Oh, that is too bad," he said, extending his hand for the
card. "May I?"

Uncertainly, Regana gave it to him, wondering at his request. Quickly perusing the card, Wesmorlen smiled.
"Your card confirms my opinion that you are indeed a
popular young lady, Miss Kently," he said, "however, I
believe I see an opportunity."

Wesmorlen drew a line on the card and then signed his
name with a flourish. "Does that meet with your approval, Miss Kently?"

He handed Regana her card, his fingers brushing against
hers in the lightest of contacts. Regana tried to ignore the
sudden sensation of warmth which suffused her, and
sought refuge in glancing at her card. She gasped when she
saw that he had boldly struck out Lord Botheringham's
name, and written his own over it.

"I think Lord Botheringham should survive with only
two dances this evening, don't you, Miss Kently?" he asked
smoothly.

Regana glanced at Emily as if for help. "I cannot think
that Lord Botheringham will be . . . pleased at your temer-
ity, my lord," she replied hesitantly, her glance returning to
his face, "though I was truly not aware Lord Botheringham had signed his name for three dances."

"I thought perhaps you were not," the earl replied.

"But what if he—" she began.

"Pray do not concern yourself with Lord Botheringham, Miss Kently," Lord Wesmorlen said dismissively.

"My concern is that *you* are satisfied with the change. Are you?"

Glancing at the card again, Regana found herself in a distinct quandary. By striking Lord Botheringham's name from her card, Lord Wesmorlen had committed a flagrant breach of etiquette. But at the same time, he had also reduced her enforced closeness to Lord Botheringham by one dance, and right now, that seemed justification enough.

"No, my lord, I confess I am not... unhappy with the altered arrangements," she replied carefully, a reluctant smile tugging at her lips. "Just a little concerned as to the possible repercussions."

Her smile broadened, and watching her, Wesmorlen drew in his breath, taken aback by her loveliness. No wonder Botheringham's face had assumed such a possessive quality when he looked at her. She inspired that sort of protective feeling. "Set your mind at rest, Miss Kently. Should the need arise, I shall see that the blame is placed squarely upon my shoulders."

His eyes glanced at her with unconcealed admiration, and Regana felt the colour steal into her cheeks. Before she had the opportunity to reply, however, a silky, feminine voice said, "Oh, there you are, Richard, I've been looking everywhere for you. Have you forgotten this is our dance?"

Regana looked past the earl to see Amanda Chadwick waiting expectantly. Up close, the marchioness was even lovelier than she appeared at a distance. But glancing into the cold suspicious eyes, Regana knew instinctively that Lady Chadwick did not welcome competition of any kind.

"Of course I had not forgotten, Amanda," Wesmorlen replied easily, seemingly unaware of the tension in the air. "I was merely renewing my acquaintance with Lady St. Hyde, who in turn introduced me to Miss Kently. Are you ladies acquainted?"

"We are not," Lady Chadwick said briefly, her manner conveying not the slightest interest in altering that situation. When introductions were effected, however, the marchioness afforded Regana the very briefest of nods.

"Richard," Lady Chadwick repeated, slipping her arm through Wesmorlen's proprietarily, "are you coming?"

The earl nodded, but turned unhurriedly back to Emily and Regana. "Until our dance then, Miss Kently," Wesmorlen said. "Emily," he added, raising her hand to his lips.

Emily watched the pair depart, waiting until they were some distance away before commenting, "Well, that was an interesting encounter. It seems that Lady Chadwick has reentered Society with a vengeance."

Regana nodded, her smile thoughtful. "It would appear the rumours surrounding their relationship have some basis in truth, though," she commented idly. "There does seem to be something between them."

"I think not," Emily remarked sagely, "or at least not in the way you may be thinking, my dear." She glanced at Regana with satisfaction. "But I certainly think *you* made an impression on Wesmorlen."

Regana hesitated, unsure of how to reply. Emily was hardly to know that she and the earl had already met, nor that their first meeting had ended so abysmally. But Regana had to confess that Lord Wesmorlen had not acted at all the way he had at the time of their first meeting. He had seemed genuinely delighted at seeing her again, and equally intent upon securing a dance. Surely he wouldn't have done that merely out of obligation to Emily.

Aware that she was engaged for the next dance, Regana bade her friend goodbye, promising to call on her the very next day. Turning, Regana smiled up into the face of her next partner, a rather dashing young captain who wasted no time in telling her how very lovely and charming she was. Regana pretended to listen, her attention wandering as her eyes sought out the tall, commanding figure of Lord Wesmorlen. She saw him dancing with the beautiful Amanda, the marchioness's smile dazzling as she laughed up into his face at something he'd said. There was no doubt they made a striking couple, and for a moment, Regana felt her heart turn over.

Then, unexpectedly, Wesmorlen lifted his head and looked directly at her, the intensity of his gaze almost taking her breath away. Guiltily, Regana averted her own eyes. But not before he'd seen the tell-tale colour stain her cheeks, the sight of which brought the faintest smile to his lips.

The next dance was the one promised to him—and to Lord Botheringham. With growing trepidation, Regana watched as Lord Botheringham approached her, intercepting the nod which passed between himself and the musicians. Regana gasped in dismay as the lilting strains of a waltz filled the room. Oh, no! She had not expected her first dance with Lord Wesmorlen to be a waltz. Now, she had no choice, unless the earl himself withdrew. And she knew instinctively he was not the sort of man to relinquish anything to which he felt he had a right!

"My waltz, I believe, Miss Kently," Botheringham said, a satisfied smile on his lips.

"I think not, Botheringham," Wesmorlen's voice cut in quietly from behind. "I believe you'll find there has been a slight change in the programme."

Regana, glancing at the baron, was startled to see the look of fear which momentarily settled upon his features as he spun round to face the earl. But then, just as quickly, it disappeared.

"Wesmorlen!" Botheringham snapped, his tone indicating that the two men were acquainted, but not favourably. "To what do we owe the honour of your august presence this evening? I understood these affairs were not to your liking."

"Generally, they are not," came the bland reply. "Though I find this evening they have taken on a charming new appearance," he continued softly, glancing at Regana.

Botheringham did not miss the heightened colour in Regana's cheeks. "We are, of course, delighted to see you," the baron lied smoothly, "but, if you will excuse us, this is my dance."

"Correction, Botheringham, it *was* your dance." The earl reached for Regana's hand. "I took the liberty of altering the order of things somewhat."

The older man blanched, then flushed with anger. "You did *what?*"

"I took the liberty of substituting my name for this dance, Botheringham."

"I think you assume too much, Wesmorlen," Botheringham retorted furiously. "The lady was promised to me this dance."

"Unless the lady is *engaged* to you, my lord," the earl replied frostily, "three dances is hardly the thing. And unless you wish to damage her reputation by causing a scene right here on the dance floor, I suggest you content yourself with two dances. Miss Kently?"

Without waiting for Botheringham's reply, the earl placed a hand lightly on Regana's waist and guided her onto the floor. She felt rather than saw the other man's rage, and was about to glance behind her.

"No, don't look around," the earl said quietly in her ear. "Botheringham is drawing quite enough attention to himself at the moment. Let people think it was he in the wrong and not you."

"But he was not in the wrong, my lord. He was coming to claim me for a dance which he had duly reserved."

The earl looked down into her upturned face, fighting a sudden, inexplicable urge to kiss that adorable nose. "Are you promised to him?" he asked abruptly.

Regana blinked, and for what seemed like the hundredth time that evening, felt her cheeks grow warm. "No, my lord, I am not."

"Then he has no right to three dances with you, Miss Kently. Unless you wish it known by your actions that you hope to be promised to him."

Unconsciously, the earl held his breath. Regana, raising her jewellike eyes to his dark ones, detected no mockery in his gaze, and her voice, when she answered, held no quaver. "No, my lord, I am not."

"Good." He carefully released his breath. "Then shall we dance, Miss Kently?" he said with a smile.

Wesmorlen drew her to him and put his arm round her waist. Unaccustomed to such close proximity with a man, Regana kept her face averted. But she was not uncomfortable. Indeed, she was at a loss to put a name to the heady emotions she was feeling. They moved slowly across the floor, his dark head close to hers, their bodies flowing in time to the music.

"*Humph,* they don't seem to be making much conversation," Lady Loring commented to Clarisse with satisfaction as they watched the pair glide by. "He was much more animated when he was dancing with Arabella."

But seeing the look on her sister's face, Clarisse put little stock in Lady Loring's pronouncement. Sometimes more was said by silence than by trivial conversation.

Regana had little memory of the remainder of the evening. The earl escorted her from the floor at the conclusion of the waltz, and bowed over her hand. "Thank you, Miss Kently. I hope you will do me the honour of more than one dance at our next meeting."

"I think that can be arranged, my lord," she responded lightly. "And without the necessity of having to alter the . . . order of things unduly."

The smile she was beginning to know so well curved his lips. "Are you concerned about Lord Botheringham?" he asked.

Regana shook her head thoughtfully. "Not for myself," she replied, "though I should be quite surprised if you don't hear from him."

"Then you have nothing to worry about," Wesmorlen replied airily. "As I mentioned, I'm quite capable of dealing with Botheringham, should the need arise."

Little did either of them know how quickly that confrontation would come about. After Regana and her family had left, Wesmorlen and Bancroft bade goodnight to their hosts and made to enter the earl's carriage, when a voice forestalled him. "Wesmorlen, a word if you don't mind."

Surprised, the earl stopped and turned to see Botheringham watching him, his expression carefully veiled.

"Rather late for a discussion, isn't it, Botheringham?" Wesmorlen said, pausing with one foot on the step.

"I think not," the baron replied mildly. "Though if you would prefer to meet me somewhere more private..." he said, indicating with his eyes the interested looks they were receiving from departing guests.

"I don't see that we have anything which needs saying, in private or otherwise," Wesmorlen said flatly.

"Ah, I beg to disagree with you, my lord," Botheringham remarked casually. "I think we have a great deal to talk about."

"Regarding?"

"Regarding Miss Kently, as I think you well know."

Wesmorlen heaved an audible sigh and stepped down from the carriage, dimly aware that his plan was already beginning to work.

"What do you want, Botheringham?" he said impatiently. He saw Lord Botheringham sneer, and willed himself not to give in to his own longing to darken the man's daylight then and there.

"I'm surprised at you, Wesmorlen," Botheringham commented. "What you did earlier this evening was hardly the work of a gentleman."

"On the contrary, Botheringham, what I did was most gentlemanly. If you had, as you'd so obviously planned, stood up for three dances with Miss Kently, it would have been tantamount to announcing to all assembled that you wished to marry the girl. And by standing up with you, Miss Kently would as much have consented."

"Did it not occur to you, Wesmorlen, that I *do* plan to marry the chit? And that, all things considered, I see no reason why she should not accept my suit?"

"No, actually it hadn't," the earl said, feigning indifference. "I thought you would have found her a trifle young for your liking."

"Not at all," Botheringham replied, smiling in a way the earl found most disagreeable. "Personally, I prefer a young wife. No bad habits to undo, and of course, she would be most biddable."

"You value obedience in a wife, I take it," the earl said, masking the anger which was growing in him by the minute.

"Most assuredly."

"I further assume that love is not an overly important requirement in your relationship?"

"Love?" Botheringham scoffed. "Since when was love a necessity in marriage? I require a gracious hostess, someone with the ability to capably look after the running of my houses, and eventually to bear my children. Miss Kently possesses such qualities."

"And what do you offer in return, Botheringham?" the earl couldn't resist asking.

"Frankly, I don't see that it's any of your business," Botheringham said curtly. "Suffice it to say she should be satisfied being the wife of an extremely wealthy man with a title and a position in Society.''

And pitied for everything else, the earl thought. Suddenly, he was weary of the entire conversation, and of Botheringham in particular. "I have no desire to linger here any longer, Botheringham," he said, turning back towards his carriage. "Have you said all you wanted to say?''

"I believe so, though I will reiterate one thing." Botheringham approached the earl and lowered his voice. "I intend to offer for the girl and I don't expect to encounter any...difficulties. Do I make myself clear, Wesmorlen?''

"Are you warning me away from her?" the earl responded, his voice carefully neutral.

"Interpret it as you will," Botheringham snapped.

With that, he turned on his heel and marched away. Wesmorlen, carefully maintaining the bland expression he'd adopted at the outset of the interview, climbed into his carriage and bade the driver set off.

"What was all that about?" Bancroft asked as soon as they were under way. Wesmorlen flicked an invisible piece of lint from his jacket and pulled on his smooth leather gloves. "Nothing of importance," he replied finally. "It seems that Botheringham is interested in Miss Kently and feels that I may afford him some difficulties in that direction."

The baronet smiled at his friend affably. "And do you?''

The earl didn't answer immediately. In his mind, he reviewed everything Botheringham had said, remembering all too well the expressions which had accompanied those words. "Miss Kently is a very attractive young lady," he finally said by way of response. "And, unless I'm mistaken, does not hold Botheringham in particularly high esteem." Wesmorlen smiled thoughtfully. "Further, it's my understanding that all's fair in love and war, Gerald.''

Bancroft regarded his friend shrewdly. "I don't doubt for a moment that this will more strongly resemble a war than anything else, Richard. But I advise you to have a care. Botheringham is not the man to cross, as well you know."

Wesmorlen slanted a narrow smile at his friend. "I'm surprised at you, Gerald. Are you not the one who's been nagging me to give some thought to settling down and installing a wife at Blackoaks? Am I not now thinking of doing exactly that? Besides, the decision will be Miss Kently's in the end, after all."

Bancroft nodded, though cautiously. "Tell me, Richard—this sudden interest in the Kently woman. It wouldn't be motivated by what Botheringham did to your brother last spring, would it?"

It was a question the earl had expected, especially given that Bancroft knew him so well. But it was not one to which he was willing to give an answer, even to his closest friend. "As I said, Gerald, I am not reluctant to further an acquaintance with a beautiful woman."

Recognizing the tone of finality in the earl's voice, Bancroft shook his head, aware that he was unlikely to learn any more. "All right, Richard, I won't presume to delve any further. I just hope no one is hurt, if you take my meaning."

"*No one* shall be hurt, I assure you," the earl said distinctly. "And if I do end up offering for Miss Kently, is it not a match that many ladies would welcome?"

"Perhaps," Bancroft replied, his voice tense, "though not if they knew they were being used in a game of revenge."

It was a daring thrust, and one which the earl would not have accepted from many. Even now, Wesmorlen's dark eyes glittered dangerously, but he willed his emotions under control. "Revenge, Gerald?" he repeated, as a picture of the beautiful lady impressed itself on his mind. "I can hardly credit my courtship of a beautiful woman as having anything to do with revenge. In point of fact, if what I heard tonight is true, Miss Kently would be freed from a relationship she neither wants nor would welcome. I see no element of revenge in that."

IN SPITE OF HER RESOLVE to rise early, Regana slept later than usual the next morning and awoke to find the sun already well risen in the sky. Donning a pale lavender morning gown, she quickly made her way down to the breakfast parlour, only to find that neither Clarisse nor her aunt was about.

"Have my aunt and sister breakfasted yet, Marie?" Regana asked, smiling at the girl as she set a silver pot filled with coffee on the sideboard.

"No, Miss Regana. Mrs. Standish is feeling a mite poorly this morning, and Miss Clarisse asked for a tray in her room," the girl informed her. "She said to tell you that she was rather tired after the festivities last evening, but that she would be down directly."

Regana nodded in satisfaction, and helped herself to a small portion of toast and eggs from the sideboard. Clarisse must have had a good time to want to take breakfast in her room. She was a confirmed early riser, and for her to linger abed until midmorning was a most unusual occurrence.

Gazing out of the mullioned windows, Regana found her own thoughts returning to the events of the previous evening, and in particular, to the Earl of Wesmorlen. She still found it difficult to accept that the elusive earl was actually the man she'd met while riding the other morning. How different he had seemed last night: so charming, and not at all like the cool, distant stranger he'd been at their first meeting. Indeed, for once it seemed the gossips hadn't exaggerated. Handsome, charming, and adept at turning even the most intimidating dowager's head, Lord Wesmorlen was everything she'd heard him rumoured to be, and more. Yet for all his qualities, he appeared remarkably unconceited. At the ball, he had moved about the room chatting

with debutante and dowager alike. He had even stood up
with Hortense Chapman once, bringing a smile of such
amazed delight to that lady's face as to render her almost
attractive. Of course, he had also danced with the accred-
ited beauties like Arabella Dalmeny, Regana conceded, remembering Lady Dalmeny's obvious satisfaction. And the
widowed Marchioness of Chadwick.

It was clear from the disapproval on many hopeful
mothers' faces that Lady Chadwick's presence at the ball
was unwelcome. Wealthy, titled and extremely available,
she had to be viewed as a formidable opponent. Even Lord
Botheringham had seemed momentarily dazzled by her
beauty, before his mask of polite indifference had slipped
back into place.

Regana allowed the hint of a smile to cross her lips as she
nibbled at her toast. Could it be that the elderly baron was
human, after all? That he was not immune to a woman's
beauty and charms, as she'd suspected.

It was an interesting idea, but one which Regana felt little inclination to pursue, and it was with some dismay that
she received Wrigly's announcement that Lord Botheringham had called and was awaiting her attendance in the
library.

"Goodness, whatever could have brought him at such an
early hour?" Regana remarked, glancing down at the gold
watch she wore pinned to her gown. "Lord Botheringham
is usually such a stickler for convention."

"He did say it was a matter of some importance, miss,"
Wrigly added.

"Oh, dear, how inconvenient," Regana muttered. "I had
certainly not thought to entertain his lordship this morning. And Clarisse is still abed."

"Would you like me to tell the gentleman that you are
not at home to visitors, miss?" Wrigly enquired hopefully,
anxious to be of service to his young mistress, and well
aware that she was not particularly enamoured of her caller.

Regana was tempted, but then shook her head. Her training would not allow her to lie or seem rude, and by not appearing she ran the risk of doing both. Besides, Clarisse would probably be down before much longer. Surely she could tolerate Lord Botheringham for a few minutes.

"Thank you, Wrigly, but no, I'll see Lord Botheringham. Perhaps you could have Marie find out how soon my sister will be down, though, and make sure she joins us as soon as possible."

"At once, miss," he said. "I'm sure Miss Clarisse will be in agreement."

Encouraged by his assurances, Regana rose and smoothed down her skirt. After waiting as long as she dared, she proceeded down the hall to the library. As she opened the door to find Lord Botheringham restlessly pacing the length of the room, she wasn't sure whether she just imagined the frown of annoyance on his features, for in an instant it was replaced by the bland, polite smile she knew so well.

"Good morning, Miss Kently," he greeted her. "You appear well rested after last evening's entertainments."

"I am, thank you, my lord," Regana replied. She forced a bright note into her voice and advanced into the room. "Did you enjoy the festivities? I thought the musicians quite accomplished."

"I suppose they were," he answered noncommittally. He hesitated as Regana settled herself in a wing chair by the French doors. "It seems you sat out very few dances."

Regana's smile remained fixed. "I enjoy dancing, Lord Botheringham. It is one of the reasons I attend the balls and parties. Besides, young ladies are expected to dance."

"Not to mention that dancing provides an atmosphere for mingling and meeting new people," Lord Botheringham continued.

Regana viewed his vaguely disapproving face mildly. "It does, but is that not the general purpose, sir?" she replied, her blue eyes sparkling. "Only think how monotonous it would be if one knew exactly who would be at every party. What, pray, would there be to discuss if not the foibles or attractions of new faces?"

"Such as the faces you encountered last night?" Botheringham suggested.

Regana glanced at him in surprise. She knew exactly what the baron was referring to, but was intrigued that he should draw attention to it. Was it possible the man was jealous?

"I encountered many new faces last evening, Lord Botheringham. Is there one specifically to whom you refer, or were you talking in generalities?"

"Miss Kently, I think you know quite well to whom I refer."

"Do I?" she replied. "Then perhaps you would be so good as to enlighten me, Lord Botheringham, for in truth you have the better of me."

"I refer, Miss Kently, to Lord Wesmorlen."

Upon hearing the name, Regana hesitated ever so slightly. "Oh, Lord Wesmorlen," Regana said, as if only just recalling his face. Her lips twitched spontaneously. "Yes, of course, now I recall—the gentleman they call the Unmarriageable Earl."

Botheringham looked at her askance. "I beg your pardon! The what?"

"Oh, did you not know that is what they have dubbed him?" Regana smiled, enjoying her game. "But no, perhaps you would not. I was only informed of it myself at the ball. And Lady St. Hyde confirmed it just after we were introduced."

The baron clearly did not share her amusement. "I see. And did *you* seek these introductions, Miss Kently?" he asked.

Regana raised beautiful eyes to his, her smile cooling ever so slightly. It was a coming question, and one which he should not have had the audacity to ask.

"As a lady, it is not my place to request an introduction, Lord Botheringham, as well *you* know," she replied quietly. "I was speaking with Lady St. Hyde when the earl approached. As he and Lady St. Hyde were acquainted, it was she who quite naturally performed the introductions. Indeed, it would have appeared markedly odd had Lord Wesmorlen continued to converse with Lady St. Hyde and ignored me. Do you not think so, my lord?"

"Miss Kently, I assure you I meant no offence, though I fear perhaps offence has been taken," he said, hastily sensing her reserve. "Please accept my apology. I should have known, of course, that *you* would do nothing untoward."

Regana inclined her head. "Thank you, Lord Botheringham, though I fail to understand your particular concern. In asking to be introduced *and* in requesting a dance, Lord Wesmorlen did nothing untoward, either."

"Nothing untoward?" Botheringham replied, astounded. "My dear girl, the man scratched my name from your dance card in a manner I can only call reprehensible. I consider that *most* untoward. And quite underhanded!"

"On the contrary, Lord Botheringham," Regana replied firmly. "It was you who acted in a reprehensible manner. You had no right to mark yourself down for three dances, and had I noticed you'd done so, I would have sought you out earlier and asked you to withdraw one. After all, to stand up with a gentleman for three dances, especially when one of them was a waltz, would have suggested there was some form of . . . attachment between us."

"And is there not, Miss Kently?" Lord Botheringham said, coming to stand by her side. "Have I not given you sufficient reason to believe that there is some attachment between us?''

Regana rose uncomfortably and moved behind the heavy, mahogany desk. She was afraid Botheringham was going to declare himself, and quite frankly, it was the last thing she wanted to hear. But what could she say to prevent him? And where was Clarisse, she wondered, casting a hopeful glance towards the library door. If ever Regana needed her sister, it was now.

''Miss Kently,'' Botheringham was saying, ''I think perhaps the time has come for me to make myself a little clearer. Pray, be seated.''

Regana hesitated. She knew it was rude to remain standing behind the desk, but she was loath to resume her chair. ''If you don't mind, Lord Botheringham, I think I should prefer to stand,'' she replied. She met his gaze levelly, wondering whether she imagined the brief flash of annoyance in his eyes again.

''As you like,'' he said dismissively. He cleared his throat. ''Miss Kently, I think you know that I have regarded you with approval for some time now. Apart from your being pleasant to look upon, your manners and conduct have always impressed me as being above reproach. As well, your inherent skill in running an establishment and of being its chatelaine are qualities I require in a wife. In short, I believe you are eminently suited to the position I have to offer.''

''You flatter me, my lord,'' Regana murmured, eyes downcast.

''Not at all. I, in turn, have much to offer you,'' Botheringham continued, drawing forth an ornate snuff box and flipping up its lid with an expert hand. ''A title, a respected position within society, houses here and in London and, of course, the wealth so necessary to maintain one's manner of living. All of these I am willing to put at your disposal.'' He paused, returning the snuff box to his breast pocket. "I admit, Miss Kently, that I have been reluctant to take a wife simply because I had not found a woman possessed of suitable qualifications. But a man in my position must marry, and you, with your beauty, intellect and remarkably practical outlook on life, satisfy all my requirements admirably."

Regana listened to the baron's recitation and couldn't help but wonder whether she was receiving a marriage proposal or a business offer. He'd neatly summed up her qualities, weighed them against what he had to offer and had come to the conclusion that they were equal. Now all he had to do was set out the terms and they could shake hands and consider it done.

"Miss Kently," he said again, "are you listening to me?"

"Of course, Lord Botheringham, every word."

"Yes, well, as I was saying, I would, of course, like to speak to Mrs. Standish and officially request her permission to address you. Until such time as I have done so, I don't expect an answer from you. Can you tell me when I might be able to speak with her?"

Aware that she was to be given a brief reprieve, Regana spoke up quickly. "Unfortunately, my lord, my aunt is not well. She suffers with headaches, and it is difficult to say when she will be sufficiently recovered to speak with you."

"I see." He was clearly not pleased. "Do you think she might be sufficiently recovered by this evening?"

On this point at least, Regana could speak truthfully. "No, my lord. Regrettably, the excitement of the ball last evening quite drained her and she has removed to her bed. Such exertion usually renders her immobile for the better part of two days."

"Ah. That is unfortunate," Lord Botheringham commented, more to himself than to her. In light of Wesmorlen's sudden and most unwelcome interest in Miss Kently, this was definitely not what he wanted to hear. "Yes, most unfortunate. I have business matters which necessitate my

leaving for the City tomorrow morning. Normally, I would
let my man of business deal with it, but I feel this situation
calls for my personal attention. I doubt I shall return before the week is out. I fear my meeting with Mrs. Standish
shall have to wait until next week.''

By not so much as a flicker did Regana betray her relief.
''I quite understand, Lord Botheringham. I would not wish
your business interests to suffer over a matter such as this,''
she replied caustically.

Missing her ironic tone completely, Botheringham nodded his approval. ''I think we shall deal very well together,
Miss Kently. You have a sensible head on your shoulders,
one not cluttered with romantic drivel and nonsensical
ideas. I can think of a few ladies who would do well to take
a page from your book. In the meantime, I hope now that
I have made you aware of my intentions, you will, er, how
shall I say, govern yourself accordingly.''

Regana looked at Lord Botheringham in bewilderment.
Either the man was very confident, or very conceited, she
thought, unable to decide which. She had granted him the
opportunity of speaking to her privately, without a chaperon, and had listened while he enumerated in the most un-
romantic manner possible, the advantages of a match
between them. He had made no mention of his feelings towards her, leaving Regana to assume that he had none, and
now had the audacity to ask her to govern herself accordingly—which, Regana knew, included turning down any
invitations which might arrive from other gentlemen—as if
they were in fact betrothed.

Well, he had a great deal to learn about Regana Kently,
she thought with annoyance. Coming round from behind
the desk, she gazed up at him, her back very erect, her chin
lifting proudly.

''Lord Botheringham,'' she said, ''I have always acted in
a manner befitting the situation, whatever that situation has
been. Such was my training, of which you speak so highly.

I understand that you came here this morning to make me aware of your intentions, and you have done so. However, I am not to consider that you have proposed. Is that correct?''

"Well, yes..." He nodded. "Not... formally, that is."

"If not formally, then not at all," she responded quietly. "Further, I understand that you wish to speak with my aunt prior to making any formal address to me, and that until you are able to do so, I am not bound by any promise to you. Is that also correct?"

"Dash it all, of course you're not bound," the baron huffed. "I simply wanted you to be... aware of my intentions."

"Which I am, Lord Botheringham. And I am, of course, flattered. However," she continued, crossing to the bell-rope, "I fear I must ask you to leave. I have been awaiting the arrival of my sister, but as I feel I have lingered as long as I dare unchaperoned, I think this meeting should be at an end. Ah, Wrigly," she said, almost laughing at the alacrity with which her butler appeared, due no doubt to his hovering nearby in anticipation of her call. "I believe Lord Botheringham was just leaving."

"I was? Ah, yes, perhaps I was," he amended, catching sight of the butler's stony face. "Well, thank you, Miss Kently. I shall call upon you again next week when it is to be hoped we may continue this discussion. Good morning, Miss Kently," he added to Clarisse as they passed each other in the doorway.

"Lord Botheringham," Clarisse said, surprised to find her sister alone with the gentleman. As soon as he had departed, she demanded, "Regana, what did I miss? What were you doing alone with Lord Botheringham in the library?" Then, she gasped and her eyes grew as big as saucers. "Oh Lord, he didn't propose, did he?"

"He did, and he didn't," Regana said, tucking her arm in Clarisse's and escorting her back to the breakfast room.

"This was not the morning for you to linger in bed, little sister," she teased, and proceded to relate the highlights of Lord Botheringham's address.

CHAPTER FIVE

As PROMISED, Regana and Clarisse set out for Emily St. Hyde's that very afternoon. Not surprisingly, Aunt Mary had begged off owing to her headache, leaving Clarisse to accompany her sister, albeit somewhat reluctantly.

"Well, Emily is more your friend than mine," Clarisse protested gently as they set off. "I thought you would have preferred to be private, to catch up on all that's been happening. After all, she has been away for quite some time."

"Which is precisely why you should come with me, Clarisse," Regana explained. She surveyed her sister's deep pink day dress with approval. "Even though Emily has been away, she has an uncanny knack of knowing exactly what's been going on in her absence. What's more, I seriously doubt we'll find her alone today: Emily seldom lacks for company!"

Regana's predictions proved to be remarkably accurate. Upon their arrival at the St. Hydes' stately Jacobean manor house, they were not unduly surprised to find that Emily already had visitors in the form of Lady Dalmeny and her daughter Arabella.

"Well, this is a pleasant surprise," Emily said genuinely, her warm smile encompassing them all when everyone was seated again. "I really didn't expect to see so many people today. I was sure you'd all be abed, recovering from the effects of a late night."

"Now, Emily," Lady Dalmeny chided, "you know me better than that. I've never been one for lying abed. Too many opportunities missed, I always say."

"Yes, you always were an early riser, Constance," Emily amended good-naturedly. "But what about you, Arabella?" she said, turning to regard the girl who looked quite lovely this morning in a gown of blue-and-white striped silk, the blue matching the colour of her eyes. "I would have thought you a little tired after the evening's festivities."

"Oh, not at all, Lady St. Hyde," Arabella bubbled happily. "I could hardly sleep at all. I tried, but I was really too excited. It was such a wonderful evening."

Her expression became rather dreamy, and Regana couldn't help but wonder whether the memory of the earl's presence had something to do with that.

The tea was brought in and placed next to Emily. While she was pouring, Lady Dalmeny steered the conversation back to the events of the previous evening. "I don't wish to give the impression I'm rushing my fences," she began, "but I do admit to feeling rather pleased that Lord Wesmorlen chose to honour us with his presence last evening. Everyone knows how few functions he attends."

"Yes, so I've heard," Emily replied, carefully hiding a smile. "To what do you attribute his appearance, Constance?"

"Well, again, I don't wish to appear beforehand," Lady Dalmeny said, visibly puffing up, "but I don't believe I'd be speaking out of turn if I were to say I think he may have come to see Arabella. She is, after all, a beautiful girl, and it's well known that his lordship is looking for a wife this Season. That's why he's taken up residence at Blackoaks again."

"Really? Now, that is strange," Emily said, pausing in the act of pouring Lady Dalmeny's tea. "I was under the impression that he was definitely not looking to marry this year, but rather that he was bringing his younger brother down to convalesce. Or was it something to do with the management of the estate?''

She pretended not to notice the sudden downturn of Arabella's pretty mouth, and fixed a bright smile on her lips. ''But then, I may be wrong. You never know which rumours to believe, do you, my dear? There always seem to be so many flying about. Regana, will you take milk or lemon in your tea?''

The conversation moved on to another topic, much to the chagrin of Lady Dalmeny, who obviously felt the topic of Lord Wesmorlen had not yet been exhausted. They were just settling in to discuss the shocking amount of money the Prince Regent was spending on his elaborate summer house in Brighton, when Evans, the butler, announced in his sonorous tones the arrival of Lord Wesmorlen and the Honourable Peter Wesmorlen.

A hush fell over the room, then Lady Dalmeny rose, moving with an alacrity Regana wouldn't have credited, given the lady's generous proportions, and exchanged places with Arabella so that her daughter should have a vacant seat next to her on the settee.

''Well, I am treated to yet another delightful surprise,'' Emily said, positively beaming as the gentlemen entered. ''I had no idea we'd have the pleasure of your company today, Richard. And Peter, dear boy, it's been an age since I've seen you. Come in, my dears, and sit down. What a welcome diversion you've provided. The ladies and I were just about to indulge in another round of gossip.''

Lord Wesmorlen smiled at her fondly. ''Perhaps you would prefer that we left you ladies to continue your chat. I should hate to think that our arrival had put a damper on the proceedings, Emily.''

''It certainly won't do that, my lord,'' Emily assured him, a sparkle in her eyes. ''We simply won't be able to discuss *you* as we'd intended, that's all. Besides, you don't think I'd actually let two of the most highly eligible young gentlemen of the ton escape my drawing-room that easily, do you? Silly boy! Now do come and sit down. And, bless me, if I'm being most remiss in my duties, not even attending to the introductions. I don't believe you know these ladies, do you, Peter?"

"Unfortunately, I have not had the pleasure, Emily." Peter smiled his confirmation.

"As I thought. Mr. Peter Wesmorlen, may I present Lady Dalmeny and her daughter Arabella. And the Misses Regana and Clarisse Kently from Grantly Hall."

Peter acknowledged the introductions, bowing slightly over each of the ladies' hands in turn. When he came to Clarisse, however, he seemed to hesitate, a sudden flush of colour infusing his cheeks as he raised her hand to his lips. His admiration was plain to see, and Regana noticed his eyes lingering appreciatively on her sister's blushing cheeks and demurely downcast eyes.

"Well, now that everyone is acquainted," Emily announced, smiling at both brothers equally, "you must sit down and join us."

"Are you sure we're not intruding?" Wesmorlen asked again, his glance touching briefly on each of the ladies present before coming to rest on Regana. "I'd hate to think we had prevented you from hearing the latest on-dits, especially as you've only just returned from Paris."

"On the contrary, Lord Wesmorlen," Regana said to cover her confusion. "I believe it will be Lady St. Hyde regaling us with the latest on-dits." She glanced at her friend affectionately. "I do not believe there's much that escapes her notice."

"You're quite right, Regana, there isn't." Emily laughed good-naturedly. "Perhaps that's what comes from being abroad. Everyone is so anxious to bring me up to date on what I've missed that I end up knowing more than the ones who've stayed. Although I hear remarkably little about you, Richard. Or you Peter," Emily said, indicating with her eyes the vacant chair next to Clarisse. "What do you do to avoid the wagging tongues so effectively?"

After a moment's hesitation, Peter settled himself in the chair next to Clarisse. He was a good-looking young man, slighter in build than his brother and fairer both in hair and in complexion. But his warm brown eyes reflected a genuine kindness, and Regana couldn't help but like him. She had been momentarily surprised to see him walking with the aid of a cane, and briefly wondered how he'd come by the injury to his leg. Now, he put the cane behind the settee, as if he preferred not to draw attention to it.

"Actually, Emily, I, like you, am only recently returned to the country. I've been rusticating in the wilds of Scotland."

"Scotland! Ah, yes, I recall your dear mother telling me about it," Emily remarked. "I understand you have a rather large property somewhere up there."

"Large and draughty!" Peter laughed, his boyish face lighting up attractively. "Mama thought I should spend some time at each of the estates once I finished Oxford. I suppose she started me with the worst so that I could better appreciate the others."

"Is it really as isolated as you say, Mr. Wesmorlen?" Clarisse asked shyly.

Peter turned to regard her, and grinned ruefully. "I suppose not," he admitted, "though compared to London and hereabouts it does seem very remote." He accepted the refreshments handed to him by Emily, and added, "I think I've seen enough moors and heather to last me for the rest of my life!"

The ladies laughed at the mournful expression on his face. "Well, that explains how you've managed to stay out of harm's way," Emily remarked. "And what about you, Richard? Are you planning to stay long at Blackoaks?"

"Yes, Lord Wesmorlen," Arabella chirped, smiling prettily in the hope that he still might sit down beside her. "Are you glad to be back in the country?"

The earl nodded, a devilish light appearing in his eyes. "Indeed I am, Miss Dalmeny. London is an exciting place, but sometimes one must remove oneself from it for a while in order to better appreciate its attractions. I also find the country very... pretty at this time of year."

The comment was clearly meant as a compliment, and, as intended, Arabella took it as one, giggling and blushing becomingly. Looking on, Lady Dalmeny beamed her approval. "Does that mean you intend to stay for a while, Lord Wesmorlen?" she asked.

Carefully hiding his smile, Wesmorlen nodded. "I think perhaps I shall. There are a number of things I hope to accomplish while I'm here, not the least of which is taking more control over the running of Blackoaks. I also admit to having been somewhat remiss in my social duties." He glanced at his brother ruefully. "So I have taken it upon myself to reintroduce Peter to Society. And I could think of nowhere better to start than with you, Emily."

"Oh, you do talk such fustian," Emily answered, though clearly not displeased. "Of course you must start with me. I would have been quite out of curl if you hadn't. And speaking of mingling," Emily said, turning now to regard Clarisse, "you were quite the success last night, my dear. I believe I saw you sit out no more than two dances all evening."

Aware that all eyes were now focussed on her, Clarisse felt her cheeks turn a becoming shade of pink. "Yes, it was a lovely ball," she replied, smiling in spite of her nervousness. "It would have been very difficult not to have had a good time."

"I hear you looked quite the thing, Miss Kently," Peter said earnestly. "I'm only sorry I wasn't there to ask you for a dance. Perhaps you will do me the honour of keeping one for me at Lady Chadwick's ball next week.''

His words fell into a startled silence, and Regana wasn't the only one to look at him in surprise.

''Amanda Chadwick is giving a ball?'' Lady Dalmeny sniffed, her eyebrows lifting until they almost disappeared. ''Isn't she being just a little precipitate? After all, she's only just out of her widow's weeds.''

''Now, Constance, you can hardly expect Amanda to play the grieving widow forever,'' Emily said, never one to fear speaking plainly. ''I'm sure it took all Amanda's resolve to wear black as long as she did.''

''I don't doubt it,'' Lady Dalmeny replied haughtily, ''but I still say she's being a mite too hasty in planning a ball.'' She looked at Emily sharply. ''Are you saying you approve of what she's doing?''

''I'm not saying I approve or disapprove, Constance,'' Lady St. Hyde replied calmly. ''But I believe it is not for anyone to judge how much or how long a wife grieves for her husband. Amanda has completed her required year and she is fully entitled to reenter Society and enjoy what it has to offer. And if that includes giving a ball, then so be it. Frankly, I'm not in the least surprised that she's giving one so soon.''

''Do you intend to attend, then, Lady St. Hyde?'' Arabella asked timidly.

''Why, yes, dear, if I am invited.''

''I have it on the best authority that everyone is to be invited,'' Wesmorlen said. ''Amanda informed me of her plans last night.''

At this, a few knowing glances were exchanged.

''Capital!'' Peter said brightly. He directed a smile at Clarisse. ''Then you will be able to have that dance with me, Miss Kently.''

Clarisse glanced up at him with a mixture of surprise, pleasure and embarrassment. "Well, yes...I should be delighted to. If we attend, of course."

"I certainly hope you shall," Wesmorlen cut in. "I too, look forward to the pleasure of a dance, Miss Kently," he said, looking directly at Regana, "and one for which I shall not be obliged to fight."

"Yes, that was a rather interesting...arrangement you made last night, Richard," Emily murmured. "Quite put Lord Botheringham out of sorts, from what I hear."

The earl shrugged eloquently. "It seemed to me the least I could do. He was, to my way of thinking, monopolizing Miss Kently in a rather presumptuous manner. And, as I pointed out to him, asking a lady for three dances is tantamount to asking for her hand."

"Well, perhaps that was his intention, my lord," Lady Dalmeny remarked matter-of-factly. "I hear through the tattle-mongers that Lord Botheringham claims himself an ardent suitor of yours, Regana."

Thoroughly discomfitted, Regana shook her head. "If he is, I am quite unaware of it, Lady Dalmeny."

"You could do a lot worse, Regana," Arabella piped up, adding insult to injury. "He is very rich, after all."

"So is the Viscount Blanchford," Emily spoke up quickly, seeing the panic in her friend's eyes. "But nobody wants to marry him."

"Well, of course not!" Lady Dalmeny informed them archly. "That's because he's an obnoxious little man who drinks too much and spends far too freely. His family quite despairs of him. And did you hear about the latest goings-on with his sister...?"

As the conversation veered off into safer channels, Regana slowly released the breath she'd been holding, aware that her hands had been gripping the delicate china saucer so tightly that her knuckles were white. Was this what her life was to be, she wondered, oblivious to the conversation

going on about her. Was she to be subjected to an endless
series of cross-examinations from friends and family alike
until she finally succumbed to whatever man happened to
be paying her court? It wasn't fair, she thought crossly.
What right did other people have to tell her whom she
should marry? She didn't even *like* Lord Botheringham, yet
it seemed to everyone present that she had no good reason
not to accept him, should he offer. Couldn't they understand that she would as lief remain single as marry a man
she didn't love?

Belatedly, she realized that the conversation had veered
once more, and that Emily was trying to recapture her attention. She glanced up guiltily, flushing even more when
she saw Wesmorlen regarding her intently.

"Regana, dear, are you listening to me?" Emily said with
a smile. "I asked if you and Clarisse were planning to go to
Lord Tyler's picnic. It promises to be quite a nice affair."

"If the weather holds," Lady Dalmeny commented
dryly. "We were rained out at Lady Montague's garden
party last week. And I in my new bonnet. Ruined. Quite
ruined."

Regana caught the sparkle in Emily's eye and hastily
averted her own, fearful lest laughter get the better of her.

"Yes, Clarisse and I plan to attend," Regana replied in
answer to the question, "though we probably won't know
until the day whether in fact we shall be able to go."

"Oh?" Peter said in surprise. "Have you conflicting
plans, Miss Kently?"

"No, not at all," Regana assured him. "It's just that
Aunt Mary has been suffering with headaches a great deal
lately. They come upon her very suddenly, oftimes without
warning. And on such short notice, it is sometimes difficult to find a suitable replacement."

"Well, I hardly see that as a reason to prevent your going," Emily said brightly. "I would be delighted to go along
and act as chaperon for the day."

"Oh, no, Emily, I couldn't impose on you in such a manner," Regana objected immediately. "What would Lord St. Hyde say?"

"Nothing, Regana, because dear Cecil advised me yesterday morning that he would be away in the City for a few days. Dear man, he asked me if I would mind being on my own for a bit. Naturally, I said I wouldn't, though if the truth be known, I'm not a great one for staying alone. You would actually be doing me a favour by allowing me to accompany you."

"But what about Elizabeth?" Clarisse asked quickly.

"Elizabeth will be in Mrs. Lindsay's very capable hands," Emily replied confidently. "As a matter of fact, it will probably do her good to see someone else for a change. She sees me morning, noon and night." Instinctively, her face softened. "Not that I'm complaining, of course. She's a little darling, and I know I shall miss her terribly, but I don't think she'll mind if I spend a day away. Now, any more objections?" she challenged.

"I say, Richard," Peter said suddenly, "since we shall all be attending this outing, why don't we make up a party and go together? The ladies could travel in the carriage, while you and I ride alongside."

Wesmorlen glanced at his brother quickly. Was this the same Peter who no more than a few days ago had complained that he would never ride again, let alone ride amongst a group of ladies; the same man who had stated his conviction to wait until his later years to wed?

"Oh, yes," Lady Dalmeny chimed in, suddenly more optimistic about the whole affair. "Perhaps Arabella and I could ride with you?"

Hiding his amusement, Wesmorlen replied, "I don't see why not. I'll arrange for a carriage."

"Oh, how wonderful!" Emily exclaimed happily. "The barouche, I hope, Richard."

"As you wish, Emily," the earl acquiesced graciously. "I'll send it round to fetch you."

"Wonderful. I know we're going to have the most marvellous day," Emily said, beaming.

"If it don't rain," Lady Dalmeny grumbled again.

DESPITE LADY DALMENY'S dire predictions, however, the day of the picnic dawned sunny and bright, without a cloud in sight to mar the cerulean sky. The air was warm, though not oppressively so, and only the gentlest of breezes disturbed the leaves of the overhanging trees.

Unfortunately, it was not the weather, nor Aunt Mary's sudden bout of megrims which prevented Regana from enjoying the much-anticipated event. To her horror, the morning of the picnic, she herself awoke feeling so dizzy and lightheaded that she could barely stand. Her head ached appallingly, and she was almost bent over with pains in her stomach.

Alarmed by her sister's dreadful pallor, Clarisse had promptly called for the doctor, who, after examining Regana, announced that she was suffering from a mild case of influenza, and that she would doubtless feel the effects for the remainder of the day.

It was devastating news, though it was hard to say which sister was the more upset. For try as she might, Regana could not persuade Clarisse to allow her to go to the picnic. Despite her assurances that she would not exert herself in any way, Clarisse would not be moved, and insisted on sending Regana back to bed. It was only after an abrupt wave of nausea made her feel quite dizzy that Regana grudgingly acquiesced and returned to bed, dimly aware that she had never felt so wretched in her life.

In spite of her weakness, however, Regana was equally adamant that Clarisse go to the picnic without her, an idea which Clarisse found most perturbing. "But Regana, how can you expect me to go and enjoy myself when you're in your sickbed? My mind's made up; I shall stay here and take care of you," she said nobly.

"Clarisse, don't be silly," Regana argued weakly. "There's no point in both of us missing the picnic. Besides, there's nothing you can do for me. The doctor said all I need is rest."

"But I won't enjoy the outing if you're not there," Clarisse moaned. "Who shall I talk to?"

"Emily, for one," Regana pointed out. "After all, she very kindly volunteered to act as chaperon for us. How do you think she will feel if neither of us go?"

"Well, I hadn't thought about that," Clarisse said, reluctant to disappoint anyone.

"And what about Mr. Wesmorlen?" Regana said, sensing she was wearing her sister down. "Imagine how disappointed he'll be if you don't appear. After all, it was his suggestion that we all go to this together."

That was probably the strongest argument Regana could have used, yet Clarisse was still hesitant. "But what if you need something?" she persisted. "Aunt Mary is still abed."

"Marie is quite capable of bringing me anything I need, Clarisse," Regana assured her. "And I have magazines and books here in abundance. Besides, I have no doubt I shall be asleep rather a lot," Regana said, not pretending to yawn. "This silly illness has me quite exhausted, and I doubt I'll want to do anything beyond read and sleep."

"Well, if you're sure," Clarrise said, giving in unhappily.

"I am. Besides, how am I to know what happens if you don't go and report back to me?" Regana said lightly.

The teasing achieved the desired effect, and when the earl's carriage arrived at the appointed time to collect them, Clarisse went on her own, assuring Regana that she would likely have a miserable time, but that she would duly watch and report all the details.

Standing by the window to view their departure, Regana tried not to let her disappointment overwhelm her. She knew she wouldn't have been able to enjoy herself feeling as wretched as she did. Still, the fact that Arabella Dalmeny looked exceptionally lovely in a white muslin gown tied with a blue silk sash and carrying a matching blue-and-white fringed parasol did little to raise her flagging spirits. With a sigh, and another painful cramp in her stomach, Regana turned to bed, and waited for the day to pass.

By LATE AFTERNOON she was feeling a little better. Marie had brought a hot brick to keep her feet warm and had kept her supplied with cool water and cloths for her forehead. Consequently, when Clarisse returned home, Regana was sitting up in bed, leafing through a copy of *La Belle Assemblée*.

"Oh, Regana, thank goodness you're awake," Clarisse said, instantly coming to her side. "Are you feeling improved?"

"Yes, much, thank you, dearest. But tell me, how was the picnic?"

Clarisse slipped off her shawl and sat on the edge of the bed, her face wreathed in smiles. "The picnic was lovely, but you'll never guess what happened!" She giggled. "Arabella Dalmeny fell into the lake!"

"Fell into the lake? Dear heavens, how did that happen? Is she all right?" Regana asked, her mind conjuring up an image of the lovely Arabella being pulled out of the water, dripping and furious.

Clarisse nodded quickly. "She's fine, but she's as mad as hops! Poor Charles Wickworth. It wasn't really his fault. If Arabella hadn't urged him to catch Lord Wesmorlen up, they never would have collided."

Clarisse went on to describe what had happened. It seemed that Lord Wesmorlen had taken Emily out for a punt on the lake when Arabella convinced Charles to take her out and row along beside them. Unfortunately, in their efforts to catch them up, the boats had collided, sending Arabella, who was in the process of standing up, into the water. Wesmorlen had quickly fished her out and rowed her the few feet back to shore, and had sent her and Lady Dalmeny home in his carriage.

Regana listened to the story, her eyes growing wider by the moment. She knew she shouldn't have found it humorous, but the thought of Arabella in her lovely blue-and-white dress being pulled from the lake, soggy and dishevelled, set her shoulders shaking.

Consequently, when the door opened to admit Lady St. Hyde a few minutes later, she was surprised to find the two sisters sitting on Regana's bed, convulsed with laughter.

"Well, I'm glad to see you're feeling better, Regana," Lady St. Hyde commented drily. "I begin to wonder whether you were ever sick at all."

Guiltily, Clarisse shook her head. "It's my fault, Emily. I was just telling Regana about Arabella. I can't help laughing when I remember how angry she was when Lord Wesmorlen fished her out of the water."

"Clarisse, I'm surprised at you," Lady St. Hyde said, trying but not succeeding in sounding stern. "Arabella might have been hurt."

"Tosh! The only thing hurt was Arabella's pride." Clarisse laughed, though not unkindly. "The boats were only in a few feet of water. Arabella could simply have stood up rather than floundering about like a herring in a net."

In spite of herself, Emily couldn't prevent a smile from dimpling her own cheeks. "That's not the point, Clarisse," she chastized. "And you shouldn't be encouraging Regana to laugh, either," she said, noticing that Regana's colour was still noticeably pale. "How are you feeling, my dear?"

"Much better, thank you, Emily," Regana said, "and I do apologize for laughing, but I just have this picture in my mind, and well—"

An abrupt knock on the door halted their conversation.

"Come in, Marie," Regana called, thinking it was Marie with her tea. But when Emily opened the door to reveal the Earl of Wesmorlen standing there, Regana gasped and drew the sheet up to her chin.

"Richard, this is highly improper!" Emily scolded. "Visiting a lady in her bedchamber!"

"From what I can see, the lady is quite respectably covered," came the amused rejoinder, "and since I'm unlikely to rip the covers off with both of you standing right there—" he smiled, ignoring Clarisse's startled gasp "—I hardly think Miss Kently's reputation has anything to fear from a brief visit. I merely wished to enquire how she was feeling."

Emily tried unsuccessfully to hide a smile and slowly turned to her friend. "Is it all right, Regana, or would you prefer his lordship to come back another time?"

Blue eyes met black across the room, and though her mind formulated one answer, her lips gave quite another. "I think it would be all right, Emily, though just for a moment," Regana replied softly. "If only to satisfy his lordship's curiosity that I shall, indeed, survive."

"You are quite right, Miss Kently," the earl said, slowly approaching the bed. "I merely wanted to tell you how much we missed your presence at the picnic and to assure myself that you were not desperately ill."

The tenderness in his voice caused Regana's heart to flutter strangely, and the reply she'd been about to utter caught in her throat. How was it that he was always able to reduce her to a helpless state of nerves like this, she wondered, gazing up at him. Why did she keep thinking she saw messages in his eyes, only to look at him again and find them gone? No man had ever affected her like this before, and she was completely at a loss to know how to deal with it.

Sensing her discomfort, Emily briskly moved forward. "Richard, I thought I heard another voice downstairs. Did Peter come with you?"

"Peter?" the earl replied blankly, reluctantly removing his eyes from Regana. "Oh, Peter. Yes, he did. He, too, was anxious about Miss Kently's welfare. I left him downstairs with Mrs. Standish."

"Mary is up? Oh, dear Lord. Clarisse, perhaps you'd better go down and rescue Mr. Wesmorlen," Emily said drily. "Mary's a dear soul, but she does tend to drive one to distraction with her chatter."

"Yes, Lady St. Hyde," Clarisse said, not quite able to mask her pleasure at being sent to entertain the younger Wesmorlen.

"And ring for some refreshments, Clarisse," Emily called after her. "I know the timing is a little late but I think it can be forgiven under the circumstances. His lordship and I shall be down shortly."

Closing the door, Emily approached the earl, a firm but sympathetic expression on her face. "You really shouldn't be here, Richard. If word of this got out, it would be deemed highly improper. And you know how damaging that could be to Miss Kently's reputation."

The earl looked as though he would argue the point, but then, glancing at Lady St. Hyde's fixed expression, changed his mind. "You're correct as always, Emily," he conceded. "But I have seen what I came to see." He turned to smile back into the turquoise eyes. "Forgive me, Miss Kently. I hope I have neither embarrassed nor discomfitted you with my visit. My intentions were, I assure you, the most honourable in nature."

Having taken advantage of Emily's diversion to gather her thoughts, Regana nodded more easily. "No apology is necessary, my lord. Your kind thoughts are appreciated.

And once again, I assure you that I am fine. Though I'm sorry to hear that the picnic came to such a precipitous end." She smothered a grin. "Perhaps under the circumstances, it's Arabella Dalmeny you should be calling on."

She was amused to see the hint of a smile light his eyes. "The thought had occurred to me," the earl admitted ruefully. "However, I felt confident that Miss Dalmeny would be resting in good hands. I would also not be fibbing if I said your welfare was of higher priority to me."

Regana, feeling her face blush crimson at his words, could think of nothing to say. "All right, Emily, I'm going!" Wesmorlen said, sensing that Emily was about to chastise him again.

The door had barely closed behind him before Emily chortled. "Just as I thought. You have scored a victory there, my dear. I've never seen Wesmorlen so thoroughly brought to heel!"

The words stayed with Regana long after Emily had left her to join the others downstairs. The great bachelor earl brought to heel? And by her? Somehow, Regana doubted it. But there was certainly no mistaking that he was being very attentive to her, or that there was a definite attraction between them. She felt it every time they were together.

But did that mean that there was anything more in his mind than just a simple flirtation?

CHAPTER SIX

REGANA HEARD no more from Lord Botheringham over the next few days, giving her to assume that he had extended his stay in the City to conclude his business. Not that his prolonged absence caused her any grief. If anything, Regana was relieved. She hadn't been able to forget the strange conversation they'd had before he had left, and though she knew that she would have to deal with Lord Botheringham eventually, his temporary removal made that a matter of future concern.

In truth, Regana was far more disconcerted by the knowledge that Lord Wesmorlen had also removed to London for an unspecified time, his absence bringing home to her with disturbing clarity just how much she'd come to look forward to his visits.

Regana was still bemused by the earl's unexpected attentions, despite her sister's assurances that there was nothing to be bemused about. Since the night of the Dalmenys' ball, Wesmorlen had endeavoured to call at Grantly Hall almost every day, whether it was for tea, or simply for a chat in the afternoon. Most of the time, he was accompanied by Peter, who continued to smile and entertain Clarisse, and it wasn't long before both Regana and her sister were moved to admit that where before the time allowed for social calls had dragged endlessly on, the same time now passed with untoward speed.

Now, as Regana knelt in the garden, the basket beside her filled with freshly cut flowers for the dining-room table, she cautioned herself not to read too much into those visits. If, as she had begun to suspect, the earl visited mainly for the purpose of furthering his brother's acquaintance with Clarisse, it would be foolish for her to entertain silly ideas regarding her own future. However, she could not refrain from indulging in pleasant daydreams every now and then about the earl's possible intentions.

To Wesmorlen, coming on her unawares, the sight of Regana in a charming white sprigged-muslin day dress with a wide-brimmed straw hat tied over those brandywine tresses was like a breath of fresh air after the endless dirt and noise of London. He sat his stallion and watched her for a moment, admiring the delicate curve of her neck and the exquisite lobe of one dainty ear just visible beneath the brim of the hat.

"Ahh, the pleasures of the countryside," Wesmorlen mused softly, "where else could I find a more lovely and winsome sight than a beautiful young lady filling her basket with flowers."

Regana looked up, the task at hand abruptly forgotten. "Lord Wesmorlen!" she said, her face lighting up with such genuine pleasure that he felt his heart turn over. Then, as if belatedly recalled to both her manners and her training, she added hastily, "That is, you...startled me, my lord. I did not hear your approach."

Wesmorlen stared down into her upturned face, conscious once again of an overwhelming desire to sweep her up into his arms and carry her off, like a knight rescuing a damsel in distress. Surprising, considering he'd never suffered from such gallant notions before. "What a pity," he said ruefully. "I thought perhaps you were glad to see me." He sprang down easily from the saddle, and bent to pick up her basket, his look becoming decidedly devilish. "Did you miss me?"

Regana started, then shook her head, her laughter low and musical. "I wasn't even aware you'd gone until your brother informed me of it yesterday,'' she fibbed outrageously. ''But once I realized you weren't about, I missed you sorely.''

''Baggage!'' he replied, feeling a headiness at being close to her again. ''Next time I'll stay away longer,'' he threatened. ''But what's this about Peter calling round yesterday? Has my brother been wearing out his welcome during my absence?''

''I don't think he could.'' Regana laughed kindly. ''And certainly not after being reprimanded by Lady Dalmeny for spending what she called an 'inappropriate amount of time with the younger Miss Kently upon the occasion of their first meeting'. I doubt he would want to draw her ire again, so they are wont to settle for a visit here, and a drive there.''

''Speaking of which,'' the earl continued, ''I wonder if you might care to join me for a drive this afternoon, Miss Kently. I have a new team in my stable and I am anxious to put them through their paces. Perhaps you would be willing to give me your opinion as to their mettle?''

The invitation was unexpected, but it was certainly not unwelcome, and Regana nodded demurely. ''I should be delighted to drive with you, Lord Wesmorlen. And to give you an honest opinion on your cattle, though I seriously doubt I should find fault with anything you might purchase.''

The earl looked at her in amusement. ''You flatter me, Miss Kently. I am not solely a Corinthian.''

''No, but your knowledge of horseflesh is widely known, my lord, and I have heard tell of more than one gentleman who has sought your guidance in the past.''

''Be that as it may,'' the earl acknowledged, ''I look forward to hearing *your* views, Miss Kently. Until this afternoon, then,'' he added, mounting and turning his horse in the direction of Blackoaks.

After the earl had gone, Regana went inside and informed Aunt Mary and Clarisse of his invitation.

"There, I knew it!" Clarisse announced with satisfaction. "Emily was right. Lord Wesmorlen is most definitely harbouring a tendre for you."

"Tosh. Lord Wesmorlen was just being kind, Clarisse," Regana insisted, setting the basket of flowers on the table. "He merely wants my opinion on his new horses."

"Balderdash!" Aunt Mary said with her usual candour. "I don't know of any man, let alone a nonpareil like Wesmorlen, who would admit to asking a woman for her opinion, especially on matters of horseflesh. Offends their masculine pride. After all, Regana, you said yourself there are few men who know their cattle better than the earl. No, I tend to agree with Clarisse. Lord Wesmorlen favours you. Asking for your opinion on his horses was nothing more than an excuse to take you driving with him."

"But that doesn't make any sense," Regana replied in mild bewilderment. "Why would Wesmorlen, of all people, need an excuse? He may invite whomsoever he pleases. Surely he knows he has no need for such pretence?"

But the fact of the matter was, Wesmorlen did not know it, and later that same day, as he drove his new high-spirited greys towards Grantly Hall, Wesmorlen found himself in a definite quandary. He had to admit he was no longer terribly pleased with his plan for wooing Miss Kently away from Botheringham. Granted, Regana seemed to be enjoying his company, and he knew that Botheringham had noticed his increased attentions to her, but what he couldn't enjoy was the deception he was practicing upon her. Regana was an innocent bystander, utterly unaware of what had happened between Lord Botheringham and his brother, and Wesmorlen was cognizant of a growing reluctance to involve her in it.

At the same time, however, he was also aware of his reluctance to give her up. The more time he spent with Regana, the more time he wanted to spend with her. And that, he knew with startling clarity, had nothing to do with Botheringham.

For her own part, Regana was still reluctant to allow that Wesmorlen held more than a passing interest in her, in spite of what Clarisse and Aunt Mary said. After all, who was she to think she might attach his affection? An earl could do considerably better than an untitled country girl with little social background and no dowry to take into her marriage.

Regana was still pondering that thought as she sat beside the earl in his dashing high-perch phaeton later that afternoon. She had changed into an ice-blue carriage dress trimmed with black frogging. It was one of her favourite dresses, and she hadn't missed the spark of admiration in Wesmorlen's eyes when he had handed her up into his phaeton.

The fine weather had brought out a spate of people anxious to enjoy the day, and as they drove through the countryside Regana was amused to see a number of envious glances being cast her way. No doubt word would very quickly spread that Regana Kently had been seen driving with the Earl of Wesmorlen.

"You seem to be the centre of attention this afternoon, Miss Kently," Wesmorlen remarked as they passed by the startled faces of Lady Dalmeny and Arabella. "Not that it surprises me, though," he added, glancing at her appreciatively. "You look exceptionally lovely in that dress. You should always wear blue."

Regana blushed and thanked him, aware that once again she was at a loss for words. She'd never felt like this before, and she wondered if she wasn't a fool for wishing the ride could go on forever. As the phaeton swayed, and the hard length of his thigh pressed fleetingly against hers, Regana tried to ignore the warmth which spread through her body like liquid fire.

Instead she concentrated on his hands, admiring how strong and capably they held the ribbons, and wondering, too, how they would feel against her skin. The unexpected thought brought the blood surging to her cheeks, and Regana dipped her head, fearing he might discern her heightened colour. Really, she must stop this most unladylike train of thought.

On the other hand, Lord Wesmorlen had been delighted to discover that his original assessment of Regana's character had been correct. Besides being beautiful, she was possessed of a lively intelligence, which he'd found so lacking in most of the young ladies he'd encountered in London. She responded to his questions easily, their shared laughter indicating a like sense of humour. Nor was she afraid to voice an opinion, even on subjects which normally would have been foreign to a young lady of Quality.

"I believe you to be something of a bluestocking, Miss Kently," said the earl with a chuckle when they had finished a mutually satisfying discussion on the relative merits of steam as a source of propulsion.

"Not at all, Lord Wesmorlen," Regana assured him, her eyes dancing. "I admit to being well read, but you must understand that my father encouraged that." She laughed fondly. "I suppose having a professor for a father does tend to alter one's upbringing somewhat. He had a natural curiosity about so many things that it was difficult for me not to share some of that curiosity."

"And your mother didn't try to dissuade you from such academic tendencies?"

"My mother realized quite early that there was little hope of curbing my predisposition towards learning. Fortunately my sister demonstrated an equally early interest in things domestic, thereby relieving some of the pressure which might have been brought to bear. I suppose Mama assumed that if at least one daughter was dutiful in following the prescribed course, the other would follow eventually."

"Which you clearly did," the earl commented appreciatively.

"Eventually—" Regana nodded "—though not before I'd enjoyed my fill of other, less conventional subjects."

"Such as?" Wesmorlen probed, genuinely curious.

Regana hesitated, fearing that perhaps she had already disclosed too much about her unusual background, and shook her head. "Nothing which I intend to discuss here and now, Lord Wesmorlen," she remarked with a gentle laugh. "Suffice it to say, however, that you may be surprised at the subjects upon which I am able to offer an opinion."

"I don't doubt that for a moment, Miss Kently," the earl replied, studying her lovely profile. "Not for a moment."

Regana smiled, revealing her irrepressible dimples. They drove on in silence for a while, content to enjoy the fine weather and each other's presence. The earl set a brisk pace, handling the ribbons with the deceptive ease only to be expected from a member of London's noted Four-In-Hand club. But given the spriteliness of the greys, Regana doubted it would be an onerous task.

"I think you need not be concerned by your purchase, Lord Wesmorlen," Regana commented with approval. "Your greys work well together, nor do they exhibit any signs of stress over the pace you're setting them. I think they will stand you in good stead for a number of years."

Aware that his own thoughts were of a similar nature, Wesmorlen complimented her on her assessment, and asked her, much to her surprise, if she would care to take a turn at the ribbons. Wesmorlen hadn't expected Regana to accept. When she did, calmly taking the ribbons from him and putting the pair through their paces with an expertise that astounded him, he was generous in his praise.

"Thank you, my lord. I was well taught."

"Many women have been taught, Miss Kently," the earl pointed out sagely. "But it doesn't mean that every woman knows how. You have to love horses to come to know them."

"And I do," Regana replied simply. "I have been driving since I was a girl."

"Another one of your father's teachings?" Wesmorlen surmised.

"My mother, actually," Regana said with a laugh. "Sang like an angel, drove like a demon. She was one of the most notable lady whips of her time."

"Good Lord," Wesmorlen was moved to say, lapsing into silence, and wondering what other delightful secrets he would discover about this enchanting creature.

It was as they were driving through a particularly picturesque stretch of countryside that Wesmorlen drew the team to a leisurely halt and stopped to glance about him with obvious pleasure. "Do you know something, Miss Kently—and I implore you not to tell my brother I admitted this, for I'd just as soon deny it—but I find I'm beginning to enjoy life in the country. The peacefulness here is an antidote to the frenetic pace we set in London. I find it very calming, somehow."

Regana turned to him in amusement. "Now you are gammoning me, my lord," she teased him gently. "Can *this* be the same Wesmorlen I've heard such stories about? The nonpareil and noted Corinthian? Claiming to find enjoyment in the simple pleasures of country life? I'd as lief believe a racehorse not wanting to run."

Wesmorlen regarded her fondly. "Saucy baggage. If you were a man, I'd thrash you for such insolence."

"How thankful I am that I am not," she declared, laughing, continuing to study him with thoughtful countenance. "Seriously though, my lord, you do not strike me as the sort of man who would feel overwhelmed by the bustle of London—or by anything else, for that matter.

Indeed, if any man is in better control of himself and all he encounters, I've yet to meet him."

The compliment was not meant to flatter. It was merely set forth as a statement of fact, and spoken with absolute conviction. The earl, for all his position and wealth, never flaunted them, nor did he follow the crowd which so ardently aped the mannerisms and postures of Beau Brummell, that acknowledged arbiter of fashion.

Glancing covertly at him now, Regana had to admit there was nothing foppish or fancy about his appearance. The buff breeches which fitted smoothly into a pair of highly polished black riding boots, were topped by a cutaway coat of dark blue superfine. Shunning the ridiculously high collar points, which allowed men neither freedom of movement nor any great degree of comfort, the earl wore a simple, though elegantly tied, cravat. He was a man who was comfortable following his own fashion, and thinking of some of the highly dandified young gentlemen she'd seen in London, Regana was glad of it.

"A penny for your thoughts, Miss Kently," the earl said suddenly, setting his team off at a brisk trot again.

Regana turned to find the dark eyes upon her, a curious twinkle in their dusky depths. She turned away and allowed an unknowingly provocative smile to touch her lips. "They're not for sale, my lord," she replied evasively. "And if they were, it certainly wouldn't be for a— Oh! my lord, watch out!"

Her cry of dismay was met with an equally surprised exclamation on the part of the earl as a horse and rider suddenly appeared, as if from nowhere, and stopped dead in front of their carriage. Pulling hard on the reins, Wesmorlen drew the startled greys to an abrupt halt, the quickness of which all but threw Regana from her seat. She might have been unseated, had it not been for the strong arm which suddenly slid firmly about her waist.

Regana's heart was pounding, though whether it was from the abrupt stop or the intimacy of Wesmorlen's grip, she wasn't sure. With her eyes still on the dancing greys, she opened her mouth to speak, but stopped when she heard the sound of soft feminine laughter. Startled, she glanced round to see the beautifully mocking face of Amanda Chadwick looking up at them from the back of her own dancing black stallion.

"Bravo, Richard, bravo! I see you haven't lost your touch."

"What the— Good God...Amanda?" The earl broke off, belatedly recognizing the incredibly beautiful woman who was sitting by calmly watching them. "What in blazes did you think you were doing, stopping in front of me like that? You might have caused an accident."

"Nonsense, Richard," the Beauty replied in a voice which sounded remarkably like warm honey. "I had no doubt a whip of your expertise could halt his team in time. And if you couldn't, I knew that my dear Satan," she added, stroking the neck of the magnificent black stallion, "could have manoeuvred me out of the way in time. So you see, darling, there was really no danger at all. To me, or to your guest," she said, her eyes going pointedly to Richard's arm which was still resting securely around Regana's waist.

Regana intercepted the decidedly mocking glance, and cursed the colour which flooded her cheeks. She felt a fool for having reacted with such alarm, even though she was hardly to know at the time that Lady Chadwick was a very capable horsewoman, and not some poor, unfortunate rider who was being carried away by his mount.

"Your faith in my ability is flattering, Amanda," Wesmorlen drawled, "but I strongly suggest you temper the methods by which you effect a meeting in future."

The Beauty's only response was a husky laugh deep in her throat. "Oh, Richard, don't be so melodramatic," she

retorted drily. "You of all people should be used to my un-
predictability. Besides, I don't know that Miss…Kently was
too upset by the outcome of my little game. From where I
sit, I think perhaps she rather enjoyed it."

If Lady Chadwick had hoped to provoke a scathing
counterattack, or alternatively a spate of embarrassed
blushes, she was to be disappointed. Regana, having
quickly regained her composure, smiled at the earl and
gently but firmly pulled away from him. "Thank you, Lord
Wesmorlen," she said clearly. "It was good of you to concern yourself with my safety when you were so clearly occupied with bringing the carriage to such a precipitous
stop." She turned cool blue eyes towards the marchioness.
"I'm only sorry Lady Chadwick's concern does not extend to the welfare of her own horse." She glanced pointedly at the prancing stallion's left hind leg. "Your mount
has thrown a shoe."

The mocking smile vanished, to be replaced at once by a
scowl of displeasure. The earl, who had quickly dis-
mounted at Regana's pronouncement, examined the stallion's hind leg, and confirmed the loss. "Better get him to
a blacksmith, Amanda," Wesmorlen advised. "And have
your groom check that hoof. I don't like the odour. I'll
wager an infection is setting in."

Returning to the carriage, he gave Regana an admiring
glance. "Good thing you noticed that, Miss Kently. I'm
sure Lady Chadwick is equally grateful," he added, looking at Amanda.

To ignore the prompt would have been a blatant breach
of etiquette, something which even the great Marchioness
of Chadwick was reluctant to commit. The acknowledge-
ment when it came, however, was little more than cursory.

"I am, as you say, Richard, grateful that Miss Kently has
such astute perception. I shall have Wiley see to it as soon
as I return. On another note," she said, effectively dis-
missing Regana, and turning the full intensity of her beauty

on him, "you still haven't told me whether you're coming to my ball, darling. You haven't forgotten about it, have you?"

Wesmorlen favoured her with a lazy smile. "How could I forget, Amanda? You sent me two invitations."

"I know." Amanda pouted prettily. "But I also know how many things you have on your mind, Richard, and I didn't want you to plan something else." Her look became suddenly intent. "You will come, won't you—you and Peter both? After all, it's been ages since I've been able to dance and now that I'm officially through my mourning, it seemed a perfect time to begin. And I thought it would be a wonderful opportunity to, how shall I say, renew our old friendship?" she added, sending a telling glance in Regana's direction.

Regana, sitting quietly by the earl's side, missed the look, seemingly absorbed in the study of the stitching on her gloves. She was, however, fully cognizant of everything going on and couldn't remember when she had ever felt more uncomfortable.

That Lady Chadwick intended to discomfit her, Regana had no doubt. What she couldn't countenance, though, was that rather than disapproving of the lady's outrageous behaviour, the earl didn't seem in the least bothered by it.

"I shall speak to Peter immediately upon my return and let you know on the morrow," he was saying now.

"Wonderful!" Lady Chadwick beamed. The earl glanced at her pointedly. Seeing the expression in his eyes, Amanda turned reluctantly to Regana. "I hope we shall see you there as well, Miss Kently."

Momentarily, the comic aspect of the situation struck Regana. This woman no more wanted to include her in the guest list than Regana wished to be included, but even the Marchioness of Chadwick could not willingly commit such a flagrant transgression of manners as to ignore her.

"Does that invitation also include my younger sister, Lady Chadwick?" Regana asked sweetly. "I'm sure she would enjoy the festivities, too."

Lady Chadwick's smile faltered for no more than a second. "Of course, Miss Kently, bring whomever you please. I daresay the house will be overflowing with people. A few more won't make any difference."

"My lady is too kind," she murmured.

Blissfully unaware of Regana's subtle irony, Amanda turned back to the earl. "I can't wait to show you what I've done to the house, Richard. I know how much you admired the abbey when you were last there, but you won't even recognize it now."

"Benton Abbey is a fine old house," Wesmorlen confirmed, by way of explanation to Regana. "One of the oldest in the area, though it was sadly in need of interior alterations when last I visited Lord Chadwick."

It seemed by his pointed use of the marquis's name that Wesmorlen intended to remove any doubt which may have lingered in Regana's mind as to the propriety of his last visit. Suspecting this was for her benefit, Regana smiled graciously. "I look forward to seeing your home, Lady Chadwick. I have heard it's quite beautiful."

Amanda looked at Regana with a slight lessening of animosity. "Thank you, Miss Kently. I admit I have worked hard on it, but it was a labour of love. Besides, I was glad of the diversion. I had so many lonely hours to fill while Tony was away."

Her face had assumed a soft, winsome expression which Regana knew any man would find appealing. And it seemed the earl was no exception.

"I'm sure you won't be lonely much longer, Amanda. I predict any number of gentlemen will be calling once they know you're out of black gloves."

"As long as *you* know where to find me, Richard, that's all that matters," Amanda whispered seductively.

There was no mistaking the invitation behind her words, and hearing it, Regana was unable to prevent the swift rush of colour to her cheeks. Thus far, the Beauty had violated every canon of propriety, from insulting an acquaintance to being outrageously forward with a gentleman. But as a bystander, Regana was somewhat at a loss to know how to deal with the situation. Should she just sit by, condoning by her silence the woman's shocking behaviour? Or should she speak up, and risk having her motive mistaken for jealousy?

In spite of her confusion, Regana knew one thing. No true lady would have dared risk her reputation by speaking so wantonly in front of another woman. Yet this one did, and with no apparent regret. Perhaps it was that which made the decision easier for her.

"Lord Wesmorlen, I think we had better be returning," Regana said, her voice soft but firm. "If you and Lady Chadwick wish to make... arrangements, perhaps you would be so kind as to do so elsewhere. Good day, Lady Chadwick."

Regana watched as the Beauty's face turned an unbecoming shade of red. "Well, I— Richard, do you permit her to talk to me like that? Richard, where are you going?"

"To take Miss Kently home," Wesmorlen said, appearing to have some trouble in maintaining a serious face. "No doubt her aunt will be wondering at her absence. Good afternoon, Amanda."

Wesmorlen flicked the reins, leaving Lady Chadwick to stare after them in impotent fury. Regana, sitting quietly by the earl's side until they were almost back at Grantly Hall, was considerably distressed by the marchioness's inexcusable behaviour. But she was even more appalled by her own shocking lack of manners. What ever had possessed her to speak so rudely, especially considering she barely even knew the lady? And in front of the earl, who reputedly held Lady Chadwick in high esteem.

"Lord Wesmorlen," Regana began miserably, "I think perhaps there is something I should say."

"If it is what I think you are going to say, Miss Kently, I don't wish to hear it."

Regana looked up at him in alarm. "Is clairvoyance yet another of your many talents, my lord?"

"I only wish it were," Wesmorlen returned, finding it more difficult than ever to hide his amusement. "I should like to know what thoughts are lurking behind those lovely eyes of yours right now."

"I think perhaps you would not," Regana demurred, hastily lowering them. "They are not particularly charitable at the moment."

"Not surprising." He chuckled appreciatively. "Amanda can be rather... provoking at times."

The fact that the earl was openly laughing at her now did little to assuage Regana's misery. "My lord, I hardly see that there is anything comical in what just happened," she said lamely. "I spoke out of turn, and in a most unforgivable manner. I only hope you can forgive my behaviour. Nor do I intend to accept Lady Chadwick's invitation. I know it was only extended because of you. I cannot imagine that she would want—"

"And I cannot imagine that I would not want," the earl interrupted, his laughter abruptly forgotten. He brought the horses to a gentle stop, and turned to face her. "Miss Kently, forgive me for laughing, and believe me when I say it was not at your expense. But if you were considering not coming to the ball, I urge you to think again. I agree that Amanda spoke without courtesy or caution just now, but unfortunately, such is her nature. I doubt she would do so in public, and I firmly believe that you and your family would enjoy seeing Benton Abbey. Nor are you likely to see much of Amanda since she has invited nearly everyone in the county. Besides,'' he added, glancing at her averted face, ''you must know that Amanda's reactions to you are motivated purely out of envy.''

''Envy!'' Regana replied, her eyes widening. ''What could she possibly have to be envious of? Lady Chadwick has been judged an Incomparable, is possessed of a title and a notable fortune and has houses here and in London. Further, as a widow she is not so strictly encumbered by the restrictions which are imposed on an unmarried lady, all of which combine to make her, I would think, a very attractive proposition to a man looking for a wife. So why, pray tell, could she possibly be envious of me?''

Wesmorlen, having listened with growing amusement to Regana's clear lack of insight into the character of Amanda Chadwick, shook his head. Taking her hand, he carefully removed her glove and then, to Regana's astonishment, placed a delightful token of his affection against the soft palm. ''Your charming ignorance and the fact that it is neither affected nor assumed is exactly what she is envious of, Miss Kently,'' he said gently. ''And now, dear lady, I wish to hear no more talk about it. I expect to see you, your sister and your aunt at Benton Abbey the night of the ball. Because if I do not, I shall come to Grantly Hall and escort you there myself!''

CHAPTER SEVEN

THERE WAS NO DOUBT in Regana's mind that she was probably the only person in Hanton-on-Grange who was not looking forward to Lady Chadwick's ball!

While there were many who said the marchioness's haste in throwing off her black gloves and in planning the elaborate affair were the height of bad taste, others merely shrugged, saying it was characteristic of the wilful, headstrong Beauty to get her own way.

Now as their carriage joined the long queue of others waiting to unload their occupants at the impressive front entrance to Benton Abbey, Regana looked up to find her sister's eyes on her, her concern evident.

"Regana, dear, you're so quiet," Clarisse remarked gently. "Are you not feeling well?"

Guiltily aware that by her very silence she had drawn attention to herself, Regana smiled and shook her head. "I'm fine, really," she assured her sister. "I was merely woolgathering."

"Could have gathered a whole sheep for the time you were gone," Aunt Mary put in tartly. "I think there's more going on in that pretty little head of yours than you're letting us know about." She glanced at Clarisse knowingly. "And I don't think it's so different from what's going on in yours."

"I can't think what you mean, Aunt," Clarisse prevaricated.

"You know exactly what I mean, young lady," she teased. "In my experience, only one thing causes a woman to go staring off into space or blushing for no apparent reason—and that's a gentleman. And from where I sit, the gentlemen who are at the root of both your blushes and silences are at the end of this journey."

"Now, Aunt, let us not get ahead of ourselves," Regana warned, her good humour returning. "I can see you are planning two weddings and it simply will not do. Granted, I think we all agree that there is a marked interest in Clarisse from the younger Mr. Wesmorlen," she said, sending a smile towards her sister, "but please do not read anything untoward into the relationship between Lord Wesmorlen and myself."

"Aha!" Aunt Mary pounced. "Then there *is* a relationship between the two of you."

"Tosh, I did not say that!" Regana retaliated quickly. "Really, at times you can be so literal, Aunt!" she remonstrated. "Lord Wesmorlen has been very pleasant to me, but I know for a fact that such is his nature."

"His nature doesn't encourage him to take every young lady he meets out driving, Regana," Clarisse pointed out casually, her supposition supported by Aunt Mary's concurring nod.

"No, perhaps it doesn't," Regana admitted. "But you seem to forget that he escorted Lady Chiltern to a musicale a few weeks ago and that he was seen to be dancing attendance upon Druscilla Bankworth at Lord and Lady Smythes' rout. Nor," she added quietly, "should you forget that much has been said of late regarding his relationship with Lady Chadwick."

"Humph! Lady Chadwick!" Aunt Mary muttered. "She's no lady, mark my words. Any woman who doesn't have the decency to observe a full year's mourning for her husband is no lady, to my mind. It's the earl's title she's after," Aunt Mary said, shaking her finger. "Amanda was used to money and position, and that's what she's after again. Well, all I can say is that if the Wesmorlen is fool enough to be taken in by such a one, he deserves all he gets!"

When Regana, Clarisse and Aunt Mary stepped through the open doors and into the brilliantly lit entrance hall, it was difficult to see anything beyond the tremendous crush of people.

"Goodness! I do believe everyone I know, and a good many I don't know, are here tonight," Clarisse whispered in her sister's ear. "Isn't it amazing what curiosity will do?"

Somewhat sheepishly, Regana nodded. "It is, but I must admit to feeling some curiosity about Lady Chadwick myself. I understand she always was a rather daring hostess, and as she has been out of circulation for almost a year, I'm curious to see what manner of ball she'll be throwing to herald the beginning of her new life."

It seemed to be a sentiment shared by many, and true to form, Amanda did not disappoint her audience. With deliberate timing, the marchioness emerged in a glittering gown of filmy silver gauze so fine as to appear almost transparent. The under-slip was scarcely a tone deeper than her own skin, adding to the illusion that she was wearing nothing at all underneath the gown. The waist was cut high, as was the style, but the décolletage dipped outrageously low, certainly lower than fashion decreed, Regana thought. And, as if to draw attention even further, there, nestled in the creamy expanse of bosom, hung the fabulous Chadwick diamond necklace, a huge tear-drop diamond set in a frame of beautifully worked gold filigree. More diamonds glittered in her hair, and Regana had to admit that the overall effect was absolutely breathtaking, which—judging by the dazzled looks on the faces of many of the gentlemen present—was exactly as Amanda had planned.

Not everyone, however, was duly impressed. Aunt Mary was positively shocked. Eyes wide, she watched the Beauty greeting her guests and turned to Regana, her grim face reflecting her disapproval.

"That is without doubt the most indecent gown I've ever seen!" she pronounced frostily. "And not even a toque as a concession to her widowhood. Where is the woman's sense of decorum? In my day, she would have been dragged from the room with a blanket over her head." Aunt Mary raised her quizzing glass and peered through it intently. "Good heavens, I don't believe the chit is wearing anything under that gown. Regana, is she wearing undergarments?"

"I believe so, Aunt," Regana replied, trying hard to suppress her amusement. "I don't think even Lady Chadwick would be so bold as to appear in public without... suitable underclothing."

"Humph!" Aunt Mary snorted, dropping her glass. "I don't know about that. Just see that you don't follow her example, Clarisse," she admonished her younger niece. "You may think the gentlemen find it appealing, but I can assure you it's not offers of marriage she'll be receiving dressed like that."

"She has been married once, Aunt," Regana reminded her tactfully. "And quite well. Obviously the way she dressed, which I feel obliged to point out has not changed greatly over the past four years, did not inhibit Lord Chadwick's suit at the time."

"Twaddle!" Aunt Mary proclaimed. "Anthony Chadwick always did have more money than sense, especially when it came to a pretty face. Followed his father that way," she grumbled. "Still, look where it's got him. He's dead, and she's living like a duchess."

That was altogether too much for Regana. Unable to contain the mirth which had been threatening to bubble over since their arrival, Regana gave in to a silvery ripple of laughter, the lightness of which earned her more than one appreciative glance.

Lord Wesmorlen, having himself turned to ascertain the source of the delightful sound, spied Regana, and caught his breath at the enchanting sight she made. Though nowhere near as immodest as Lady Chadwick's, Regana's gown of deep apricot silk drew almost as many admiring glances. It, too, was styled in the fashion of the day, though the front hem was raised slightly to display a pair of dainty feet encased in matching silk slippers. Delicate pearl drops adorned her earlobes and tiny seed pearls sewn on an apricot velvet ribbon caught up the richly glowing tresses which Marie had arranged in a deceptively simple yet elegant style. The warm shade of the gown seemed to enhance the clear blue of her eyes and Wesmorlen couldn't help but think that he had rarely seen such perfection of face and form.

Intent on his study, Wesmorlen failed to notice Lady Chadwick's approach, nor did he see the darkening of her features as she realized where his attentions lay.

So, that was the way of it, Amanda fumed, dismayed to discover that Wesmorlen *was* pursuing Regana Kently, and that she had been foolish enough to let him manoeuvre her into inviting the woman here.

Amanda closed her fan with a snap, aware that her anger was smouldering dangerously close to the surface. It was no secret that Amanda Chadwick wanted the Earl of Wesmorlen—she always had. No other man had ever set her on fire the way he did, and she seriously doubted any other man ever could. They had courted ardently during her first Season, and it was thought by many that the dashing young viscount would take the beautiful Amanda Lyndhurst for his wife.

But Amanda had been younger then, and foolish, too easily swayed by the lure of a title. At the time Richard had been a mere viscount, whereas Anthony, having already succeeded to the title, was the Marquess of Chadwick. So it was hardly surprising that when Chadwick had turned his attention towards her and begun paying her court, Amanda had been flattered. It was only after she had encouraged Chadwick, hoping to inflame Wesmorlen's jealousy, that she had realized her mistake. Wesmorlen had not been willing to play her game, and had withdrawn his suit. Consequently, when Chadwick had offered for her, she'd had little choice but to accept, or pay the unwelcome price of sitting on the shelf and looking a fool for all her trouble.

When Anthony had been killed in France, Amanda had grieved for a time. Then, she'd begun to hope that Wesmorlen, now the earl and as yet unmarried, might still be harbouring some feelings for her. But she'd known better than to appear eager. Dutifully, she had played the grieving widow and suffered her blacks for a year. Towards the end of that time, however, she had taken pains to show Wesmorlen, as tactfully as she could, that she was still very interested in him. And she thought she'd succeeded in capturing his affections.

Until now. From the unguarded expression Amanda saw on his face, it was quite clear where his affections lay. But she was damned if she was going to lose him now, especially to that little nobody. But how was she to prevent it? Amanda wondered, her mind racing. She knew she wouldn't sway Wesmorlen by railing at him or exposing him to jealous tantrums. He'd turn away from her even more. No, somehow she was going to have to divert his attention away from Regana, to cast Regana in a bad light. Though how one did that to someone so disgustingly unblemished, Amanda wasn't sure. If only there were some hint of scandal that she could dredge up, or an involvement.

An involvement! But that was it! Amanda brightened, a calculating smile curving her lips. How could she have forgotten the conversation she'd overheard just the other morning at the modiste's in Hanton-on-Grange? Thanks to the gossipy Lady Loring, she had all the ammunition she required.

"Ah, there you are, Richard," Lady Chadwick purred, composing her features and coming up behind him. She touched his arm lightly with a gloved hand and smiled up into his face. "Have you forgotten we have the next dance?"

The earl smiled lazily, and turned away from his study. "Of course not, Amanda. I was just coming to find you."

Wesmorlen escorted her onto the floor, cognizant of the envious glances he was receiving from the flock of young bucks in the room. "Have I told you how dazzling you look this evening?" he said.

Lady Chadwick laughed huskily. "No, you haven't, you naughty boy, and I was quite prepared to take you to task if you hadn't. You know how unsure a widow can be. Especially when she's surrounded by so many beautiful younger women."

"I doubt there are many who could outshine you this evening, my dear. Especially dressed like that." His eyes did a leisurely perusal of her attire, the look in their depths sending an unmistakable quiver down her spine. "That gown is quite spectacular, not to mention indecent, Amanda. But then, I'm sure you knew it would be."

Amanda tilted her head back provocatively, the movement drawing attention to the smooth whiteness of her slender throat. "Can you blame me, Richard? I feel like a butterfly bursting forth from its cocoon. Besides, I chose this dress for you, didn't you know? You always used to say you liked me best in white."

Wesmorlen acknowledged the compliment. "I'm flattered you remember."

"I remember everything you ever said to me," Amanda replied softly. "As if it were yesterday instead of four years ago. I only hope you can forgive some of the things I said to you, and mark it down to the naïveté of youth."

"There is nothing to forgive, Amanda," the earl replied, though not unkindly. "If you are referring to your preference for Lord Chadwick over myself, it is a matter of little consequence now. You had your reasons, and I accepted them. I had no choice."

"And now?" she asked, looking up at him alluringly. "Now that I have gained wisdom, and a second chance, are there not some new choices we might make?"

Wesmorlen made no reply, unwilling to compromise himself with an answer he might regret later. Amanda also dismissed the subject, afraid lest she appear too eager. She had to move slowly, cautiously, until she was more sure of her ground.

"The two Kently girls look lovely this evening," she said, changing the topic in a seemingly innocent manner. "Indeed, your brother Peter seems quite dazzled by the younger one. He's scarce left her side since they arrived."

The earl nodded with satisfaction. "I'm delighted to see him take up with someone so charming. I was beginning to despair of his ever looking at a young lady again after his accident."

"Well, I don't think you need concern yourself about that. The young lady seems as interested in Peter as he is in her. And why wouldn't she be?" Amanda pointed out in a logical manner. "I'm sure the aunt would be delighted to have her make as successful a match as the elder sister has."

The remark quite naturally startled him. Amanda had uttered the words as though they were common knowledge. Had something happened since he and Regana had last spoken? Had Botheringham actually managed to steal a march on him?

Wesmorlen schooled his countenance into a look of polite enquiry. He'd been caught with his guard down once this evening; he had no intention of allowing it to happen again. "Really, Amanda? I wasn't aware the elder sister was already betrothed. Did I miss something?"

"Well, the betrothal hasn't officially been announced," Amanda conceded reluctantly, "though I understand from

Lady Loring that Lord Botheringham approached Miss
Kently before he removed to the City. From what I gather
they came to a kind of understanding."

"An understanding," Wesmorlen repeated blankly.
"What kind of an understanding?"

"I don't know, really. Something to the effect that they
would formally announce their engagement upon his return."

"Then he's already proposed?" Wesmorlen said more
sharply than he'd intended.

"Well, Lady Loring couldn't say exactly whether he had
or not. She merely said that he'd spoken to Regana and that
they had come to an understanding."

Amanda, watching him from beneath her lowered lashes,
tried to gauge the effect her words had had. She felt sure his
look of studied indifference was just that, but she had to
admit she was disappointed that her ruse hadn't achieved
more definite results. In truth, Wesmorlen hardly seemed
to be interested at all. Still, he had questioned her about the
proposal; perhaps the game wasn't over yet. Her thin smile
flashed as she prepared for another assault. "I suppose she
considers that it was worth turning down all those gentlemen last Season," she continued, as if merely imparting
gossip. "By waiting, Miss Kently has no doubt attached one
of the wealthiest men in London. And I believe that was
one of her particular requirements. I suppose that large
amounts of money could help one to overlook the man's
obvious...deficiencies in other areas."

"You are unkind, Amanda," the earl chastised her in a
lazy drawl, his indifference masking a growing concern.
"Miss Kently does not strike me as the mercenary sort."

"Ah, but you don't know Regana Kently well, do you,
Richard?" Amanda purred. "Suffice it to say that the
young lady is not as innocent as she might lead you to believe. She's been playing the fickle miss, leading half the ton

on a merry chase and then dashing their hopes when they offer for her."

Their conversation broke off as the steps of the dance took them apart. Left to his own wanderings, Wesmorlen mulled over the news Amanda had imparted. He found it difficult to credit that Regana was at all mercenary, as Amanda would have him believe. He'd found nothing in her character to lead him to suspect that money was a primary factor in her quest for a husband, or in fact, that she was in search of a husband at all. And if money and a title were the criteria, surely *he* was the better candidate. After all, the extent of his wealth was widely known, and there was no question that his family was of higher rank and social standing than Botheringham's.

No, the more Wesmorlen thought about it, the more he was inclined to believe that the whole story was nothing more than a fabrication on Amanda's part, contrived to make him change his opinion of Regana. And if that was her intent, he was determined not to show any feelings one way or another.

When the dance brought them together again, Amanda searched his face to see if she had discomposed him. Unfortunately, it seemed she hadn't. And when she tried to reopen the subject of Miss Kently, Wesmorlen forestalled her, saying casually, "Amanda, why don't we just leave the topic alone? What Miss Kently does and whom she accompanies is certainly her own affair."

Wesmorlen appeared genuinely unconcerned and took care to look everywhwere but at Regana. Decidedly put out that her gambit had elicited no response, Amanda pouted prettily. "I'm surprised to hear you say so, Richard. I thought you harboured a tendre for the young lady. You seemed quite protective of her that afternoon I came across the two of you driving."

"Well, naturally I would be solicitous of the young lady, Amanda," Wesmorlen responded, one dark eyebrow lifting. "Any lady I take out is in my protection, if you will, while she is with me. What kind of gentleman would I be to act otherwise?"

Amanda didn't reply, reluctantly aware that everything Wesmorlen said made sense. Nor was there anything in his manner now to indicate that he had more than a passing interest in the young lady. Either her instincts had led her astray, or the earl was a very convincing dissembler, Amanda acknowledged, neither of which were pleasing possibilities. However, able to do little beyond accepting the fact, the marchioness let the subject drop for the moment, and decided that the wisest thing she could do was to remain awake on all suits.

Wesmorlen, watching the play of emotions across the Beauty's face, allowed himself the satisfaction of having bested her. Although Amanda's initial pronouncement had caused him considerable distress, he was now more convinced than ever that the story was nothing more than a wholecloth to lure him away from Regana. He knew that Amanda would stop at nothing to get what she wanted. She never had. So it followed that if Amanda thought that by casting doubt upon Regana's character she could accomplish what she set out to do, Wesmorlen knew she wouldn't hesitate.

Thus, when Wesmorlen approached Regana a short while later, he felt no compunction to question her about Lord Botheringham or their so-called understanding. "Good evening, Miss Kently," he said, bowing from the waist. "You're looking very lovely and festive this evening."

Regana sensed rather than heard his approach and turned to smile up into the dark eyes with a look which did the strangest things to his equilibrium. "Thank you, my lord. I confess to feeling rather festive tonight." She glanced at the throng around them in amusement. "I think Lady Chadwick may rest assured that her first venture back into Society has met with resounding success."

"It would seem so," the earl confirmed, "though I doubt Amanda troubled herself to think it would be otherwise."

Regana laughed indulgently. "It must give one a great sense of security to know that everything one attempts will turn out well. I know if I were to plan a ball as elaborate as this, I should be in such a state of nerves for weeks beforehand as to render myself quite useless for anything else."

"Now that I find utterly incomprehensible," the earl replied without hesitation. "You have always struck me as the sort of lady who could accomplish anything she set her mind to, and with the utmost aplomb." He looked directly into the azure eyes. "Or have I made a grave error in judgement?"

Regana gave a low gurgle of laughter. "For me to agree with your compliments would be to laud my own abilities, Lord Wesmorlen, and I am loath to do such a thing. Suffice it to say that I can do a creditable job of arranging things when I have to."

The earl smiled to himself, finding her candour quite charming. He knew Amanda would have been only too happy to regale him with examples of her many talents, as doubtless would most of the other young ladies with whom he was acquainted. That Regana shied away from such ostentatious displays only served to reinforce the earl's opinion that she was anything but mercenary or fickle.

"I hope, Miss Kently, that you have not forgotten my request for a dance." His eyes flashed wickedly. "I should hate to incur Lord Botheringham's wrath yet again by having to alter the order of things."

"You need not concern yourself with that, my lord," Regana said with a chuckle. "Lord Botheringham will not be in attendance this evening, and since no other gentleman has been so bold as to attach me for more than two dances, I do have a few spaces left on my card which you may claim."

She handed him the dance card and tried to hide her pleasure when she saw him mark himself down for two dances, one of which was the supper dance. No doubt that would put Lady Chadwick in high dudgeon.

"You said Lord Botheringham would not be in attendance this evening," Wesmorlen observed conversationally as he secured a glass of punch for her. "Does he always advise you of his comings and goings?"

"No, not really," Regana replied, unaware of how carefully he watched her. "It is simply that he came to see me last week and during the course of the visit advised me that he would be in the City for a time. Normally, I have no more idea of his whereabouts than anyone else."

Her voice was completely without guile, and though she spoke of Botheringham, her eyes were on the floor, following the movements of the dancers. Her lack of interest in the portly baron was obvious, but the fact that Botheringham had been to see her at all irked Wesmorlen. Could there be some truth in what Amanda had said about there existing some kind of understanding between them?

He had no opportunity to question Regana further, however, and had to be content to watch her take her place for a country dance with a handsome young buck whom Wesmorlen didn't particularly care for. It suddenly occurred to him that he spent a great deal of time lately watching this enchanting creature in the arms of gentlemen whom he didn't particularly care for.

"*Now* what's causing you to look so thunderous, darling?" Amanda teased softly, her voice close to his ear. "If I didn't know better, I'd say you were looking a trifle jealous, Richard."

Wesmorlen studiously removed his gaze from Regana once again. *Damn Amanda,* he cursed silently. Did she have nothing better to do than to watch his every move?

"Hardly that, Amanda," he replied in an offhand manner. "I was merely thinking it ironic that for a party to be hailed as a success, it must become such a suffocating crush."

Amanda adopted an offended pose. "Are you not enjoying my little party, Richard?" she asked, pouting. "I've spent weeks planning this, you know. I wanted everything to be perfect. Just for you."

Wesmorlen decided to ignore the last remark. "And it is perfect, Amanda," he said in a conciliatory tone. "No doubt it will be talked of for weeks to come."

"But not by you," the Beauty observed, her green eyes cooling ever so slightly.

"I am not the standard by which to judge your success, Amanda. The decor is exquisite, the food delicious, and the wine in abundant supply—all the trappings of a gala ball. It's merely that I find my tastes changing towards smaller, more intimate gatherings."

Amanda moved closer to the earl, her fragrant perfume filling his nostrils. The bodice of her gown barely covered the creamy expanse of bosom, and as she leaned closer to him he was given a tantalizing view of soft pink skin.

"If that's what you prefer, darling, we can arrange as intimate a gathering as you like. You have only to tell me where and when."

The invitation was so blatant that for a moment Wesmorlen couldn't help but smile. Looking down into the beautiful face raised to his, seeing the full, ripe lips, the dark smouldering eyes filled with longing, Wesmorlen suddenly wondered how he had ever been foolish enough to be attracted to Amanda. He knew he had only to nod his head and she would willingly go to his bed. But hers was a hollow beauty, he realized now. There was no gentleness or softness in her nature. Amanda was solely concerned with Amanda, and for that reason, Wesmorlen knew she would never be his wife.

Regana, choosing that very moment to look up in response to something her partner said, was sadly unaware of the direction of Wesmorlen's thoughts. Had she been, the sight of him standing beside Lady Chadwick, their eyes smiling into each others', their bodies so close as to be almost touching, would have given her little cause for concern. As it was, the sight which met her eyes caused Regana to gasp as though someone had dealt her a physical blow. She tried to look away but it was as though she were suddenly turned to stone. The smile faded from her lips and she was aware of nothing more than a throbbing ache in her heart.

Her body carried her through the rest of the dance mechanically. Fortunately, her partner, oblivious to her sudden silence, kept up a stream of one-sided conversation until the dance ended and Regana could make her escape. She had no desire to mingle; she needed to be alone with her thoughts, to deal with her pain and to sort out her tumultuous emotions.

Slipping through the open French doors onto the terrace, Regana followed the path down through the gardens, her steps illuminated by the silvery light of the full moon. The cool evening air was like balm to her heated cheeks and she drew deep breaths of it into her hot lungs. By now, tears trembled in her eyes and, blindly, she stumbled along until the music became no more than a distant sound. Descending farther into the garden, she stopped finally at the rotunda by the edge of the pond, where the only sound was the trickle of water in the fountain, and the occasional chirp of a night insect.

Lowering herself onto the cold stone bench, Regana closed her eyes. What a coil she'd made of this, she thought, her eyes misty with unshed tears. She'd stupidly allowed herself to fall in love with the Unmarriageable Earl, a man who had stolen more hearts than she even knew about, and who now added hers to his list.

Yes, she loved him, Regana admitted, finally allowing herself to put a name to this emotion which had taken control of her senses despite her futile attempts to deny it. She loved him. It was as simple, yet as complicated, as that. He was the man she had been looking for, waiting for all this time. And now that she'd found him, she had to accept that he loved another.

Regana felt strangely numb at the prospect, as though all emotion had been drained from her. Had she just imagined that he was developing a tendre for her? Had she misread all the signs—the lingering glances, the warm smile he seemed to reserve for her alone? Or were those things he shared with every woman he met? Perhaps he was no different from the other gentlemen of the ton, after all, Regana thought dismally, perhaps he was as dishonest and idle as the rest of them, concerned with himself first and foremost. And if that were the case, then obviously she had been the greater fool for having allowed herself to believe that he, the great Earl of Wesmorlen, scion of a great and noble family, and confidant of the Prince Regent, would deign to care for someone like her. It certainly seemed that way now, she thought, recalling the way he'd been looking at Lady Chadwick.

And what of the future? Regana mused, finding these thoughts even more oppressive. If by chance Clarisse should marry Peter Wesmorlen, Regana knew that she would be forced into contact with the earl whether she wanted to be or not. Which also meant she would see him married to Amanda Chadwick, and eventually to see the children they would have together.

Abruptly, Regana recalled the conversation she'd had with Lord Botheringham. He'd said they had an understanding—but an understanding of what? Was she affianced or not? Had they parted on the assumption that she would marry him, or simply that he would ask her to marry him upon his return? And if that was the case, what would she say, now that it was clear that Wesmorlen did not want her? If love was not to be considered, did it really matter whom she married?

"No, no! Please don't let this happen!" The words broke from her in an anguished whisper, a cry from the heart which echoed in the stillness of the night. Hearing them, Wesmorlen stopped dead in his tracks. He'd seen Regana slip from the room and had waited until Amanda was suitably occupied with her next partner before slipping out to find her. Now, however, watching Regana as she sat on the bench, her head down, the normally vibrant face curiously vacant, he felt an overwhelming sense of disquiet.

"I'm beginning to think we share a similar disdain for these functions," Wesmorlen said quietly. "It seems we both felt the need of some fresh air."

Regana was so startled by the sound of his voice that she jumped up from the bench and drew back against the marble pillar, her heart beating like a drum. Her eyes were wide, and her expression, momentarily unguarded, reflected all the pain and disillusionment she was feeling. Wesmorlen flinched, shocked that he should see her suffering so. What had happened to take the laughter from her face and extinguish the sparkle in those expressive eyes?

"Miss Kently, I've startled you—forgive me," he said huskily. "I could see you were deep in thought and should have realized you would probably not hear my approach. Please," he said, indicating the vacated seat, "will you not sit down and tell me what troubles you?"

Regana stared back at him, dimly aware that he had no knowledge that the sight of him and Lady Chadwick was the cause of her distress. For that at least she was thankful. She would not allow him to see how much she loved him. Nor would she suffer his pity.

"I...did not hear your approach, Lord Wesmorlen," she answered as calmly as her emotions would allow. "I was, as you say, lost in thought. Pray forgive my unexpected reaction."

Regana sank down onto the bench again, her eyes still carefully averted. She opened her fan and held it to her face, striving to regain her composure. "I find the rooms stuffy," she replied eventually, anxious to fill in the awkward silence. "So overcrowded with people. I think perhaps I am becoming more like my sister used to be, preferring the company of a few close friends to these suffocating assemblies." She laughed in a self-deprecatory manner. "But I'm sure I'm in the minority on that head."

Aware that Regana had almost echoed his very words to Amanda, the earl nodded in commiseration. "The things we do in the pursuit of pleasure," he said, chuckling, hoping to alleviate some of the tension which still marred her lovely features.

But Regana failed to respond. The tension was still present. So much so that it seemed almost a tangible thing between them, and whereas their past conversations had been of a light-hearted and easy nature, this one felt terribly stilted and awkward. Somehow a different quality had entered their relationship. Not dislike, exactly, the earl decided, but rather a kind of indifference. And suddenly he wondered if that weren't much worse. "Miss Kently... please..." he began, hoping to break through the barrier. "I can see that something has caused you great distress. Will you not tell me what it is?"

"No, I...think not," Regana replied. She rose, praying that her legs would not give way under her. "I think I should return to the house, Lord Wesmorlen. I don't think it...proper that I be out here alone with you."

Her voice was soft, almost inaudible, yet it cut him to the core. "Why not?" he asked gruffly. "Are you afraid of me, Regana, or is there some other reason for your concern?"

She dimly registered the use of her first name, but it was not uppermost in her mind. His question had struck too close to home, and in her present state of mind, she had no desire to delve into a subject which could only bring her more pain. "No, my lord, I do not fear you. You've never given me any reason to. As to asking me why I shouldn't be out here alone with you, I really don't think I need explain that. I'm sure you're just as conversant with the edicts of Society as I."

"If I were to propose to you, Society would have nothing to say about it, would it?"

CHAPTER EIGHT

THE WORDS were uttered almost before he realized it, but having said them, Wesmorlen knew he had no regrets. They were the very words he had been longing to say. Regana, hearing them spoken in such a matter-of-fact manner, wondered if she'd heard him correctly. "Propose?" she repeated, hating the way her heart leapt into her throat. "I'm ... not sure I understand, my lord."

"Do you not?" he replied, the smile she knew so well tugging at his lips. "Then perhaps I should say it a little more succinctly."

The earl took one of her hands in his and gently pressed her back onto the bench. His eyes never left her face, and to Regana's amazement, Wesmorlen dropped to one knee beside her. "Miss Kently," he began, "I know this may seem rather sudden, and I know our acquaintance has been short, but I profess that I have never felt for any woman in my life, what I feel for you. Your beauty, your goodness, everything about you endears you to my heart, and I find that I want you very much to be a part of my life. Dearest Regana, would you do me the honour of becoming my wife?"

Regana gazed back at him, rendered quite speechless. How could he be proposing to her when she'd just seen him speaking so intimately with Lady Amanda?

"My lord," she said finally. "I don't know what to say, though to say that I am shocked would indeed be putting it mildly."

"Does my proposal offend you, Miss Kently?" he asked quietly. "For I assure you, no offence was intended."

"On the contrary, my lord, you flatter me," Regana corrected, the hint of a smile warming her eyes. "It's simply that you caught me unawares. I thought your affections lay...elsewhere."

The earl watched the colour stain her cheeks, and slowly, comprehension began to dawn. So that was it! What a fool he had been not to realize sooner. She had obviously seen him standing with Amanda and had misunderstood their closeness. That would explain why she had fled the floor immediately upon her acquitting the dance. It also explained the change in her behaviour to him. But was it the reason for the pain he'd glimpsed in her eyes earlier? For if it was, did that not indicate some degree of affection towards him?

"Regana," he said gently, still holding her hand. "I think perhaps there is something I should say, and I shall be very honest with you." He paused, aware that what he was about to say had to be phrased very carefully. "Lady Chadwick is a beautiful and desirable woman, and I shan't pretend she isn't. No, wait, hear me out!" he urged, pulling her back even as she would have fled. "Nor shall I pretend that at one time there wasn't an involvement between us. But," he said, stressing the word, "I also know that we would never suit as husband and wife. I'm telling you this because I believe you may have misunderstood something you saw earlier and I would like very much to put your mind at ease. Regana?" he said, squeezing her hand. "Regana, are you listening to me?"

Regana nodded, not trusting herself to speak. She'd heard every word he'd said but she was still in a quandary. Dared she believe that there was nothing between him and Lady Chadwick? She wanted to—desperately. Just as she knew she wanted to accept his proposal. But what if she were wrong? And what of Lord Botheringham and his strange declaration? Need she tell the earl about that? What if Botheringham believed them to be engaged, only to come back to find that she had accepted another man—and a man that he would certainly take exception to. He would be furious, and Regana was suddenly fearful as to what direction that anger might take.

"Lord Wesmorlen, I appreciate your candour in explaining the situation between yourself and Lady Chadwick. I confess I did...misinterpret what I saw earlier, and your explanation has certainly helped to set my mind at rest." She hesitated for a moment, then decided for her own peace of mind, she would have to empty her budget entirely. "My lord, I value honesty above all things. It's very important that you understand that. If I thought for a moment that you were lying to me about Lady Chadwick, I would turn your proposal down without a second thought."

"Then set your mind at rest, my dear, for I am telling you the truth," Wesmorlen assured her. "There is nothing between Amanda and myself."

His fingers were tracing a circular pattern on Regana's wrist, arousing the most curious sensation in her stomach. "Yes...I do believe you. But there is something I must say to you, and I admit it has me in rather a tizzy."

The earl watched the adorable face, aware that she'd made no move to pull her hand away. "Yes, Miss Kently?"

"Well, it's rather awkward, really. I don't quite know how to put it."

"I've always found the straightforward approach to be the best," Wesmorlen advised. "Please, Regana, tell me what's troubling you."

Lulled by the charity in his voice, Regana took a deep breath and then recounted the details of her meeting with Botheringham and of their subsequent understanding. She found the telling somewhat embarrassing and had to be urged to continue a number of times. Wesmorlen listened with growing interest, and though his face betrayed nothing, his mind locked away every bit of information with satisfaction. So, the rumours of an understanding were not misplaced. Silently, he sent his apologies to Amanda. It seemed in that at least, she was not incorrect.

From another vantage point, however, Wesmorlen realized that his moment was almost at hand. He had Botheringham exactly where he wanted him. Now, all he needed was Regana's consent to marriage and his revenge would be complete. But why was he feeling curiously flat about the whole thing? This was what he'd waited for—wasn't it?

"And so you see, my lord," Regana concluded, "I am in a bit of a quandary as to whether I am even in a position to entertain your proposal."

"And if I were to tell you that you most decidedly are, what would you say?" Wesmorlen asked.

"I'd ask you how you could be so sure," Regana responded. "How do you know that Lord Botheringham did not intend what he said as a proposal?"

"Because I know Lord Botheringham well enough to know that when he does something, he leaves no room for doubt in anyone's mind as to what he means. If Botheringham had intended to propose, he would have done so in a most forthright manner and it would have been left for you merely to answer yes or no."

"And the fact that he told me to govern myself accordingly?"

The earl shrugged expressively. "Was simply to make you think that you were his property even though you were nothing of the kind. He had no leave to ask it of you though it doesn't surprise me that he did."

Regana sat quietly for a moment, mulling over everything Wesmorlen had said. She had to agree that he'd made perfect sense, and that she had no reason not to believe him. Indeed, if what he said was true, she was really under no obligation to Botheringham, not even to wait for his official proposal.

"And you really don't think Lord Botheringham will think himself made to look like a fool?"

It took only the briefest of moments for Wesmorlen to overcome his conscience. "Why should he?" he replied. "The only thing he'll feel foolish about is that he didn't ask you to marry him when he had the opportunity. Because if I have anything to say about it, he shall never have the opportunity again."

Wesmorlen took Regana's other hand and raised both of them to his lips, kissing first one and then the other. He saw the pulse beating in her throat and knew she was not unaffected by his nearness. "So, my dear Miss Kently—Regana," he said quietly, smiling up into her eyes. "I ask you again. Will you do me the great honour of becoming my wife?"

There was little reason for Regana to hesitate this time, but for some reason, she did. Was she still harbouring doubts about Amanda, despite his assurances to the contrary, he wondered. She continued to look silently into his face, as if memorizing every feature. Then, breathing a tiny sigh, Wesmorlen heard her say, "Yes, Lord Wesmorlen, I will be your wife. I should be very proud to be your wife."

Wesmorlen had not anticipated a negative answer, but in those brief, agonizing moments when Regana had hesitated, he'd experienced the strangest constriction in his heart, as though someone were holding him round the chest and squeezing with all his might. The relief and joy he felt upon her answer made him almost lightheaded.

Suddenly, and with startling clarity, Wesmorlen realized that he was utterly in love with this woman who had just consented to be his wife. Love had crept up on him and caught him unawares. And to think it had all started out as a quest for revenge!

Belatedly, the earl recalled Regana's words about honesty, and knew a moment's remorse. But then, he reasoned, revenge might have been his original motive in pursuing Regana, but love had long since taken its place. Had he taken her from Botheringham strictly out of a desire for revenge, he would have suffered her anger willingly. But not for anything would he hurt her now; nor would anyone else.

Aware that he was still holding her hands, Wesmorlen drew Regana closer. As his lips touched hers for the first time, Regana felt a warm glow spread through her body, awakening sensations and feelings she'd never thought to experience. Gradually, his kiss grew more demanding, and Regana was amazed to find herself returning those kisses with an ardour which matched his own. It was only when she felt his fingers lightly caressing the satiny skin on her bare shoulder that Regana drew back, dimly aware that she should hardly be allowing him to kiss her so wantonly in such a public place.

"My lord..." she said breathlessly, her pulse racing.

"Richard," he corrected, his own voice husky.

"Richard." She smiled happily. "I really think we had best return inside. If people were to see us..."

"Oh, blast the other people!" Wesmorlen grumbled. "I happen to like kissing the woman I intend to spend the rest of my life with."

"And I hope you will continue to do so," she replied, blushing in spite of herself, "but not, I think, at this time or in this place."

Reluctantly, Wesmorlen accepted the wisdom of her advice. Offering her his arm, the earl pulled her to her feet, gently drawing her to him.

"I love you, Regana," he whispered, lifting her chin so that he could see those glorious eyes. "Never forget that."

They shared one last kiss, their bodies lightly touching, before Wesmorlen slowly drew away and escorted her back up to the ballroom.

From her concealed vantage point on the balcony, Amanda Chadwick watched the pair stroll contentedly back to the house, her beautiful face set in a hard, angry mask. So, Richard had betrayed her, after all, she thought, her eyes glinting like chips of emerald ice. Betrayed her for a little nobody like Regana Kently. And judging by the besotted look on the chit's face, he might even have proposed marriage.

Well, he wouldn't get off lightly this time, Amanda vowed, angrily turning on her heel. "You'll be very sorry you did this to me, Richard," she whispered under her breath. "As shall you, Regana Kently. Just see if you're not!"

THE EARL DID NOT announce their engagement that night. Though he longed to shout it to the world, he knew it was only proper that he formally ask Regana's aunt for her niece's hand in marriage. Once they had her consent, they would tell Clarisse and he would advise his mother of the news—which would doubtless ensure her happiness for many days to come—following which a notice would appear in the *Gazette*.

Before they parted company that evening, Regana sought out Wesmorlen one more time to ask what she should say to Botheringham.

"Why don't you leave that to me?" Wesmorlen offered casually. "I wanted to see him on another matter in any case, so I can discuss this with him at the same time. When did you say he was to return?"

"Tomorrow, I believe."

"Excellent. I'll call round to see him after I speak to your aunt." His eyes crinkled in amusement. "You don't think she'll send me off with a flea in my ear, do you?"

"I hardly think so," Regana replied with a laugh. "Unless she knows some deep, dark secret about you which precludes your eligibility."

Wesmorlen laughed in genuine amusement. "Nothing for which I haven't already been reprimanded, my darling girl."

After Regana and her family had left, Wesmorlen returned to the ballroom. He had not seen much of Amanda after he and Regana had returned from the garden. When he had, it was to see her laughing provocatively into the face of whomever she happened to be dancing with. Therefore, he didn't expect the stinging tone in her voice when she bade him goodnight.

"By the way, Richard, are congratulations in order?" she said, walking with him to the door.

"Congratulations, Amanda? Whatever for?"

"Oh, I don't know," she replied, shrugging diffidently. "I just thought you seemed rather buoyant after your walk in the garden with Miss Kently. Perhaps I was mistaken." Her eyes glittered maliciously. "Good night, Lord Wesmorlen."

The earl glanced at her sharply, aware that the eyes looking back at him were as cold as ice. Had she seen them kissing in the garden, he wondered. If so, why was she being purposely evasive about it now? What was Amanda hiding?

Regana, too, had felt the sting of Lady Chadwick's tongue. As she was about to depart, the marchioness had floated up to her, her keen eyes missing nothing.

"Leaving so soon, Miss Kently?"

"I'm afraid so, Lady Chadwick. My aunt tires easily, and if we linger, she will be that much worse for it tomorrow."

"Yes, of course," Amanda murmured sympathetically. "Too much excitement isn't good for any of us, is it, Miss Kently? But then, I'm sure I don't need to tell *you* that... after tonight."

There was no mistaking the animosity in her voice, and Regana wondered if her brief interlude in the garden with Lord Wesmorlen might have been witnessed. There was no opportunity to find out, however, as Amanda turned away to see to another departing group. But then, what did it matter if Lady Chadwick did know? If all went well tomorrow and Aunt Mary gave her consent, the announcement of their engagement could be made public, and a chaste kiss in someone's garden would be of little consequence.

REGANA AND CLARISSE were in the morning room when Lord Wesmorlen arrived the following day. The sisters had been discussing the events of the previous night in great detail, when Clarisse, who happened to be standing by the window, said in surprise, "Why, I believe you have a visitor, Regana. And a very handsome one at that."

Regana joined Clarisse at the window and watched the earl ride past, proudly thinking that no man could look more dashing in his coat of dark blue superfine, ivory breeches and polished black Hessians. An elegant diamond-and-onyx pin nestled in the folds of his neckcloth, skilfully arranged in the dashing but casual Mailcoach style, while the sun glistened off his shiny black beaver.

"My, he is handsome," Clarisse sighed. "Almost as much so as his brother."

"Hush, goose," Regana admonished, returning to her chair. "And do sit down, Clarisse, it won't do for Rich... Lord Wesmorlen to see us both gawking at him from the window."

"Rich?" Clarisse said in confusion. "Who is...?" Suddenly, her eyes widened. "You were going to say Richard, weren't you? You're on a first-name basis with Lord Wesmorlen, aren't you, Reggie?"

"I am?" Regana replied, feigning innocence.

"Tosh, Regana, of course you are. That's why he's here so early. He's coming to talk to Aunt Mary about you, isn't he? And then he's going to ask you to marry him!"

"Well, not exactly," Regana hedged.

"Not exactly. What do you— Oh!" Clarisse gasped, then smiled from ear to ear. "He's not going to ask you to marry him because he's already proposed, hasn't he? That's why you looked so radiant last night."

"Clarisse, I—"

"Regana, I truly am out of all patience with you!" Clarisse declared. "Wesmorlen proposed to you at the ball last night and you didn't even tell me, you naughty girl. Well, he did propose, didn't he?"

"Clarisse, I really should wait until—"

"Until I have your aunt's permission to announce our betrothal," the earl finished for her from the doorway. Both girls swung round, unaware that Lord Wesmorlen and their aunt had joined them. Regana held her breath, afraid to ask but longing to know. Then, seeing the smiles on both their faces, she jumped up and hurried to greet her fiancé.

"Darling," he murmured, as she slipped into his arms.

"Come along, Clarisse," Aunt Mary said, pulling the still-beaming girl out of the room. "I think we'll give these two a few moments alone. But only a few, mind, Regana," she added with a wink.

When they were alone, the earl tipped Regana's head back and placed a full, lingering kiss on her lips. His hands cradled her face as though it were his most precious possession, and when Regana's lids finally fluttered open, it was to gaze into eyes which were glowing as brightly as her own.

"I assume this means that Aunt Mary agreed," she whispered mischievously.

"Only after a great deal of convincing," Wesmorlen teased, brushing her lips again. "In the end, she had to agree that I was a sterling fellow and quite fit to marry her niece. Speaking of which," he said, leading Regana to the love seat, "I have something for you."

Wesmorlen sat down next to her and pulled an intricately worked jewel box from his breast pocket. "This has always graced the hand of the eldest Wesmorlen's bride. I give it to you today, Regana, as a token of my love and esteem."

Regana caught her breath as he opened the lid to reveal a magnificent diamond-and-sapphire ring cushioned against the deep black velvet. Breathless, she watched as he took it from the box and slipped it on to her finger and then lifted her hand to his lips.

"Now it's official," he whispered, taking her lips again. "All that's left now, my lady, is to set the date."

Lost in the wondrous pleasure of his kiss, Regana didn't hear the door open. It wasn't until she heard Clarisse's tactful "ahem" that she reluctantly drew away from Richard.

"I take it our few moments are up," Richard murmured, releasing her, albeit reluctantly.

"Congratulations, dearest," Clarisse whispered as Regana embraced her, tears of joy springing to her eyes. "I'm so very happy for you."

"Thank you, Clarisse, though I don't imagine it will be long before I'm saying exactly the same thing to you."

Regana then turned to embrace her aunt. "Congratulations, my dear," Aunt Mary said, holding her tightly. "I know you shall be very happy. Oh, dear, these things always make me so dashed sentimental," she added, dabbing a handkerchief at her eyes. "Now where is Wrigly with that champagne? Wrigly!"

THERE WERE TWO more people Wesmorlen intended to inform prior to his engagement being made public. He had already sent a note to his mother, the countess, informing her of the news of his impending betrothal and advising that he would be arriving with his fiancée in a few days' time. The second person, and one he would only see in person, was Lord Botheringham.

True to his word, Wesmorlen had gone to Tewkehurst House, Lord Botheringham's country residence, immediately upon leaving Regana. At his knock, an elderly butler had opened the door, and after giving his name, Wesmorlen had been shown into Lord Botheringham's library, there being advised that his lordship would be along directly.

Glancing round the huge book-lined room with its high ceilings and panelled walls, Wesmorlen couldn't help but feel that the inside of the house echoed the sombre mood of the outside. The library was dark and surprisingly Spartan, furnished only with a massive mahogany desk and two leather armchairs. Dark velvet curtains hung at the windows, as though the occupant couldn't abide the brightness of the sun. Even the fire burning in the blackened grate was not enough to stave off the chill which permeated the room.

When Botheringham finally entered, Wesmorlen was standing by the window. There was no trace of welcome on the baron's face, nor did he waste time with pleasantries. He sat down at his desk and pulled a sheaf of papers from a drawer.

"What do you want, Wesmorlen?" he asked without preamble. "I don't have a great deal of time, nor can I think of any good reason why you'd be here."

"Normally I'd agree with you, Botheringham. Today, however, I come as a favour to another and to make you aware of some news."

"Oh? What favour, and what news?"

Wesmorlen had waited a long time for this moment, and had anticipated deriving a great deal of satisfaction from it. Now that the moment was at hand, however, he found the victory strangely hollow. He took no particular pleasure in imparting the news and did so with no other thought in mind but to have done with it and leave. Was this the sweetness of revenge he'd heard so much about, Wesmorlen wondered briefly.

"I came to inform you of my impending betrothal," he said quietly.

The grunt which met his words was hardly congratulatory. "Your betrothal," Botheringham sneered. "You flatter yourself, Wesmorlen. What makes you think I have any interest in whom you leg-shackle yourself to?"

"Because the lady in question, the lady who has consented to be my wife, is Miss Regana Kently."

A stunned silence greeted his words. Slowly, Botheringham stopped shuffling his papers and peered up at Wesmorlen in disbelief. "What did you say?"

"I think you heard me, Botheringham," Wesmorlen replied. "I have asked Regana Kently to be my wife and she has consented."

"The devil, you say!" Botheringham stormed, slamming his fist down on the table. "She was to have been mine. Damn it, we had an understanding."

"No, *you* had an understanding, Botheringham," the earl pointed out. "You went to see her and discussed her suitability, after which you advised Regana that you would call upon her again when you returned from the City."

"Exactly." The baron nodded. "I was to do so today, at which time she was to entertain my proposal and deliver me her answer."

"And so she has, Botheringham," Wesmorlen said, "except that it is being delivered through me. And the lady is, of course, quite unable to accept any proposal you may put forward, as she has already accepted mine."

The older man glared at the earl ominously. "I warned you to stay away from her, Wesmorlen. I told you that I intended to offer for her and I did."

"No, Botheringham, you did not," the earl said, keeping his voice level. "What you did was discuss the possibility that you might offer for her. As I pointed out to Miss Kently when she broached this subject with me, since you did not ask for a definitive yes or no, I don't see that a formal proposal was ever made. Nor did you approach her guardian to elicit her permission for such a proposal to be made."

"You're playing with words, Wesmorlen," Botheringham said, waving his hand as if to dismiss the objections. "The intent was there and you damn well know it. But you pursued her anyway."

The earl shrugged negligently. "You are entitled to your opinion, Botheringham."

The baron lifted his large frame out of the chair and moved to stand by the window. "I fail to see why you made such a point of pursuing her, Wesmorlen. She is, after all, without notable family connections. I would have thought that point alone would have put her well below your lofty requirements."

"It didn't seem to deter you," Wesmorlen pointed out sagely.

"I, alas, am not as young or as...virile as you," Botheringham sneered, making the word sound like an insult. "As such, I am hardly likely to attract a great number of ladies to pick from. Besides which, what woman would not choose the coronet of an earl as opposed to that of a mere baron."

"I thought you considered your great wealth and social standing as suitable recompense," Wesmorlen sallied. The half smile on his face did little to hide his tangible dislike, and suddenly, a gleam of comprehension dawned in Botheringham's eyes.

"By God, it's revenge, isn't it?" he said incredulously. "Revenge for what I did to that simpering brother of yours last year. That's what sparked this sudden interest in the

Kently woman. As soon as you learned that I was courting her, you took it upon yourself to seduce her away from me. Am I correct?''

Wesmorlen turned away, feigning interest in a book he saw upon the shelf. "Have a care, Botheringham," he murmured, a steel edge audible through the silken tone. "Although I feel inclined to be somewhat more charitable towards you for having introduced me to my betrothed, I fear I am still not overly tolerant as regards your attitude towards my brother."

A silence hung between them, broken only by the measured ticking of the mantel clock. When eventually the earl turned back to the other man, his face was set in an inscrutable mask. "I've said what I came to say, Botheringham. I'll show myself out."

"Oh, yes. Spoken like a true man of honour," Botheringham spat out. "Is that how you work, Wesmorlen? Seducing another man's betrothed while he's away and then gloating over it? Hardly the honourable thing to do."

Abruptly, the earl turned, his eyes like glittering steel lances. "Was it, I wonder, any less honourable than calling a man a liar and a cheat to his face when you knew damn well he wasn't? Was it honourable, I wonder, to disgrace him publicly when in fact it was your own cowardly way of punishing him for having let slip a few careless remarks about your less than gentlemanly behaviour to a serving wench a few years back."

Wesmorlen paused, aware by the stricken look on Botheringham's face that his arrow had hit home. "Oh, yes, I knew, Botheringham," the earl continued softly in the face of the other man's silence. "Not that night at Lord Montrose's house, mind you, when I could have spoken up and prevented what happened and made you look a fool into the bargain. Unfortunately, I didn't find out until recently. But I did find out, Botheringham. I knew there had to be more to it than a simple dislike of my brother."

The earl walked slowly across the room. "You did an admirable job of covering your disgrace up, I'll give you that, but you made a few careless mistakes. And when I set out to find something, I make use of every mistake I can. The loose ends you left were only too happy to fill in the details... for the right price. In the end, I had a pretty complete picture of what happened."

Shaken, the older man drew in his breath slowly, but his gaze did not falter. "It was a long time ago," he said heavily. "It was an error in judgement, I admit it. But surely you can't hold that against a man for life. Besides, I didn't kill your brother when you know damn well I could have."

"No, you didn't," Wesmorlen acknowledged slowly. "And you can be thankful that you didn't, Botheringham, because if you had it would be more than Miss Kently you'd be forfeiting."

Botheringham flinched. "Beware, Wesmorlen," he growled. "I don't take kindly to threats."

"Nor do I, Botheringham. And I can assure you I would be a far better opponent than my brother, were it to come to that." Wesmorlen paused in the act of opening the door. "I wouldn't guarantee that you would fare so well were you to match your skills with me. Do you take my meaning?"

Botheringham didn't reply, but it was clear from the whitening of his knuckles on the chair back that he understood.

"Perhaps you forget it wasn't I who issued the challenge, Wesmorlen," Botheringham threw back at him. "Your brother did that."

"Yes, he did," Wesmorlen replied tightly, "after you provoked him and goaded him until he had little choice but to challenge you. And don't think for a moment that you played me for a fool, sir. I know that you had no intention of killing my brother. You're far too good a shot for that. No, you thought to leave him with an injury he might sustain all his life, didn't you? An injury which would make him less a man. Well, I'm sorry to disappoint you, my lord," Wesmorlen said bitingly, "but fortunately, that's not going to be the way of it. Not only is my brother's leg healing perfectly, but he has also met a young woman who loves him in spite of it. And now, as I've said all I ever intend to say to you again, Botheringham, I bid you good day!"

With that, Wesmorlen closed the door and left the forbidding house, feeling that for the first time in a long while, the debt to his brother had, at least partially, been repaid.

CHAPTER NINE

IT WAS ARRANGED that Peter would accompany Regana, Clarisse and Aunt Mary to Blackoaks in order that Regana might meet her future mother-in-law, the Countess of Wesmorlen. The earl had gone on ahead, saying he had some business to attend to prior to their arrival.

Regana regarded the coming visit with an anxiety not at all in keeping with her normally calm, unflustered disposition. She'd heard Lady Wesmorlen's name mentioned at any number of assemblies, and though she was always spoken of in the most respectful way, it was not without a certain wariness, for it seemed that the countess, despite her sixty-odd years, was still as sharp and discerning as she'd been as a young girl making her debut at Court.

Hers had been a charmed life, so Regana had been informed. Married after her first Season, the countess had produced two fine sons and sadly, one daughter who had died before the age of two. That death had sparked the family's removal from London to their country house in Gloucestershire, where they had raised their sons in an atmosphere of horses, hunting and love.

Two years ago, Richard had succeeded to the title when his father had passed away after a brief illness. All of this Regana had learned from Emily St. Hyde, and now, as the carriage bearing the Wesmorlen coat of arms made its way towards Blackoaks, Regana was grateful for the knowledge. Richard had assured her that his mother was looking forward to meeting her and that they would get on famously. But then, Regana thought with some amusement, men always suffered from the misplaced notion that all women got on equally well.

It was about four o'clock in the afternoon when they finally arrived at Blackoaks. As the carriage turned in through the massive stone gates, Regana caught glimpses of a large, stately house well ahead, its solid stone walls glowing a warm gold in the late-afternoon sun.

The last hoof had barely fallen before a liveried groom appeared to hold the horses, followed almost as quickly by a footman to pull down the steps and unload their baggage. When the beautifully carved front door swung open and Richard emerged, the smile of warmth on his face did much to allay Regana's fears.

"Ladies, welcome to Blackoaks," he called, helping Aunt Mary and Clarisse to alight. Then, when he extended his arm to Regana, the look in his eyes was for her alone. "I've missed you," he said quietly, lifting her hand to his lips.

"And I you," Regana replied shyly, feeling a tingle all over as he pressed a tender kiss against her fingers. He'd only been gone a few days, yet it felt like an eternity. Whatever would his mother think of her, blushing like a schoolgirl every time her son set foot in a room.

"Come on, you two," Peter called teasingly from the doorway. "You'll have plenty of time for that later."

Wesmorlen laughed, while Regana felt her cheeks flush brightly. He did not relinquish her hand, however, merely tucking it securely into his arm.

As they stood admiring the magificence of the main hall, Regana became aware of the presence of another person and, turning, caught sight of a woman who could only be the Countess of Wesmorlen.

There was no doubt in Regana's mind that the stories of the countess's youthful beauty had not been exaggerated. She was possessed of great beauty still, though one now mellowed with the gentle passage of time. She was taller than Regana had expected, and moved with a quiet dignity which only time and breeding could instill. Her grey eyes, not unlike Clarisse's in colour, were bright and inquisitive, and Regana sensed that a lively sense of humour lurked behind the dignified exterior.

"Ah, Richard, I see our guests have arrived," she said, her voice pleasantly low and well modulated. Her radiant smile encompassed each and every one of them.

"Mother, may I present Mrs. Standish and her younger niece Miss Clarisse Kently," the earl said, drawing them forward.

"Mrs. Standish, I hope you did not find the journey tiring," the countess said.

"Not at all, Lady Wesmorlen," Aunt Mary replied brightly. "The carriage was a delight to travel in, though I fear you may have spoiled me for anything else."

The countess smiled, a twinkle appearing in her eyes. "My late husband greatly disliked travelling. He never rode when he could drive, nor drove when he could be driven. And he was most particular about his conveyances. He used to say that if a person had to subject himself to the inconveniences of travel, he might at least do so in comfort."

Regana smiled to herself. It was clear from the countess's tone of voice that there had been a great deal of affection between her and her late husband, and she was suddenly reminded of her own parents and the happiness they had shared.

"And Miss Kently," the countess continued, looking at Clarisse. "I'm delighted to meet you both."

"And this is the young lady I told you about, Mother," Wesmorlen said, drawing Regana forward. "This is Miss Regana Kently, my fiancée."

The hand which enclosed hers was firm, and Regana saw genuine warmth in the clear grey eyes. "You've made my son very happy, my dear," she said softly. "And in doing that, you've made me very happy, as well. I am delighted to welcome you to our family. May I call you Regana?"

"I would be honoured, my lady," Regana replied, moved by the sincerity of her welcome.

"Good. I hope you will forgive my tardiness in not being here to greet you," the countess apologized to them all. "But I was going over the arrangements for dinner. Now, I'm sure you would like to rest after your journey. Mrs. Dobbins will show you to your rooms. I hope you will be comfortable and trust you will let me know if there is anything you require."

She smiled again at Regana. "I thought that in honour of your engagement, we would have a special family dinner tonight. Nothing elaborate, you understand, but perhaps a trifle more festive than usual. If you don't feel you'd be too tired, of course," the countess added kindly.

"I'm sure we will feel quite refreshed once we have removed the traces of our journey, my lady," Aunt Mary assured her. "Do you dine at six?"

"I can advance that time if you prefer, Mrs. Standish," the countess said with a smile, "though personally, I prefer to dine at eight."

Seeing their aunt's look of surprise, the countess laughed. "One of the customs I carried over from my time in London, Mrs. Standish. I prefer to dine at a later hour, and I see no reason to alter that simply because we're in the country."

"Eight o'clock will be fine," Aunt Mary said, liking the woman's clear, forthright manner.

"That sounds delightful, Mother, thank you," Wesmorlen said. Then, turning to Peter, he said, "I told Robert Mortimer I'd drop by and have a look at a new horse he's just brought down from London. He's hoping to enter it at Cheltenham. Care to come along."

"Goodness, Robert Mortimer," Peter said with a smile. "Yes, I'd like that very much. Splendid chap, Robert. I haven't seen him in years."

"Good," Richard said. "I told him we'd be along this afternoon. He's asked me to give him my opinion, though why he'd want it I'm not sure. Mortimer's one of the shrewdest judges of horseflesh I've ever met."

He turned to Regana, his glance decidedly wicked. "Perhaps I should take you with me, as well. I do believe you possess as discerning an eye as any."

Regana laughed at him and shook her head. "Alas, I must confess my expertise does not extend to the subject of racehorses, my lord. Mayhaps you can enlighten me over dinner."

"Just make sure you *are* back in time for dinner, Richard," the countess said with a twinkle in her eye. "As I recall, Sir Robert pours a rather generous toddy when he has guests, and I don't want to have to send Buckers down there looking for the two of you."

"Have no fear, Mother, I won't let you down," Richard replied with a laugh. "I learned long ago how to make Mortimer think I was keeping up my end." He winked at Regana. "I used to pour my drinks into the rosebushes when he wasn't looking. Poor old Dudgeon always wondered why that particular bush had such an unusual fragrance."

"You mean he didn't recognize the smell of liquor?" Aunt Mary asked in surprise.

"Not likely," Peter said with a laugh. "Dudgeon never touched the stuff!"

"He did have the best roses in the county, though," the countess said thoughtfully.

As the gentlemen took their leave, the ladies followed Mrs. Dobbins up to their rooms. Located on the same floor, the three rooms were adjoining, all giving view onto the magnificent formal gardens. As in the main hall, Re-

gana was struck by the opulence of the decor, each room
being furnished with fine antiques and paintings by Gainsborough, Rubens and Poussin. Her bedroom was deco-
rated in shades of pale peach, the velvet curtains and
bedspread being of a deeper apricot colour. On the floor
was a thick Aubusson carpet. A magnificent four-poster
bed dominated the room, while a peach-and-cream striped
love seat and chair were set in the window alcove.

Aunt Mary had brought Marie along to act as ladies'
maid to all three of them, but the countess, feeling that one
maid between three simply would not do, had sent her own
maid along to tend to Regana. Yvette was a diminutive
creature, but Regana soon discovered that like the rest of
the Wesmorlen staff, she was well trained and very good at
what she did. Thus, regarding her reflection in the mirror
as she prepared to go down for dinner that evening, Regana thought her hair had never been dressed so elegantly,
nor her toilette attended to with such particular care.

For her own part, Marie, having one fewer lady to dress,
had been able to give extra attention to both Clarisse and
Aunt Mary. As a result, the three ladies descended the
grand circular staircase in fine looks. Buckers, the Wes-
morlens' head butler, awaited them at the foot of the stairs.
"Her ladyship asks that you join her in the green room,
ladies, if you please."

The green room was actually a small reception room off
the dining room, done in shades of pale green, yellow and
white. Regana saw the countess, elegant in a gown of fine
French silk, chatting amiably with her two sons, both of
whom looked most distinguished in evening attire.

Immediately, Regana crossed to the countess. "Thank
you for sending Yvette to me, my lady," she said quietly.
"It was good of you."

The countess waved her hand as if to dismiss her generous gesture. "Yvette is a treasure. And I thought perhaps
as your own maid would have her hands full attending to

three of you, a little help would hardly go amiss. I don't know how she manages."

Regana didn't feel it necessary to inform the countess that since the three of them seldom went out at the same time, it wasn't too great a problem for Marie. For now, she decided to simply enjoy the luxury of a personal maid.

Dinner was a delightful meal. They dined by the light of three exquisite crystal candelabra, and though later, Regana couldn't remember having seen the servants, she knew that her glass was always full and that each deliciously prepared course flowed smoothly after the other. As expected, Lady Wesmorlen was a skilled hostess, adept at drawing out her guests and in keeping the flow of conversation lively. Wesmorlen was his usual charming self, regaling them with lighthearted stories of his travels in Europe. While he spoke, his eyes often strayed to Regana, his admiration there for all to see.

At the conclusion of the meal, the countess gave the signal and the ladies left the gentlemen to their port and cigars. As there were only the two of them, however, they quickly rejoined the ladies for coffee and cards in the drawing-room.

"Now that dinner is over, but before we retire," the countess said, making sure she had their attention, "I would like all of you to know that I am giving a ball in honour of my son's betrothal to Regana, and that it would give me the greatest pleasure if all of you would attend as my honoured guests."

A ripple of anticipation met her words, and Wesmorlen glanced at Regana proudly. "Thank you, Mother. I think I speak for Regana and myself when I say that we are honoured."

"Good. Then it's settled. Now," she said, rising, "since my days are going to be rather full, I think I shall say goodnight and leave you people to your pleasures."

"I think I shall do the same," Aunt Mary said. "Good-night, my dears," she said, kissing both her nieces. "See you on the morrow."

With the somewhat surprising departure of both the countess and their aunt, Regana looked at Clarisse guiltily. "I suppose we should follow their example," she admitted. "I hate to admit it, but I am feeling rather tired."

"Then by all means go to bed, my dear," Wesmorlen said solicitously. "Peter and I have a full day planned for you ladies tomorrow, and you'll need a good night's sleep if you are to keep up with us."

Both sisters glanced at him with renewed interest. "Are you going to tell us what manner of excitements you've planned?"

The earl looked at Peter, and saw the younger man shake his head. "It would seem not. You'll just have to go to your beds curious."

"I will tell you, however," Peter added, "that you shan't be disappointed."

"Well, I suppose we can't ask for more," Clarisse said, smiling at Peter. "I'll say good-night."

When just Regana and the earl were left, he crossed the room slowly and took her into his arms.

"You really oughtn't to be doing this," Regana objected, nevertheless loving the feel of his arms about her.

He bent his head and dropped a kiss on the tip of her nose. "Miss Kently, have I ever told you how adorable your nose is?"

Regana laughed. "No, my lord, I don't believe you have."

"Well, I'm telling you now."

He looked into her eyes, his own darkening at the love he saw reflected there. "Then, have I ever told you that you have the most beautiful eyes I've ever seen?"

He placed a gentle kiss on each of the closed lids. Regana, finding it harder to concentrate with every moment, shook her head and whispered huskily, "No, my lord, I don't believe you have."

"Well, I'm telling you that now, too. And, have I told you, my darling Miss Kently, that you are driving me to distraction and if I don't marry you very soon I shall go completely mad?"

"No, my lord, I don't—"

Her answer was cut off in midsentence as the earl's lips came down on hers, effectively ending the conversation. As she gave herself up to the sheer pleasure of his kiss, Regana wondered if any woman could be happier than she was tonight.

TRUE TO THEIR WORD, Richard and Peter did their utmost to entertain their guests, planning activities which would interest everyone, including Aunt Mary. There were picnics in the park, long leisurely walks through the gardens, trips to the neighbouring spa town of Bath, and any number of other festivities planned to occupy the daylight hours. In the evening, there were numerous parties to attend as word of the earl's betrothal spread. Most of the neighbours were delighted to hear the news and were eager to entertain the newly engaged couple. Only one person was conspicuous by her absence, Regana realized as she sat in front of her dressing table one evening: the Marchioness of Chadwick.

Since the night of Amanda's ball, Regana had been moved many times to recall the woman's parting remark. She had mentioned it once in passing to Richard, but when he had brushed it off, saying it was of no consequence, Regana had similarly given it little more thought.

She might have forgotten it completely, had she not encountered Lady Chadwick at the modiste's in the small village of Kenby while she and Clarisse were shopping for some ribbon to trim Regana's new bonnet. Browsing amongst the well-stocked shelves, Regana turned, startled to find herself looking into the cold green eyes she remembered so well.

"Well, if it isn't the celebrated Miss Kently," Lady Chadwick said mockingly. "I might have known we'd encounter each other eventually."

Regana inclined her head in the briefest of greetings. "Lady Chadwick," she said, preparing to turn away. But Amanda had not finished.

"I believe congratulations are in order, Miss Kently," she continued smoothly. "I understand you are to be married."

"Thank you. Yes, I am," Regana replied warily.

"How wonderful for you. You must pass along my congratulations to Lord Botheringham when next you see him."

Regana felt her cheeks grow hot. The woman was obviously trying to cause mischief. "I'm afraid you don't understand, Lady Chadwick. It's not Lord Botheringham I am to marry. I'm engaged to Lord Wesmorlen."

Amanda affected a look of perplexed surprise. "Lord Wesmorlen! But how can that be, Miss Kently? I understood from Lady Loring that you were promised to Lord Botheringham. How is it you come to be engaged to Lord Wesmorlen when you were already spoken for?"

Regana looked at the woman, trying to hide her growing dismay. By now, everyone in the shop was listening to their conversation, Lady Chadwick having made her pronouncement in a rather loud voice.

"You must be mistaken, Lady Chadwick. I was not promised to Lord Botheringham at all."

"Really? How strange," Amanda replied, continuing to look puzzled. "Then I wonder why Lord Botheringham was saying that you and he were affianced."

"I couldn't say, Lady Chadwick," Regana replied, feeling the heat steal into her cheeks. "Lord Botheringham neither asked me to marry him nor sought my aunt's permission to address me."

"Ah. Then I suppose what Lord Botheringham has been saying about there being a reason why Lord Wesmorlen pursued you so ardently is equally untrue."

That brought Regana's head up sharply, and she glanced at the woman, dismayed to see the gleam of victory in her eyes.

"I think the reason was quite obvious, Lady Chadwick," Regana said brusquely, aware of a trembling in the pit of her stomach. "At least it was to me. Come along, Clarisse."

Before the spiteful woman could make any further remarks, Regana and Clarisse made their escape, even though Regana felt sure that Lady Chadwick hadn't planned to say any more. It was enough that she had embarrassed Regana in public by her announcement of her supposed broken engagement. No doubt that juicy bit of gossip would be circulating within the hour.

In the carriage on the way back to Blackoaks, Regana was noticeably withdrawn, her normally smooth brow furrowed.

"Regana, you don't really believe anything that woman said, do you?" Clarisse said finally, aware of her sister's despondency. "She was just being vindictive because you are going to marry Lord Wesmorlen and she isn't."

But Regana shook her head, her blue eyes clearly troubled. "It's not her envy that worries me, Clarisse," Regana said, breathing a heavy sigh. "That I can understand. What concerns me is her implication that Lord Wesmorlen had a reason for courting me. What did she mean by that? What possible reason could he have had other than loving me?"

"None at all," Clarisse replied firmly. "Lady Chadwick was just being spiteful. Surely you can see she's consumed by envy?"

Regana could certainly see that, but the thought that there might be something else behind the earl's courtship stayed with her like a thorn pricking relentlessly in her side. Hadn't she herself said that Wesmorlen had not seemed interested in her upon their first meeting? It wasn't until after he saw her dancing with Lord Botheringham that he had approached her, Regana remembered. Could Lord Botheringham have had something to do with this? She knew he and Lord Wesmorlen were not the best of friends. Was that also why he had wanted to tell Botheringham of their betrothal rather than let her do so?

It made more sense than Regana cared to admit, but she was at a loss to know how to verify her suspicions. Dared she bring the subject up with Wesmorlen? Would he admit to deception, even if it were true? Worse still, how would *she* react if he did? She loved Richard, but if she discovered that he didn't really love her, or that he had lied to her, could she go ahead and marry him anyway?

THE QUESTION was still unanswered as Regana proceeded downstairs the following morning. She was surprised to find the house empty, and enquired from Buckers as to the whereabouts of everyone.

"Lord Wesmorlen went out early this morning, miss, and asked that I let you know he would probably be away until late afternoon."

"And my sister?"

"I believe she joined Lady Wesmorlen and Mrs. Standish on a shopping expedition," Buckers said impassively. Regana glanced at the butler in surprise. "A shopping expedition. But why didn't they ask me to join them?"

Buckers looked a trifle uncomfortable. "I...believe that might have stemmed from the fact that the shopping was for...someone, miss."

"Oh, I see," Regana said, her lips twitching at the butler's obvious reluctance to spoil her surprise. "Then I certainly would have to be excluded from that, wouldn't I?"

"Indeed, miss, I should think you would."

"And Peter?"

"Has also gone riding, miss."

Thanking the man, Regana sighed, and made her way towards the library. Since she didn't feel like riding, and there was little else for her to do in the absence of any other company, she decided to catch up on some reading. Hence, comfortably curled up in a window seat with a romance novel from the circulating library, Regana occupied her time until Peter came in a few hours later, still dressed in his riding attire.

"Aha! So I've not been totally deserted, then," he cried, his boyishly handsome face lighting up. "I couldn't find a soul about the place."

"That's because there aren't any," Regana acknowledged with a laugh. "Aunt Mary, Clarisse and your mother went shopping, and Richard has not yet returned. I believe he's out visiting some of the farms."

"That doesn't surprise me," Peter said, pulling the bell rope. "One of my brother's more admirable traits is his concern for the people who earn their living from this land. As good as my father was to them, I sometimes think Richard is even better. Even though he's not been here overmuch, he's still managed to increase their standard of living, as well as ensuring that their houses and gardens are better tended and maintained. Not to mention seeing to the health of their families."

"You really care about him, don't you?" Regana said, aware for the first time of the deep bond of affection between the two brothers.

"I do," Peter said affably, "though I take pains not to let him see it. Richard's not one for sentimentality and all that. He'd cut me up royally. Ah, Buckers, could you bring some refreshments, please? Will you have a sherry with me, Miss Kently?''

Regana thanked him but refused. The butler returned with Peter's refreshment a moment later.

"Tell me, Miss Kently," Peter said after enjoying a mouthful of the amber liquid, "how did you and my brother meet? Have you known each other long?"

Regana paused, her mouth curving in a smile of fond recollection. "No, not really." She set her book aside and gazed into the fire. "Offically, we met at Lady Dalmeny's ball."

"Officially?" Peter teased. "What's this? Was there another meeting you're keeping mum about?"

Regana responded to his good-natured teasing with a laugh. "It was all quite innocent, I can assure you. We actually met while out riding one morning, but I didn't know who he was until we were introduced at the ball."

"Ah, so you rode with a stranger that morning." Peter grinned. "I had no idea you were so wicked, Miss Kently."

"Neither did I," Regana replied, laughing. "But I hadn't really expected to see your brother again. I was quite surprised to discover who he was when we were introduced by a friend of mine at the ball."

Peter walked to a chair and sat down. Not for the first time, Regana noticed his limp.

"So, you went to the ball looking for a prince," Peter announced, his cheeks dimpling.

"Not exactly," Regana demurred. "I was in fact being courted at the time."

"Ah, the mystery deepens," Peter laughed. "So you met my brother, were introduced and from there he proceeded to sweep you off your feet, ending with a romantic proposal over a candlelight dinner?"

"In a garden, actually," Regana said lightly, recalling the moment.

Peter smiled and rose from the chair. Watching him, Regana found it interesting that although Peter was unable to stand for any length of time, he soon got restless when seated. It led her to assume that he was not used to the inactivity brought about by the leg injury.

"This other gentleman must have been rather crushed to find that he waited too long," Peter said, lifting his glass. "I assume he was planning to offer for you?"

"Apparently," Regana answered carefully, "though the offer was never offically made."

It was still not clear in her mind exactly what had happened that day with Botheringham, though she preferred to believe Richard when he said that she was not bound to him in any way.

She heard Peter chuckle. "It must have come as a shock to him when you told him you were marrying someone else."

"As a matter of fact, I didn't tell him," Regana replied awkwardly. "Richard very kindly offered to speak to him. I never saw Lord Botheringham after—"

"Botheringham?" Peter interrupted rather abruptly, "Bertrand Botheringham?"

Regana glanced up at him, startled by the intensity of his response.

"Why, yes. Is he a friend of yours?"

"A friend? No, I wouldn't say that," Peter replied distantly. "We are . . . acquainted, but not as friends." He hesitated again, as if something were weighing on his mind. "Did my brother not . . . tell you of his association with Lord Botheringham?"

Unwillingly reminded of her conversation with Lady Chadwick, Regana felt herself begin to tremble. "No, he didn't," she replied slowly. "I have reason to believe they are not overly fond of each other, but I did assume them to be acquaintances. Am I mistaken?"

"They played cards together on a few occasions," Peter replied mechanically. "In London."

"Recently?" Regana asked.

"No...some...time ago."

Something in Peter's manner disturbed her, though Regana was unable to put her finger on exactly what it was. He seemed wary all of a sudden, as though afraid of saying something out of turn. Glancing at his face again, Regana was alarmed to see how white it had become.

"Peter, are you all right?" Regana asked in concern. "Shall I call someone?"

Her eyes beseeched him, and it was all Peter could do not to ask the question which sprang unbidden to his lips. But caution held him back, and he began to wonder if there wasn't more to this relationship than he'd thought. Why had Richard suddenly decided to marry this particular young woman, charming though she was, when he could have had his pick from amongst any number of well-dowered, titled young ladies in London? Was it her budding relationship with Botheringham which had sparked Richard's initial interest? And if so, why? Why hadn't he told her of his past involvement with the baron, unless it had to do with the reason he was courting her?

Peter drained the contents of his glass, trying to ignore what his mind was telling him. There was no doubt in his mind that Richard loved her; he knew his brother too well to mistake the intensity of his emotion. And surely if the motive had been something other than love, Richard wouldn't have been able to carry off such a pretence. Nor would he mislead the lady by playing her false...or would he?

By the time Richard arrived home, the conversation had reverted to more practical matters concerning the estate and its farms. But not for a moment was Regana fooled into believing that the first issue had been resolved. Peter was

still too reserved, and seemed to be paying little attention
to what was going on about him.

"Peter, are you listening to me?" the earl said patiently
when his brother failed to answer him for the third time.

As if miles away, the young man glanced up at his
brother, his eyes blank. "I'm sorry, Richard, what did you
say?"

"I said," Richard repeated with a tolerant smile, "that
Lord and Lady Bewdley have invited us to dine with them
tomorrow night. Wake up, man. Didn't you hear any of
what I just told Regana?"

"No...no, I'm afraid I didn't," Peter stammered, his
gaze going from one to the other and then back again. "I'm
sorry, I was thinking about something else."

His voice faded away, and Regana glanced at him again
with renewed concern. This was not at all like the Peter she
knew. She'd never seen him in anything but the best of
spirits; yet now, he suddenly seemed withdrawn and
moody. She glanced at Richard and saw that he, too, had
noticed his brother's strange demeanour. Before either of
them had a chance to say anything, however, Peter rose and
leaned heavily on his cane. "Please forgive me, Regana, but
I fear my leg pains me today. Perhaps a few hours' rest will
help."

"Yes, of course," Regana said quickly. "We'll call you
in time for dinner."

Regana watched the younger man leave and then turned
a troubled face to the earl. "Oh, Richard, I feel so terribly
sorry for him. I've never seen Peter so bothered by his leg
as he was today. How did he come to injure it?"

Evasively, Richard shrugged. "It was an unfortunate
accident," he replied simply. "Some days it troubles him
more than others."

"It bothered him more today than I've ever noticed. And
it came on so suddenly."

"Oh?" Richard asked, rising to pour himself a drink.

"Well, yes, we were sitting here having a lovely chat when all at once I noticed Peter's face had gone rather pale and he became very quiet."

"What were you talking about?"

"Nothing of great significance. I was telling him how we met at Lady Dalmeny's ball."

If Regana hadn't been so concerned over Peter's behaviour, she would have noticed the earl's sudden wariness.

"I'm sure it's nothing to be concerned about, my dear," he said dismissively. "The pain will go away in time."

"Perhaps," Regana murmured, clearly not convinced. "Though I can't help thinking it was more than just the pain in his leg. One minute he was fine, laughing and teasing the way he usually does, and the next, all the good humour was gone. I wonder if it was something I said. Perhaps I offended him, somehow."

Regana reviewed the conversation in her mind again, unaware that Wesmorlen had gone very still. "Yes, now that I think about it, he began to act strangely after I told him that Lord Botheringham had been courting me." Regana glanced up at the earl. "He seemed surprised that you hadn't told me something about Lord Botheringham. Was there something you were going to tell me, Richard?"

Wesmorlen looked down at the trusting face in front of him, the face that he loved so much—and shook his head, hating himself for doing so. "No, nothing," he said decisively. "And you've no need to worry about Peter. The doctor warned me that the increased activity would start his pain up again, but assured me that it would eventually ease as the leg gets stronger. So you see, there's nothing to worry about. Peter will be fine. As for his reference to Lord Botheringham, I've no idea what he was talking about. Perhaps you just misunderstood him."

But Regana knew she hadn't. And with a sinking heart, she realized that Richard wasn't telling her the truth. What she didn't know was why.

However, there was little Regana could do at the moment but accept Richard's assurances. Lord knew she wanted to. If she could only have dismissed the little voice in her head that whispered there was something going on, she might have been happy.

CHAPTER TEN

REGANA TRIED NOT TO DWELL on the conversation she'd had with Peter the previous afternoon, deciding that there was little to be gained from endless speculation. By dinner time, Peter's normally ebullient spirits seemed to have been restored, and Regana began to wonder whether she hadn't merely imagined his earlier reticence.

Perhaps she was just being an ostrich burying her head in the sand, she admitted reluctantly, but to be truthful it seemed her doubts had little basis. Richard had been more attentive to her than before, lavish in his gifts and showing his love more openly than ever, even to the extent of kissing her in front of the countess, much to that lady's startled pleasure.

When it finally came time to dress for the ball, Regana couldn't ever remember having felt so nervous. She was thankful that Lady Wesmorlen had generously allowed her maid to assist Regana with her toilette once again, but this time, Regana was glad of the girl's efficient and competent help. Her fingers were shaking so badly that she could scarcely fasten a single button.

"Ah, Miss Kently, you are nervous, *non?*" Yvette had asked in her sweetly accented voice.

"Yes, Yvette, I suppose I am." Regana nodded self-consciously, adding with a rueful laugh, "I've never been engaged before."

The little French girl winked knowingly. "You 'ave nossing to worry about, Meez Kently. I am going to make you *la plus belle dame.* And your 'andsome earl, 'e will 'ave eyes for no one but you!''

True to her word, Yvette worked her magic as never before. When at last Regana was ready, Yvette stood back and admired her work, declaring that ''never 'ad Miss Kently looked more *charmante.''* Taking one last look in the cheval glass, Regana had to admit that the young girl was right. The dress was perfection, the deep midnight blue enhancing the colour of her eyes and setting off the beautiful sapphire-and-diamond ring on her finger. Yvette had dressed her hair *à la greque,* a style which flattered her high cheekbones and finely shaped nose and chin, and had darkened her long curling lashes to accentuate their length, while a discreet touch of rouge brought a becoming rosiness to her cheeks.

''Très charmante!'' Yvette murmured, nodding her head in satisfaction. *''Tout à fait.''*

Hearing a light tap on the door, Regana turned, expecting to see Clarisse, and answered, ''Come in.''

But it was not her sister who opened the door and stood gazing at her from the threshold. Regana caught her breath as she saw Richard standing in the doorway, resplendent in black evening coat, white satin knee breeches and soft shoes. ''Good evening,'' he said, his voice husky with emotion. ''I thought I might escort you downstairs, if you're ready.''

He glanced briefly at the maid, waiting as she hastily curtsied and scurried out, before slowly advancing towards Regana. His eyes seemed to glow as he raised her hand to his lips. ''You look beautiful, though—'' he hesitated, studying her appearance ''—I think there's something missing. Perhaps this will do the trick.''

As Regana watched, Richard drew forth a long velvet box from within his coat and held it out to her. As she recognized the name of the jeweller appointed to the Crown on the lid, Regana's eyes widened. ''Oh, Richard, I couldn't—'' she stammered, glancing down at the box, almost afraid to open it.

"No? Well, then I have a better idea," he said. He led her to the mirror and stood her in front of it. "I thought you might need a little something to complete your outfit," he whispered, opening the box and taking something from it. As Regana watched, Richard fastened a magnificent diamond-and-sapphire collar around her throat, the perfectly matched stones identical to the ones in her engagement ring.

"There, now you're ready," he murmured, placing a tender kiss against the soft skin on her shoulder.

Touching the sparkling jewels reverently, Regana felt the sting of tears behind her eyes. And while she was overwhelmed by the splendour of the gift, it was the fact that Richard loved her enough to honour her with something so beautiful that truly touched her.

"Thank you," she whispered tremulously, smiling up into his face. "It's lovelier than anything I could have ever imagined."

"No, my love, that distinction belongs to you," Richard replied. "Now, shall we go down and greet our guests?" he said, offering her his arm.

By the time the first guests began to arrive, Regana was ready, having assumed her position in the receiving line next to Richard. Lady Wesmorlen stood at the head and provided introductions where necessary. Judging by the endless flow of guests, Regana was sure that no one had refused the countess's invitation, some of them having come long distances, anxious not to miss the opportunity of meeting and currying favour with the future Countess of Wesmorlen.

Only once did Regana's composure fail her. Turning to smile up into Richard's face, she had been momentarily nonplussed to see Lady Chadwick walk in on the arm of Lord Askew, looking, if possible, even more radiant than usual. Regana knew that the marchioness had not been invited on the express wishes of the earl. But she also knew that they couldn't very well prevent Lord Askew from bringing a companion, and it appeared that Lady Chadwick was quite aware of the fact.

However, there was nothing Regana could do about it now, and seeing the smugness on the Beauty's face as she approached, Regana fixed a smile firmly on her lips and steeled herself for the inevitable confrontation. But to her surprise, there was no need. Amanda moved past her in the receiving line, doing little more than incline her head at Regana, and smile narrowly at Wesmorlen before continuing on into the ballroom. Even her gown was somewhat subdued, Regana was forced to admit, though she seriously doubted many women could have worn the brilliant rose colour with such success.

When all the guests had finally been welcomed, Wesmorlen drew Regana to one side. "Darling, I'm so sorry," he whispered in her ear. "I had no idea Amanda would be here. I wasn't aware she was seeing Lord Askew."

"Please, Richard, don't give it another thought," Regana replied, trying to reassure him with her smile. "There is nothing she can do to spoil our happiness now. Perhaps the fact that she's here means that she has accepted our engagement. She certainly didn't seem upset."

But the fact that the marchioness appeared resigned counted for very little. Had Regana been more familiar with the Beauty's character, she would have recognized the schemings of a jealous woman.

Lady Chadwick moved into the reception room on the arm of Lord Askew, content in the knowledge that she now had the upper hand. Tonight, when the time was right, she would play her trump card and watch the earl's house of cards come tumbling down about his head. Oh yes, she could do it, Amanda knew, dazzling a passing young buck with her smile. Her brief visit to Lord Botheringham had given her more than enough ammunition with which to effect the damage.

Bitterly angry at what he had referred to as Wesmorlen's villainous treachery, Lord Botheringham had been only too happy to reveal what had happened between himself and Peter Wesmorlen, and to relate his recent interview with the earl. Not that Amanda blamed Wesmorlen for what he had done, she admitted reasonably when she'd had a chance to assess the situation. Revenge was something she understood. Nor did she delude herself that Botheringham had been completely honest in the recounting. She had little doubt that certain details pertaining to his conduct had been withheld. But that was of little consequence, for she had obtained the information she needed.

Her next problem had been to secure an invitation to the ball, a feat which had proved remarkably easy once she'd discovered that her ever-faithful Askew had been invited. He had been only too happy to take her to the ball as his guest, blissfully unaware that she and Wesmorlen were on the outs. Now, all she had to do was wait to play her card. In the meantime, she thought, accepting a glass of champagne from a passing servant, why not enjoy herself?

On the dance floor, Regana was doing her best to do exactly the same. Though the marchioness's arrival had briefly disconcerted her, she had quickly regained her composure and carried on, accepting the warm wishes of her friends and dancing with all the young men who said their hearts would never mend knowing that the incomparable Miss Kently was lost to them forever.

Regana took it all in stride, finding that the bantering words came easily to her now. How ironic that she should see the humour in their words now that she was engaged and not viewing each of them as a prospective husband.

When a waltz was announced a little later in the evening, Regana allowed Richard to lead her onto the floor, thrilling at the feel of his arms around her. She could not help but smile when she saw some of the other young ladies laughing and blushing as their partners led them out. Even though Lady Jersey had been seen to enjoy a waltz at Almack's, that most venerable of establishments, Regana knew that many still felt the dance to be distinctly compromising.

"Do you know, I think I rather like this being engaged," the earl said, glancing down at Regana's flushed cheeks wickedly as he whirled her round the floor. "One doesn't have to attend to the proprieties quite so rigidly. I should have listened to my mother and done this years ago."

Regana laughed up into his eyes. "Are you referring to doing it with me or with some other desirable young lady, my lord, for therein lies a considerable difference."

"As if there could be anyone else in my life but you," Wesmorlen whispered against her ear, aware of a marked feeling of relief.

Though he wouldn't have admitted it, Amanda's appearance at the ball had caused Wesmorlen considerable alarm. Like Regana, he hadn't forgotten Amanda's parting remark the night of her own ball, and though he had taken pains to reassure Regana that she needn't worry about it, he was unwilling to believe that Lady Chadwick would let him escape that easily. However, as the evening wore on, Wesmorlen began to wonder whether he hadn't misjudged Amanda. She was surprisingly discreet, arousing no more than her usual share of envious looks, and tending to stay quite close to Lord Askew, causing Wesmorlen to speculate on the possibility of that match actually taking place. Silently he wished Askew luck: he'd need it if he was going to take that little handful to wife.

"Regana, your party is going quite splendidly," Clarisse said a bit later, appearing at her sister's side. "And everyone says you look absolutely stunning!" Her envious glance dropped to the glittering necklace. "Did Lord Wesmorlen give you those tonight?"

Regana nodded. "Just before we came down. I admit I was dizzy as a goose when he did. I hardly knew quite what to say."

"I'm not surprised. I was rendered quite speechless by them myself. But they truly look wonderful on you! And you look so gloriously happy!"

Regana emitted a silvery ripple of laughter. "I hope that means I may bid goodbye to my unflattering sobriquet. I must remember to ask Jane that the next time I see her."

"I'm sure there won't be any need," Clarisse assured her with a giggle. "Look, even Aunt Mary is dancing!" Both girls watched as their aunt, blushing like a schoolgirl, was whisked away to dance a quadrille. "La, I daresay this will cast even Lady Chadwick's rout into the shade."

Something in her sister's manner caught Regana's interest. "Clarisse, I vow you're positively beaming tonight. Has something happened that I ought to know about?"

To her surprise, Clarisse reached over and gave her a hug. "I really shouldn't say anything, but I must admit I'm in a fidge to tell you." She glanced about, as if fearing someone might be eavesdropping, then said, "I think Pet...that is, Mr. Wesmorlen, is going to speak to Aunt about addressing me!"

Regana gasped, her eyes widening in delight. "Oh, my dearest girl, I'm so very happy for you," she whispered. "No wonder your head is in the clouds."

"I admit it is." Clarisse beamed. "I'm so happy I could burst. He's so wonderful, Regana. But the worst part is I can't say anything to anyone because it's not official."

Regana patted her shoulder reassuringly. "Never mind, pet, it will be soon enough. When did Mr. Wesmorlen say he would approach Aunt?"

"Tomorrow, if she isn't too tired," Clarisse said. "I just pray she isn't taken down with one of her megrims in the morning. You know how she suffers after these festivities."

Regana laid a reassuring hand on her sister's arm. "I'll tell Marie to make sure she takes some camomile tea before she retires. That usually soothes her."

Clarisse awarded her sister a grateful look. "I do hope so. Oh, Regana, I never thought this would happen to me. Just think, now we're going to be sisters-in-law, as well as just plain sisters. Isn't it just the most wonderful thing?"

Over dinner, toasts were raised to the happy couple and more champagne corks flew. Regana lost count of the number of times she was kissed and congratulated. It seemed her glass was never empty. It was hardly surprising, then, that by midnight, she was beginning to feel a trifle unsteady and slipped out to the conservatory for a moment's respite from the noise and crush.

The conservatory at Blackoaks was a wonderful place: a vast, domed room with wide expanses of glass, and filled with every variety of plant imaginable. Flowers of many and varied hue thrived in the warm, moist air, filling the room with their fragrance. It was a peaceful room, and one to which Regana had often found herself drawn to escape for a time from the bustle of wedding preparations. At the end of the conservatory was a smaller room which opened out onto the rose garden. Noticing that the door was open, Regana glanced into the garden, where she could just make out two figures seated on the bench. A rendezvous, perhaps? she mused.

But as she moved closer to the door, Regana quickly realized her mistake. Though their outlines were hazy, the figures' voices travelled clearly on the night air, and Regana smiled as she recognized the sound of Richard's deep, baritone voice, and the lighter voice of his brother. Perhaps they, too, had felt the need of a few moments' peace. Or could it be that Peter was talking to his brother about his plans to marry Clarisse?

Deciding that might indeed be the case, Regana was about to return to the ballroom, when the sound of her name on Peter's lips stayed her.

"Is it true, Richard, what Regana told me about Botheringham yesterday afternoon?"

There was a curious pause before the earl responded. "What did she tell you?"

"That she knew him," Peter said. "More than that, that he had offered for her. Is it true?"

"It's true that she knew him, but not that he offered for her," Wesmorlen explained. "Botheringham seemed to think that by informing Regana of his intentions to marry her, he had in fact singled her out as his exclusive property."

"But she *had* been seeing him to the extent that he planned on proposing?"

"I suppose so."

"Then why the sudden transfer of affections to you?" Peter asked reasonably. "Regana doesn't strike me as the sort of lady to jilt one man for another. Too damn fine for that."

A rather regretful tone could be heard in the earl's voice. "You're quite right, Peter, she is too fine to do such a thing. And knowing that full well, I had little recourse but to seduce her away from Botheringham."

"Seduce her!" Peter said, clearly amazed. "'Pon my word, Richard, that was hardly an honourable thing to do. Not your style at all."

Hearing Botheringham's words repeated almost verbatim, Wesmorlen smiled sardonically. "It would seem you are not alone in your opinion, little brother. However, as I recall, his treatment of you last year was hardly honourable, either. Or have you forgotten?"

"No," Peter answered bitterly. "I'm not likely to forget the man who nearly cost me my life."

Regana bit her lip, stifling the exclamation of shock before it escaped. So there had been more to Peter's strange behaviour yesterday afternoon than merely pain brought about by his injury. She'd thought as much. Something of a serious nature had occurred between Peter Wesmorlen and Lord Botheringham in the past. But exactly what had happened, and what part Richard had played, she was still at a loss to understand. Nor did she understand what it all had to do with her.

Glancing down at her hands, Regana saw that they were trembling. She knew she shouldn't stay here any longer, aware that no good ever came from eavesdropping. But she also knew with certainty that she couldn't move away. She had to know the truth.

Belatedly, she realized that Peter was continuing.

"...but both you and I know that problem was resolved a long time ago."

"To your satisfaction?" the earl interrupted grimly.

"Of course not!" Peter snapped. "But to the apparent satisfaction of the others concerned." Regana heard the bitterness in the young man's laugh. "I was allowed to escape with my life, wasn't I? That my leg was all but useless was of little concern." Peter hesitated, and then added ironically, "I would have lost that leg but for you. I thought about that a great deal while I was recovering in Scotland, you know. Poor Richard," he went on sadly, "you were the very person who tried to dissuade me from giving challenge, only to be the one to pick up the pieces and carry me away after the duel. Hardly suitable recompense for all your trouble."

The earl shrugged eloquently. "A man's honour is not to be lightly dismissed. I was wrong to try to discourage you at the time."

"Even if you knew it might cost me my life."

"Even so. You would not have had it any other way," Richard replied quietly.

"And Regana," Peter continued softly, "did she become part of the reclamation of my lost honour?"

When the earl didn't answer, Peter sighed in exasperation. "Damn it, Richard, why did you have to involve her in this?"

"She was already involved," Richard replied, his voice curiously flat.

"Not intentionally. She had no knowledge of what happened between Lord Botheringham and myself." Peter hesitated and his voice was curiously bleak when he spoke. "Did you do it to hurt her?"

The earl's voice sounded ominous. "Of course I didn't!" he replied darkly. "And she hasn't been hurt. Why do you think I went to talk to Botheringham about our betrothal? Do you think I was going to risk having him tell her his version of the story? Can you imagine the manner of lies he would have told her?"

When Peter didn't answer, Wesmorlen continued, though in a more subdued voice. "No," he said, "Regana knows nothing of what happened, and as far as I'm concerned I don't ever intend that she shall."

Peter sighed heavily. "I hope not, Richard. For your sake," Peter said quietly. "God knows, I don't like to think what might happen if she ever discovers you romanced her away from Botheringham out of a desire for revenge."

The conversation continued, but Regana heard none of it. Her head was spinning, her ears filled with a curious ringing that threatened to blot out all other sound. As darkness began to descend, Regana closed her eyes, willing herself not to faint. *I mustn't collapse now,* she thought, struggling to regain control of her tortured breathing. *I can't!*

Regana dropped her head, drawing deep draughts of the cool night air into her lungs. Finally, as the mists began to clear and the ringing in her ears subsided, Regana raised her head, aware that, for the moment at least, she wasn't going to faint. But the realization did nothing to ease the dreadful ache in her heart. That remained, a bitter reminder of everything she'd just heard. "Oh, Richard, why?" she whispered, fighting back the tears. "I thought you loved me. And all the time it was nothing more than a lie."

Fearful now lest her presence be detected, Regana turned on her heel and made her way quickly back to the main house. She needed some time alone. Time to sort out her emotions. With luck, she could slip quietly up the stairs before anyone had a chance to notice her. But, as is so often the case, Fate would have it otherwise.

"Ah, Miss Kently, I've been looking for you everywhere," Lady Chadwick purred. "Surely the bride-to-be is not tired of her own party?"

The marchioness's voice was honied, but Regana wasn't fooled for a moment. Lifting her chin, she turned to face the other woman, striving for a measure of calm she was far from feeling. "On the contrary, Lady Chadwick. I am simply not accustomed to crowds, and felt the need to have a few moments alone."

Amanda pointedly ignored the hint, and laughed. "Yes, you and Richard both seem to shun crowds. Now, that is. He never used to, you know," Amanda informed her archly. "When we were courting, he loved parties, the bigger the better. He used to say you could get lost in a crowd and never know it."

"He was younger then," Regana commented.

"Weren't we all?" the Beauty stated flatly. She turned to regard Regana in the manner of a cat toying with a mouse. "Have you given any thought to what I said the other day, Miss Kently?" Amanda asked softly. "About Lord Wesmorlen's reasons for wanting to marry you?"

Regana didn't reply for a moment, aware now that her earlier charitable feelings toward Lady Chadwick had been misplaced. How naive she'd been to believe that just because a cat's claws were sheathed, there were no claws at all!

"Lady Chadwick, why don't you simply say what you came to say?" Regana suggested calmly, turning back to face her opponent. If Richard had given her only one thing tonight, it was the power to stop the marchioness dead in her tracks. "Since I now recognize that *was* your reason for coming this evening."

Regana watched as a slow, malicious smile spread across the other woman's face. "Oh, come now, my dear, it's not really as bad as all that. If you had been in Wesmorlen's place, you might even have done the same thing. After all, blood is thicker than water, isn't it? And knowing that, I felt it incumbent upon me to inform you that Wesmorlen did have a reason for pursuing you so ardently. After all, you wouldn't want to marry him without being fully aware of the facts, would you?"

"Of course not," Regana replied, her tone crisp. "But as I told you in the shop, I already knew the reasons for his courtship, Lady Chadwick. However, as you'd no doubt like to tell me about it yourself, why don't you just get on with it?"

The marchioness hesitated, and glanced at Regana uncertainly. The girl seemed to possess a kind of grim determination she hadn't noticed before. And what of this bluff that she knew Wesmorlen's motives? Surely she couldn't have entertained his suit knowing full well the reasons behind it.

"Are you trying to tell me that you knew what happened between Peter Wesmorlen and Botheringham?" Amanda challenged boldly.

"You mean the duel? Of course I knew," Regana replied. "Do you think me a complete fool?" She felt a hollow victory as she saw Amanda's face blanch.

"You knew?" the Beauty gasped incredulously. "Yet you still agreed to marry him?"

"Why shouldn't I?" came the brittle response. "He had to marry someone. Why shouldn't it be me?"

"I don't believe you," Amanda spat out. "Do you expect me to believe that you knew why he went to see Botheringham after he'd proposed to you?"

"Naturally. I was, of course, quite grateful for his offer to intervene on my behalf," Regana replied in an offhand manner. "It spared me the necessity of an...unpleasant confrontation."

Regana hardly recognized the cold, controlled voice as her own. She felt hollow, numb, as though all emotion had been drained from her. Nor did she feel any compunction about lying to Lady Chadwick. She knew all too well that the marchioness would have suffered no such pangs of remorse in telling her of Wesmorlen's treachery.

"You surprise me, Miss Kently," Amanda tossed back at her archly. "I wouldn't think you'd have settled for a marriage of convenience."

Regana shrugged delicately. "It is not without its compensations, Lady Chadwick, as I'm quite sure you're aware. His lordship is not an unattractive man, and I am not loath to wear the coronet of a countess and assume the style of life associated with it."

Amanda's eyes widened in disbelief. "My God! you really did know all along, didn't you? You played the innocent to trap him, while all the time you knew exactly why he was courting you. He played right into your hands!"

The words cut through Regana like a knife, but not for the world would she have allowed her adversary to see just how much they hurt. "I don't delude myself that love was the great motive in *your* pursuit of the earl, Lady Chadwick," Regana replied. "And, if money and position are all you require, I'm sure Lord Askew will provide you with more than enough of both."

Regana waited, feeling a churning in the pit of her stomach and wondering how much longer she could sustain this pose.

Amanda laughed, but it was not a pretty sound. "You're quite the cool one, aren't you, Miss Kently? Perhaps it's time the earl heard exactly how cool. I'll wager he doesn't know just how thoroughly he's been outwitted. Perhaps I should tell him precisely what you've just told me."

Regana returned her gaze steadfastly. "I don't think so. And I think it would be best if you left now, Lady Chadwick," she said with remarkable composure. "I shall find Lord Askew and advise him that you have a touch of the headache and wish to leave. If you are wise, you will go with him quietly."

Amanda looked at the imperturbable face before her and laughed uncertainly. "You don't really expect me to leave now, do you?"

"Yes, Lady Chadwick, I do." Regana's expression never faltered. "Furthermore, if you attempt to humiliate me in the future, I shall tell everyone and anyone who will listen that not only were you unfaithful to your husband while he was away fighting, but that you carried on an illicit affair even during the time you were together at Benton Abby."

Amanda's face paled. "You wouldn't dare!" she snapped. "It's not true!"

"Isn't it?" Regana asked, raising her brows. "Are you so sure there wouldn't be a great number of people willing to believe it, given your rather... amorous tendencies?"

Amanda drew herself up haughtily, not willing to accept that she was beaten. "Don't think yourself so righteous, Miss Kently," she spat out. "I'll go, but not because you're telling me to. And as far as Wesmorlen is concerned, you're welcome to him. May you have many years of happiness together!'' she added with a spiteful laugh, and marched from the room, leaving Regana little fear that she would ever see the tempestuous Lady Chadwick again.

CHAPTER ELEVEN

IT WAS ONLY as a result of her carefully instilled training that Regana was able to carry out her functions for the remainder of the night. When she came downstairs after spending a few brief moments in her room, no one looking at her would have guessed at the ragged state of her emotions, nor at how close to tears she felt. She smiled and nodded as though nothing were amiss, accepting the congratulations and good wishes of her guests with such aplomb that even Clarisse failed to detect her despair.

To Wesmorlen, she was politely correct, though slightly withdrawn. Upon his remarking that she appeared a trifle pale, Regana replied that it was nothing more than the lateness of the hour and the excitement of the party. She was careful to spend as little time as possible in his company, though being equally careful not to draw comment as to her lack of attendance. To those watching, it appeared that Regana was like a beautiful butterfly, moving amongst her guests with a grace and charm most becoming to the future Countess of Wesmorlen.

It was almost two hours before the last of the guests took their leave, finally allowing Regana, standing alone in the empty hall, to close her eyes and breathe a heartfelt sigh of relief. Thank goodness it was over! What had started out as the happiest night of her life had ended up as the most miserable, and her nerves were in shreds. She wanted nothing more than to escape to the solitude of her room and the welcome void of sleep.

Unfortunately, she had reckoned without the presence of the earl, who suddenly appeared like a ghost out of the semidarkness. When he caught sight of her poised at the foot of the stairs, his face lit up with pleasure.

"Ah, Regana, I thought you'd gone to bed."

"I was just on my way, my lord," she replied distantly.

"Yes, no doubt I should be, too. Gad, that was quite an evening," Wesmorlen said, running a hand wearily through his dark hair, "no doubt to be hashed over for some time in the drawing-rooms of the ton." He glanced round the empty hall, and laughed drily. "I'd almost forgotten how it looked when it wasn't bursting at the seams with people. I believe a drink would be just the thing now." He smiled at her invitingly. "Would you care to join me in the library for a nightcap?"

He ran a finger lightly along Regana's arm, only to glance at her in surprise when she jerked away from him as though burned. "Regana, what's wrong? Are you feeling quite well?"

"Why shouldn't I, my lord?" she replied, fighting to suppress the ripple of hysterical laughter which welled up in her throat. "I've just had a wonderful betrothal party and am the envy of all. What more could I ask for?"

Her tone was brittle, unnatural, and Wesmorlen knew it. "You are many things, Regana, but a good dissembler is not one of them. What has happened to upset you so?"

As quickly as it had come, the hysteria passed, leaving Regana feeling weak and dangerously close to tears. "I think if you don't mind, Lord Wesmorlen, I'll just go upstairs to bed. The hour is late."

"Not so late that you can't explain a remark such as you just made, Regana," Wesmorlen said, his tone deceptively calm. "Didn't you enjoy your engagement ball?"

"My engagement ball? Of course," she said, forcing a false note of gaiety into her voice. "I found it very *revealing,* if you will."

Wesmorlen looked at her sharply. "Revealing? Regana, either I'm rather foxed, or you're not making a great deal of sense. Which is it?"

Regana sighed, aware of a weak, sinking feeling, as though she had awakened from a dream, only to be pitched into a nightmare. "Lord Wesmorlen, there is no need to continue this charade any longer. Your game is played. I can only be thankful that the deception was discovered before it was too late."

Wesmorlen's eyes widened at her strange pronouncement, scarcely able to believe that the cold, distant woman in front of him was the same laughing girl he had held in his arms only hours before. "Regana, I'm beginning to lose patience with you. You're not making any sense. If you have something to say, then say it. This…roundaboutation is not like you at all."

"Isn't it, my lord? Then perhaps you don't know me as well as you think," Regana flung at him harshly, "or as well as you'd like to think. Because unfortunately, I find that I do not know you. Not at all!"

REGANA LAY AWAKE most of the night tossing and turning, her dreams punctuated by painful images of Amanda Chadwick's laughing face, quickly followed by Botheringham's sneering one, until eventually she gave up the idea of sleep altogether, and lit the candle by her bedside. Staring into the flickering shadows, Regana drew the blankets round her body, trying to make some sense of it all. Nothing in her life had ever cut her as deeply as the words she'd heard tonight. *Seduced her away from Botheringham out of a desire for revenge.* The words stabbed at her heart. She had trusted Wesmorlen, willingly given of her heart, only to find that it was not her heart he was after.

He had used her from the start to get revenge on a man for something which she had no knowledge of and which she'd played no part in. And now that her usefulness was done, she could be tossed aside like a cheap penny novel. Or perhaps worse, Regana amended with a sob, *married* and tossed aside, dimly aware that those seemed to be the earl's intentions.

Catching sight of herself in the mirror, Regana was dismayed to see the dark, violet smudges beneath her eyes, and the ghastly pallor in her cheeks. Thank goodness Yvette had left some of her toiletries from the previous evening. At least she could attempt to cover up the worst of the damage. If only she could erase the damage to her own feelings as easily.

Regana thought long and hard after she rose, deciding at last that there was nothing left for her to do but break off the engagement and leave Blackoaks immediately. Perhaps she would be better off with Botheringham; at least he had never pretended to love her. He, at least, had been honest with her.

When Regana went downstairs, she found Clarisse and the countess enjoying a pleasant chat in the morning parlour.

"Well, good morning, Regana," Lady Wesmorlen greeted her brightly. "You were a great success last night, my dear. Cards have already been arriving to thank you and to extend reciprocal invitations."

Regana smiled weakly. "Thank you, my lady. It was a lovely party."

Clarisse, who had been watching her sister since her arrival, remarked in some concern, "Regana, are you all right this morning? You look dreadfully pale."

"I'm fine, Clarisse," Regana said, signalling to the maid for coffee. "I'm a little tired, that's all. It was a late night."

"Yes, it was," the countess acknowledged, sipping her tea. "Though Richard didn't seem bothered by it. Do you know, he was out riding first thing this morning. I don't believe he's back yet. Oh, for the stamina of youth!"

Suddenly wishing that she might escape on her own little mare, Regana nodded wistfully. "It's an excellent way to clear the mind after a late night, my lady. I miss riding very much."

The countess looked at her in surprise. "Well, why didn't you say something, Regana? There's no reason for you not to ride whenever you wish. We have an abundant supply of horseflesh in the stable, and one little mare in particular I think you would enjoy very much. I'll send word down that she be made ready for you whenever you like. After all," she added with a smile, "this will be your home, and I want you to be happy here, my dear. Please don't hesitate to say if there's anything you want."

The countess's tone was so genuine that Regana felt the prick of tears behind her eyes. "Thank you, my lady, but I don't want to put you to any trouble."

"My dearest girl, it's no trouble at all. I'm just delighted that Richard has found someone so lovely." She turned to smile at Clarisse kindly. "And I think that my younger son has not done so badly, either. I hope we shall have another announcement very soon."

Regana flushed, and quickly raised the cup to her lips, hoping to cover her dismay. Goodness, she'd almost forgotten about Clarisse's disclosure last night. Her sister was going to marry Peter Wesmorlen, no matter what happened between herself and Richard. And if Clarisse did marry Peter, that meant that Regana would be forced into occasional contact with Richard, whether she liked it or not!

The thought was intimidating, and it raised yet another difficulty. How would Clarisse feel once she knew that Regana was breaking her engagement? Would she go ahead and announce her own betrothal regardless, or would she postpone it? Knowing Clarisse, Regana felt sure her sister would be reluctant to flaunt her own happiness when Regana had so recently lost hers.

But would Peter understand why Clarisse was hesitating, or would he mistake her reluctance for a sudden loss of interest in himself?

"Lady Wesmorlen," Regana said, suddenly overwhelmed by the complex tangle of her thoughts. "I think I will take you up on your offer to provide me with a mount."

"I'm glad to hear it, my dear. Now you just tell me when you want to ride, and I'll instruct the stables to have Starlight made ready."

"Now, if it would not be inconvenient, my lady." Regana smiled hesitantly.

The countess looked at her in surprise. "Now? Oh, well, of course, my dear. If that is what you wish." She called for the butler, instructing him to send word to the stable to prepare a mount for Miss Kently.

"Thank you, Lady Wesmorlen," Regana said gratefully. She quickly finished her coffee and left the room, studiously avoiding Clarisse's eye. She knew all too well that her sister's suspicions had already been aroused. Clarisse had always been surprisingly perceptive when it came to her moods, but the last thing she wanted to do at the moment was discuss her dilemma. The wound was too fresh, too painful. She would first come to terms with it in her own mind and then speak with Lord Wesmorlen, advising him that the engagement was at an end. Then, she would have a quiet word with Clarisse and Aunt Mary, and finally, speak with the countess. She was not looking forward to any of it, but she knew it all had to be done.

Consequently, when the earl returned from his ride sometime before lunch, he was surprised to learn from Buckers that his fiancée had gone out riding and that she had not informed anyone of her intended destination, nor of when she might be expected to return. Turning on his heel, Wesmorlen cursed himself for not having waited until she'd come down. Something had happened last night to upset Regana very much and the sooner he found out what it was the better.

When lunch was announced and Regana still hadn't returned, Wesmorlen's unease turned to alarm. Neither the countess nor Clarisse could shed any light on her whereabouts, and though he knew Regana to be a fine horsewoman, he couldn't understand why she would have gone for such a long ride without him.

When Regana returned to the house just after two o'clock, Wesmorlen was on the verge of saddling up his horse and riding out in pursuit of her. His relief at seeing her lovely face in the hall was quickly replaced by concern at her obvious coolness.

"Good day, my lord," Regana said quietly, the natural colour brought back to her cheeks by the invigorating exercise. "I trust your morning went well."

"My morning was fine, until I returned home to discover that you had gone out without informing anyone of your intended destination, nor of when you might be expected back," he said in clipped tones.

"I beg your pardon, my lord," Regana returned, equally cool. "I was not aware I was required to keep everyone informed of my whereabouts. I simply decided to take advantage of your mother's generous offer to ride. I found myself in need of fresh air."

"I see," Wesmorlen replied carefully. "And have you had your fill of fresh air?"

"Indeed. Now if you will excuse me—"

"No, I will not excuse you!" Wesmorlen said, his eyes steely. Then, in an exasperated tone, he added, "Regana, why are you addressing me as though we were strangers? Have I offended you in some way?"

Regana lifted her chin, hoping the action might lend her strength. Her heart was pounding with such force that she felt sure he could see the movement of it beneath her dress. She hadn't thought to broach the subject with him so soon, hoping to wait until her own emotions were more in hand. But it seemed time was a luxury she was not to be afforded. "Lord Wesmorlen, I wonder if you might be able to spare me a few minutes. There is something I should like to discuss with you."

Regana's voice was admirably controlled, but the earl noticed the slight tremble of her lower lip.

"Regana, you may discuss whatever you wish with me, you know that." He opened the door to the blue sitting-room. "After you, my dear."

The gentleness in his voice was very nearly her undoing, but knowing that there was no room to prevaricate, Regana drew a deep, steadying breath and preceded him into the room. The earl closed the door and moved to stand beside her. Turning, Regana caught her breath, closing her eyes against the sight of that beloved face so near to hers. "Lord Wesmorlen, please . . ." she said, "if you wouldn't mind . . . sitting down."

The earl glanced at her with a bemused smile. "As you like." He took a seat, as she directed, and looked up at her expectantly. Regana regarded his darkly handsome face, and wished she could do anything but what she was about to do. It tore her apart to leave him, but he had lied to her, and that above all else, she could not forgive.

"Lord Wesmorlen, this is not easy for me to say," she began, avoiding his eye, "but I fear I must . . . break off our engagement."

The earl continued to look at her. "Break off our engagement? Regana, surely you jest?"

"I do not, my lord," Regana replied firmly. "Certain matters have . . . come to light which prevent me from continuing in this relationship, and I think the sooner our removal from Blackoaks can be effected, the better for all concerned."

The smile rapidly faded from Wesmorlen's face. "What are you talking about, Regana? What 'matters'? Has this something to do with the way you were behaving last night?''

She nodded tightly. ''It has. And I refer to matters which lead me to believe that your . . . intentions towards me were not always . . . what they seemed.''

''Intentions? Blast it, Regana, my intentions towards you have always been exactly what they seemed. Why do you think I proposed to you?''

Regana bit her lip and closed her eyes. ''Frankly, my lord, I wonder. I thought it was for love, but I have since come to view that belief as false.''

''False?'' Wesmorlen repeated, aware of a growing prescience of disaster. ''Am I to be permitted to ask what has happened to make you think so?''

Regana nodded, finding the words almost too painful to utter. ''I find there is a little matter of which you neglected to inform me. Namely, Lord Botheringham . . . and your brother's duel.''

Wesmorlen started, the confused look on his face slowly giving way to one of anger. ''My God. What do you know of that?'' he asked her tightly. ''Who told you?''

''It doesn't matter how or where I found out, my lord. The fact is that I did.'' Regana raised eyes clouded with pain and disillusionment. ''You lied to me, Richard. You led me to believe you loved me. Why didn't you tell me right from the start why you wanted to marry me?''

''Regana, I want to marry you because I *love* you!''

''I think not,'' she replied, shaking her head. ''You wanted to marry me for your own selfish purposes—so that you could have your revenge on Lord Botheringham.'' She looked at him bleakly. ''Am I wrong?''

''Regana, you don't understand . . .'' the earl began.

Regana closed her eyes and shook her head, refusing his excuses. By his very inability to deny the accusation, he had confirmed her worst suspicions. ''No, I don't understand,'' she said, her voice dropping. ''I don't understand how you could say you loved me when you didn't. I don't understand how you could use me as though I were some object without feelings or pride, nothing more than a puppet dangling from your fingers. What did I do to you to deserve such treatment, my lord?'' she cried.

"Listen to me, Regana, I *do* love you. I love you with all my heart!'' Wesmorlen said fervently. "No woman in the world has ever meant what you mean to me.'' Suddenly, it was the most important thing in his life that Regana should believe that. Grasping her by the shoulders, he said, "I never lied to you about how I felt, Regana. When I first saw you that morning on horseback, I was fascinated by you. Yes, against my will, I admit it, but fascinated nevertheless. I wanted to know more about you. Then, when I saw you at the ball, I watched you, followed you. I had to talk to you again.''

"Yes, you wanted to talk to me after you realized that Lord Botheringham was courting me,'' Regana said accusingly. "Before that you made no move to approach me.''

"Regana, you're not listening to me....'' Wesmorlen said, fighting an urge to shake her to make her understand.

"No, my lord, I'm not,'' Regana said as the tears finally spilled over and rolled down her cheeks. "I don't want to hear your excuses because I know what happened.''

"How can you say you know what happened, Regana?'' he growled. "Are you so willing to believe what other people say? Are you so willing to believe Lord Botheringham—or Lady Chadwick—that you would take their word over mine?'' the earl said angrily. "Why don't you ask me what really happened?''

Regana's voice broke on a sob. "Because I didn't hear it from Lord Botheringham,'' she choked out, pulling away from him, her eyes like those of a wounded animal. "Or from Lady Chadwick. Don't you understand? That's what makes this so hard, Richard. I heard it from— Oh, *damn you!*'' she said, sobbing.

With that, she ran from the room, leaving the earl standing alone in the middle of the floor, his hands by his side, still wet with her tears.

THEIR DEPARTURE was effected quickly. After her meeting with the earl, Regana broke the news to Clarisse and her aunt, explaining only that she had changed her mind and decided not to marry the earl. Both ladies had been considerably shocked, and had pleaded with Regana to reconsider, assuring her that whatever had happened was no more than a lovers' quarrel.

But Regana had remained adamant, and in the end, Clarisse and her aunt had retired to their rooms to pack, dismay and confusion clearly written on their faces. Wesmorlen had gone out shortly after their interview, dressed in riding clothes and with a look of such thunderous foreboding on his face that no one dared to ask him when, if ever, he would return.

Regana had not spoken to Lady Wesmorlen, preferring to wait until their departure was imminent. She had come to care for the earl's mother very much. As well, she respected her, and guessed that she was a shrewd judge of character. Regana knew that in her present state of mind, she would collapse under the countess's gentle scrutiny.

Instead, Regana waited, and sought her out that evening before she went to bed. As they planned to depart early in the morning, Regana knew it would be her last opportunity to speak with the countess alone. She found her in the salon, sitting quietly and working a beautiful piece of embroidery. Regana hesitated for a minute, not sure how to begin, when the countess looked up and saw her.

"Come in, my dear, come in. I know what you've come to tell me," she said sadly, putting her needle aside. "Richard spoke to me this afternoon before he went out.

Or stormed out, rather. I fear Buckers may need to bolster the hinges on the door."

Regana breathed a sigh, but it was not one of relief. "Please understand, my lady, there are reasons why I must do this. And they weigh heavily on me, for I love your son very much."

The countess nodded, not unsympathetically. "I know you do. I have only to look into your eyes to see it. And into Richard's." She hesitated, and glanced at the old-fashioned ring on her finger. "I won't presume to ask what happened, my dear. That is between Richard and yourself. I would only ask that you look deep into your heart, and ask yourself if what happened is reason enough for both of you to abandon this love forever. I've seen many marriages in my time, Regana, both good and bad. And believe me, when I say I know a good one when I see it. Yours would have been a good one."

"I thought so." Regana nodded sadly. She went to say more, and then stopped, lest she disclose too much. She had no intention of telling the countess what had actually passed between herself and Richard. For one thing, she had no way of knowing if Lady Wesmorlen was even aware of the duel which had taken place between her younger son and Lord Botheringham. Judging by the lengths to which Richard had gone to conceal it, Regana was inclined to believe she was not. Consequently, Regana felt it was much simpler just to let things stand as they were.

"Thank you for everything, Lady Wesmorlen," Regana said regretfully. "I am truly sorry that things have ended thus."

"As am I, Regana," the countess replied, "though I am a great believer in Fate. I shan't give up hope yet."

The countess's words surprised her, and for a fleeting moment, Regana wondered if she might be giving up hope prematurely. Then, recalling the anger she'd seen on the earl's face when she had broken the engagement, Regana

quickly banished the thought. The sooner she left Blackoaks, the sooner she would learn to live with the heart-
break. For Regana held no false hopes that it would go
away quickly.

CHAPTER TWELVE

REGANA'S DAYS PASSED with predictable slowness, a testament to the lethargy which seemed to have invaded both her body and her soul. She occupied her days with long solitary rides over the nearby hills, or with the occasional visit to Emily St. Hyde. Her evenings were spent working on her embroidery or in reading, though of late, the romantic novels which she had previously read so avidly seemed curiously flat and unappealing.

Surprisingly, news of the broken engagement did not spread quickly, mainly owing to the fact that since her return, Regana had taken to declining most of the invitations which arrived, especially those to large assemblies and balls. She pleaded illness as an excuse, and indeed, many who saw the pale, withdrawn girl were moved to remark that she seemed to be suffering from some sort of malaise.

Clarisse, having watched her vivacious sister change almost overnight into a pale shadow, was at a loss to know what to do or say to comfort her. Regana had not spoken a word to anyone about what had transpired between herself and the earl. She moved through her days in a quiet, composed manner, utterly unlike the vibrant, sparkling girl she'd once been. Only when she was alone at night in the privacy of her room, did she finally allow herself the tears which flowed unabated until eventually she drifted off into an uneasy sleep.

Of the earl, they heard nothing, other than what Peter was able to pass along during his frequent meetings with

Clarisse. It seemed that Wesmorlen, too, spent most of his time riding about the estate, seeing to numerous repairs and improvements to the tenant farms, or closeted in the library with the estate books. He seldom went out with friends, and generally seemed to have withdrawn into himself, causing Lady Wesmorlen considerable concern that her eldest son was in danger of becoming a recluse.

Of her own involvement with Peter, Clarisse was careful to mention very little. She longed to share with her sister the secrets of her blossoming relationship, but hesitated, aware that it would only bring painful images of the earl to mind.

All in all, it was an uncomfortable situation for everyone, as Clarisse pointed out to Emily St. Hyde as they sat together at Lady Riggerton's musicale the following week. Since their return from Blackoaks, Clarisse had taken it upon herself to inform Emily of the situation, thereby saving Lady St. Hyde the trouble of having to find it out for herself. Emily, like Clarisse, had been shocked by the news of the broken engagement. She knew that Regana loved Wesmorlen with all her heart, knew too that the earl was equally in love with her. What had happened, she wondered, casting about in her mind for likely explanations; how could things have gone so very wrong so abruptly?

Aware that she wasn't likely to stumble upon any plausible explanation, Lady St. Hyde, in her usual practical manner, decided to pursue another tactic. If she couldn't arrive at a reason for their parting, perhaps she could be of more use in trying to effect a reconciliation.

"I think, Clarisse, it's time we planned a little diversion," Emily announced one afternoon as she and Clarisse enjoyed a cup of tea on the terrace, "and one to which both our concerned parties must come. And," she said, glancing pointedly at Clarisse, "I can only think of one kind of function which would bring both of them out without causing any undue speculation."

Clarisse nodded, and waited for Emily to continue. When she didn't, Clarisse glanced up to find her friend watching her in a highly speculative manner.

"Emily!" Clarisse gasped, her eyes widening in sudden comprehension. "You're not thinking what I think you're thinking, are you?"

"Probably," Emily said gaily. "Is it not a perfect idea? After all, what better way to get both of them out than for me to throw an engagement party for you and Mr. Wesmorlen? There would be no question of Regana and Richard not attending."

"But you can't throw an engagement party where there is no engagement!" Clarisse spluttered in dismay. "Mr. Wesmorlen has not yet asked me to marry him."

"Tosh. A mere oversight, I'm sure," Emily said, quite unconcerned by this slight impediment. Then, glancing at her blushing companion, she added, "He is planning to, isn't he?"

"Well, yes, I certainly hope so. The night of the engagement ball, he did give me to believe that he intended to speak to Aunt about it the next day. But then, all this happened with Regana and somehow, the timing never quite seemed right."

Emily nodded. "Understandably. But the important thing remains that the intent is there, and both Regana and Richard are aware of it. So it won't come as a complete surprise to either of them when they hear the step has officially been taken. Good. Now all you have to do is tell dear Peter to be quick about making it official," Emily continued, as if it were the simplest of undertakings.

"Emily, I can't do anything of the sort!" Clarisse replied, clearly aghast at the notion of doing something quite so presumptuous. "He'd think I was being terribly forward. It's just not done."

"Of course it's done. It's done all the time. You just have to know how to do it." But seeing that Clarisse was mortified by the idea, Emily relented. "All right, my dear, don't worry about it. You don't have to ask him to marry you before he's prepared to. But," Emily added, her smile full of mischief, "what if we asked him to pretend just for the sake of his brother and your sister? Do you think he might agree to it then?"

Clarisse bit her lower lip and considered the new suggestion. "He might, though I do think it would sound better coming from you than from me. I wouldn't want him to think it was in any way my idea."

"Don't worry, my dear," Emily said, squeezing Clarisse's hand encouragingly. "By the time I finish with Peter Wesmorlen, I'll have him thinking this was all *his* idea!"

THE PARTY WAS ARRANGED for a week's time, Lady St. Hyde considering that the slight delay would give everyone enough time to carry out their parts in the subterfuge. Immediately after discussing her plan with Clarisse, she had spoken to Peter and had been delighted by his willingness to accommodate her. Accordingly, he had "proposed" to Clarisse in the presence of Lady St. Hyde, and Clarisse had "accepted," each hastily assuring the other that it was simply for the purposes of the plan. It didn't prevent them, however, from grinning and blushing quite charmingly whenever their glances happened to meet.

Hence, when the news was imparted over dinner at two separate houses the next evening, the desired results were achieved.

"Congratulations, dearest," Regana said, pressing a kiss against her sister's cheek in response to the not unexpected announcement. "I told you it wouldn't be long in coming."

"Thank you, Regana." Clarisse dimpled. "You don't mind, do you? And please be honest with me, for I should hate to think you were dissembling."

"Dissembling? Good heavens, dearest, why should I mind? You love him, don't you?"

"Well, yes, of course I do," Clarisse answered, blushing.

"Then nothing else matters," Regana replied firmly, well aware of what Clarisse was referring to. She sat back in her chair and lifted the crystal water goblet to her lips, hiding the slight tremor in her smile. How could she possibly express anything but the happiest of sentiments to Clarisse when the girl was so clearly over the moon about the betrothal?

In truth, Regana was genuinely happy for her sister, relieved that she was to marry such a gentle, kind man as Peter. The fact that he happened to be the earl's brother was an unfortunate, but irrevocable fact, and one which she would have to come to terms with. But then, Regana assured herself, her contact with Richard would be slight, no doubt restricted only to those times when the family was obliged to come together for holidays or special events, and merely for the sake of appearances.

At Blackoaks, the news was received with equal enthusiasm, both the countess and the earl expressing their delight at Peter's choice.

"Goodness, it's about time, stripling," the earl teased his brother affectionately. "I was beginning to wonder if you weren't indeed intending to emulate Lord Cheddarbrook and wait until your dotage to settle down. Now at least I shan't have to worry about you any more."

The countess cast a rueful glance his way. "Now the only one we need to worry about is you, Richard," she said meaningfully.

Wesmorlen studied his wineglass intently. "Rest assured, you need not concern yourself about me, Mother," he replied obliquely. "I'm quite happy to let Peter take the limelight. In fact, I'm rather relieved—now I can devote my time to the estate. And you can't offer any objection to that, now can you?" he added slyly.

The countess shook her head ruefully. "I am touched by your sense of duty, Richard, but since the estate has survived this long without your undivided attention, I don't imagine it will suffer unduly from a brief continuation. Your welfare is far more important to me."

"As it is to me, Mother," Wesmorlen replied, proffering his wineglass to be refilled, "and for that very reason I intend to devote all my time and energies to Blackoaks, which I daresay shall leave me precious little time for anything else."

"Not even for the ladies?" Peter teased him.

"Especially not for the ladies," Wesmorlen replied quickly, his expression purposely devoid of emotion. "At present, I find I have neither the inclination—" he paused, his eyes clouding with pain "—nor the desire to pursue that particular pastime."

The countess cast an anxious glance at her elder son, before returning her attention to her meal. Richard's sudden penchant for solitude was a growing concern to her, but like Clarisse, she was at a loss to know how to manage it.

The next day, the parties to the scheme were able to inform Lady St. Hyde that the first step had been accomplished without mishap.

"Excellent," Emily said with evident satisfaction. "Now if I can accomplish the second step with as much success, I shall be happy."

The second step involved the issuing of invitations to Miss Regana Kently, Mrs. Mary Standish, the Countess and the Earl of Wesmorlen to attend an intimate dinner party given by Lady St. Hyde in honour of the newly engaged couple at her home the week following this.

Regana and her sister had just returned from church when the invitation was delivered. The heavy cream parchment envelope embossed with the crest of the St. Hyde family. In a simple gown of white jaconet muslin, with no adornment other than her own loveliness, Regana looked as fresh and appealing as a spring day. No one looking at her could have guessed at the sudden dread which welled up within her as she saw her name on the envelope, written in Emily's fine, flowing script. The invitation could mean only one thing: Emily was planning a party—and Regana had little doubt as to its purpose.

Quickly scanning the enclosed message, Regana closed her eyes, and felt the familiar trembling in the pit of her stomach. It was as she had feared. Emily wished her to attend an engagement party for Clarisse and Peter the following week. And seeing a similarly addressed invitation to her aunt, Regana could only assume that like invitations had also been extended to Wesmorlen and his mother.

Despite what had passed between them, Regana knew that Richard would be at the party. As Peter's only brother, how could he not attend? But how could she be present at the same time, without causing herself more grief? Could she pretend for the sake of her sister that all was well? Or should she just decline the invitation and not attend at all?

No, that would not be possible, Regana realized with a sigh. She glanced at the invitation reluctantly. Whatever her own feelings for the earl, they would have to be put aside for Clarisse's betrothal party. It was only one night, Regana told herself; surely she could put on a brave face for a few hours.

At Blackoaks, surprisingly similar thoughts were running through Wesmorlen's mind as he beheld the open invitation in his hand. He wondered fleetingly if the dinner party were merely a ruse to bring him together with Regana, but then banished the thought as churlish. Emily was planning this in honour of his brother and Clarisse's engagement, and the countess might have done the same herself, had she not feared her elder son would be sour and uncommunicative.

The more he thought about it, the more remorseful Wesmorlen felt. Regana's rejection had put him in a frame of mind he never would have considered possible. He, Earl of Wesmorlen—nonpareil and noted man about Town, who had always prided himself on his ability to control his own emotions and ultimately, his own destiny—had in the course of a single day, been turned upside down by a delicate, beautiful creature whom he loved more than words could say. Worse, by wallowing in his own anger and misery, he'd cast a pall on Peter's happiness, the very thing he'd been striving so hard to achieve. And now he was contemplating letting his brother down even further by not attending his betrothal dinner.

Well, he certainly wasn't going to disappoint his family this time, the earl decided, quickly taking up a pen to scrawl his acceptance of the invitation. Whatever had happened between himself and Regana could be put aside for one evening. Regana was too much a lady to cause a scene, and he was determined to be as pleasant to her as she would allow him to be. Perhaps the mere sight of her would fill some of the emptiness within him, he thought, pulling the bellrope for Buckers. This much at least, he could do for his family. And for himself!

WHEN THE EARL'S acceptance finally arrived, Lady St. Hyde breathed a heartfelt sigh of relief. She had known that if her plan was going to fail anywhere, it was at this critical stage. But as she held all the acceptances in her hand, with Regana's and Wesmorlen's uppermost, she began to hope that her plan might succeed, after all. At least if they were in the same room together, they would have an opportunity to talk.

It was arranged that Peter would escort Clarisse, Regana and Aunt Mary to the St. Hydes', and Lord and Lady Wesmorlen would arrive separately. Mrs. Standish and the countess had been let in on the secret of the engagement so that, should anything go amiss, they could play along as necessary. Emily also advised her husband of the plan.

"Emily, one day your meddling will get you into trouble," Lord St. Hyde warned, chucking her under the chin affectionately. "Besides, what makes you think this plan of yours will succeed?"

"I know Regana," Emily replied, brushing a thread from her husband's perfectly tailored coat. "And I think I know what she needs."

"But you don't know Wesmorlen," Lord St. Hyde pointed out practically, "or perhaps not as well as you think. He may not take kindly to your interference, my dear, especially when he discovers that his brother's engagement was contrived only to bring him and Regana together."

"Tosh, Cecil, I sometimes think there's no romance in your soul at all," Emily said playfully, her gaze adoring as she looked up at him. "For every prize worth winning, there must be a gamble, and to me, this is certainly worth the gamble. Besides, as regards the contrived engagement, it is only a matter of time before Peter does officially propose to Clarisse, and it will then be a moot point. I simply accelerated the process a little for our purposes. And as for Regana and our dear Wesmorlen, I have little fear the meeting will be acrimonious. Wesmorlen is a gentleman. If nothing else, they will be civil to each other. And if they can be civil, perhaps they can talk."

"Have you ever considered, my dear, that perhaps it's not civil they need to be?" Lord St. Hyde asked with a wink. "Perhaps what they need is to have it out and clear the air."

Emily looked at her husband in amusement. "This isn't Gentleman Jack's, darling. But I promise you, if my way fails, I'll clear off the dining table and suggest a boxing match. Goodness knows, I'm willing to try anything to get them back together."

With that thought in mind, Emily diligently set to work, overlooking no detail towards the evening's success, right down to the formal pink table linens and sparkling crystal candelabra. Roses were brought in by the dozen to decorate the room, and Emily reminded Evans to make certain there was plenty of champagne on hand. Thank goodness it was an engagement they were supposedly celebrating and not just an ordinary dinner party, Emily thought, casting a critical eye over the menu. No one attending this party could doubt for a moment that it was planned with anything other than romance in mind.

Clarisse, meanwhile, having convinced her sister that they must both have new gowns for the party, had taken Regana, albeit reluctantly, to a new French modiste in the nearby town, who was touted by all as the *only* acceptable dressmaker this side of London.

"Really, Clarisse, I don't understand why you're in such a fidge to go to the added expense of Madame Charpelier," Regana pointed out as they sat in the atelier awaiting the notable Frenchwoman's arrival. "I thought you were quite happy with Mrs. Whitwell's work."

"I was," Clarisse conceded. "But for this occasion, I want something really special, Reggie. And I've heard Madame Charpelier makes the most exquisite gowns. Perhaps if I like what she creates for this, I'll consider commissioning her to make my wedding dress."

Regana started to comment upon the extravagant prices the French modiste charged, and then thought better of it. Why shouldn't her sister have what she wanted, and be dressed by whomever she wished, for this happy time? If she and Aunt Mary had to live more frugally once Clarisse had gone, so be it. Now was not the time to quibble.

As a result, by the time the sisters left the tiny salon, Regana's head was spinning. Never had she seen such a vast array of exquisite materials presented for their approbation nor such varied and beautiful colours of fine French silks, lustrous velvets and glowing satins. They had each been draped, pinned, turned and fussed over by the sharp-eyed Madame Charpelier, until Regana lost count of what they had purchased. When they had finally left, it was with madame's assurances that the gowns would be delivered the next day, with the remainder of the items to follow a few days later.

After leaving Madame Charpelier's, the two girls had then paid a visit to the glovers across the street for each of them to be measured for the requisite long white gloves, and then on to a nearby shop for a dozen pair of silk stockings each. It was, Regana thought reminiscently, not unlike the preparations for her first Season, remembering, too, that she had been just as weary then as she was now.

In the carriage on the way home, Clarisse chatted excitedly about their purchases, and about the forthcoming party. Regana, while silently sending prayers for forgiveness to heaven for the amount of money they had just spent, was secretly delighted by the outcome of their morning's shopping. There was no doubt that Madame Charpelier's designs were exceptional, and Regana felt sure that no London lady could be more finely attired than they would be. In particular, the gown Regana had ordered for the engagement dinner was spectacular, and though nothing would have induced her to admit as much, Regana was longing for Richard to see her in it.

Allowing herself a tiny sigh, Regana shook her head. Was she never to be able to keep her thoughts from straying to that man? She knew there was no point in trying to fool herself that she wasn't still in love with Richard. Not a day went by that she didn't recall something about him: his handsome face, the tenderness of his voice when he spoke to her, or the wonderful feeling of his lips pressed gently against hers. At times she had to shake herself to stop thinking about him.

But that part of her life was over, she chided herself firmly! And she was not foolish enough to believe that Richard might still be harbouring any affection for her. After all, he had made no effort to see her since they had left Blackoaks, nor had he passed along any messages for her through Peter. It was, she thought sadly, as though they had never known each other at all, let alone been briefly engaged.

In spite of all that, however, Regana couldn't quell the feeling of nervous excitement which grew day by day as the night of the party approached. If nothing else, she would see him again, talk with him, hear the sound of his laughter, and, perhaps, feel the touch of his hand as they exchanged greetings. Was that asking too much, she wondered. Was she being a hypocrite for wanting merely to see the man she loved again?

AT BLACKOAKS, Wesmorlen sat at his desk in the library, his gaze focussed on the fields beyond the mullioned windows. The account books lay open before him, their pages unturned in the past hour. The engagement party was this evening, and though he wanted to say otherwise, Wesmorlen was worried. It would be the first time he and Regana had communicated since she and her family had left Blackoaks. Would she be polite and carry out the expected social niceties? Or would she snub him, giving him the setdown he so richly deserved.

"Oh, Regana, what have you done to my heart?" he murmured, finally throwing down his pen in abject frustration and rising from the desk. He stood by the open window, hands thrust deep into his pockets, his eyes fixed on something none but he could see.

Why hadn't he told her the truth about Botheringham when he'd first realized he was falling in love with her? Wesmorlen cursed himself, realizing all too late what a fool he'd been to hold back. If he had admitted everything to her right at the start, she would have been hurt, yes, but it would have been a hurt he could have set about righting. But by withholding that information, all he had done was to drive away the only woman he'd ever loved, without even having made an attempt to win her back. Abruptly, Wesmorlen recalled his assurances to Gerald Bancroft that night in the carriage when he had first devised his plan. No one would be hurt, he had said, remembering how smug and self-assured he had sounded. But how very wrong he had been, Wesmorlen thought bitterly now. He had succeeded in hurting almost everyone he cared about, and in particular, the sweet, gentle woman who had captured his heart.

Well, there was nothing else for it, Wesmorlen decided abruptly. He simply had to make the attempt to win her back. He had to make her see that she was wrong about him—that he had courted her out of love and not out of some silly desire for revenge.

But most important, he had to make her believe that he hadn't lied to hurt her. But would she believe him?

"She *must* believe me!" the earl exclaimed with startling conviction. "As God is my witness, I'll make her believe me!"

CHAPTER THIRTEEN

THE ST. HYDE HOUSE was ablaze with lights when the Wesmorlen coach pulled up. The earl, helping his mother to alight, tucked her hand into the crook of his arm and escorted her up the steps to the front door.

"Regana's just as nervous as you are, Richard," the countess whispered, feeling the tension in his body. "Don't think she isn't."

The look he gave her was grim. "*She* has nothing to be nervous about, Mother. It is *I* who stand to lose everything."

"I think not," came the thoughtful reply. "She knows what she's giving up, too, my dear. Regana is no fool. She's a loving, generous girl, who happens to love you. Very much, if I'm not mistaken."

"I fear I must differ with your opinion, Mother," Wesmorlen said bleakly. "Regana may have loved me once, but I seriously doubt her feelings towards me now have anything to do with that noble emotion." He hesitated, and glanced at his mother gravely. "I've good reason to believe she hates me now."

If the countess was startled by the revelation, she gave no sign. "The presence of any strong emotion signifies strong feelings, Richard," she pointed out casually. "And Regana loved you very much. Are you so sure you're not mistaking the intensity of one emotion for another? Perhaps she's simply covering her wounds by displaying an angry face. It's been known to happen."

"Then how do I win her back, Mother?" Wesmorlen asked with a crooked smile. "If what you say is true, what words do I use to reverse the damage?"

Lady Wesmorlen smiled and gently squeezed his arm. "You'll know what to say when the time is right. Believe it in your heart and the words will come to you, my dear."

Inside, Regana heard the carriage arrive, and felt her heart begin to flutter like the wings of a bird caught in her breast. A pulse trembled under the soft skin, and a faint flush suffused her cheeks.

Regana had purposely arrived early at Lady St. Hyde's, hoping to compose herself before Richard and the countess arrived. She knew that nothing was more unsettling than arriving late to a function one was anxious about attending in the first place. But now, as she sat back and waited for the salon door to open, Regana realized that nothing could have prepared her for his arrival. Just the thought of seeing him again cast her already tumultuous emotions into a further tizzy, and brought the colour surging into her cheeks.

The moment Wesmorlen entered the room, his eyes sought her out. God, she was beautiful, he marvelled, feeling himself dazed by the sight of her. In a room filled with delicate pink and white roses, she appeared to him the most beautiful rose of all.

She had risen to greet the countess, looking a vision in a striking deep red gown, the tunic cut away to reveal an underskirt of pure white silk shot through with silver. Her arms were encased in long white gloves while her gleaming hair was drawn up and back to display the perfection of her classically beautiful features. When she moved, the diaphanous material swirled about her like a gossamer mist so that she seemed more angel than woman. As she curtsied gracefully to his mother, her face was as warm and as beautiful as he remembered it. Her voice fell like balm on his tortured heart, and he drank in the sight and sound of her like a parched man drinking water.

When finally she turned to greet him, Wesmorlen wasn't sure whether he saw the brief flash of pain which darkened her eyes, or whether he just imagined it, for in a moment it was gone, to be replaced by the cool, composed smile he knew so well. "Lord Wesmorlen," she said, offering him her hand.

Her voice was quiet, distant, and with sinking heart, Wesmorlen realized that their time apart had not changed her mind, nor weakened her conviction. She held him away with her eyes, as firmly as though she'd placed her hands upon his arms.

But Wesmorlen was not to be deterred. He had not expected her easy capitulation. "Miss Kently," he said, lifting her hand to his lips. His mouth lingered for no more than a second against her gloved hand, but it took every ounce of will Regana possessed not to snatch her hand away from him. Even through the soft material, she could feel the warmth of his lips, aware of a lingering glow as her hand dropped back to her side. The look in his eyes was searching, questioning, and Regana hastily lowered her gaze, afraid that he might see too much. She couldn't give in to him. She wouldn't! He had lied to her and she was not willing to forget or to forgive him for that. But for goodness' sake, why did she have to keep reminding herself of it?

Watching the two of them from the corner of her eye, Emily St. Hyde felt her breath catch in her throat. They were so much in love that it almost hurt to watch them. *Damn their pride, anyway,* she fumed, moving forward with a purposely bright smile on her face. "Lady Wesmorlen, Lord Wesmorlen, I'm so glad you could come."

"We wouldn't have missed it, Emily," Wesmorlen said, dropping an affectionate kiss on her cheek. "Shockingly bad ton to miss your only brother's engagement party," he joked lightly.

"Glad you realize it, old man," Peter said, coming forward with Clarisse. The earl kissed Clarisse on the cheek. "Congratulations, my dear," he said, then added, "and not so much of the 'old man,' if you don't mind, stripling. I can still give you a run for your money when I have to."

Peter smiled. "I don't doubt it. Ah, wonderful, champagne. Will you have a glass, my dear?" he said, taking one for Clarisse.

"Of course she will," Emily said, making sure everyone had one. "It's time for a toast. Richard, will you do the honours for us?"

The earl took a glass, and after a moment's hesitation carried a second one to Regana. "Will you join me in a toast to their happiness, Miss Kently?" he asked softly. Their fingers brushed in the lightest of touches as she accepted the glass, and Regana was dismayed to feel the heat creep up into her face as she nodded.

"To Clarisse and Peter," the earl began, his deep voice sending shivers down Regana's spine. "May they know only happiness in the love they've found together, and may they continue to grow in that love every day of their lives." He turned and looked directly at Regana. "For in finding love, they have truly found the door to happiness. May they travel forward through that door, and continue to find the contentment they know today."

His eyes drew hers like a moth to a flame, and Regana was helpless to look away, staring up into the smoky depths of his eyes like a lost soul. Why was he doing this to her, she moaned inwardly. Did he not know how hard she was trying to resist him?

From a distance, Regana heard someone calling her name, and belatedly realized that Clarisse had come to stand beside her.

"I'm…sorry, Clarisse, what did you say?" Regana said, shaking her head. "I fear I must have drunk my champagne too quickly."

"That's all right, dearest, I just wanted to show you my engagement ring," Clarisse said, proudly holding out her hand. "Peter's just given it to me."

Regana looked at the ring on her sister's finger and fought back an overwhelming urge to cry. Emeralds and diamonds. Was this another trinket from the Wesmorlen family vault, she wondered bitterly.

"It's lovely, Clarisse," she heard herself saying as if from far away. "Truly lovely. I know you'll both be very happy."

"May I add my sentiments to that, Clarisse," the earl said quietly. "Peter is a very fortunate young man."

Clarisse beamed at them both and moved off to stand beside her fiancé, who seemed to be playing his part with a great deal of enjoyment. Watching them, Regana was aware of a strange feeling of detachment. This was a time for happiness and for good wishes, yet she no more felt like laughing than a mother who watched her child leave home for the first time. It was all she could do to keep the smile on her face. Her heart was breaking, and she was very much afraid lest someone, especially Richard, should see it.

If the earl did see it, however, he gave no indication. He acted the gallant elder brother to perfection, laughing with his future sister-in-law, and teasing his brother about his upcoming nuptials. He was solicitous of Aunt Mary, frequently bringing a smile to that lady's face, and always gracious to the countess. Over an exquisitely prepared dinner he shared memories of his time in Paris with Lord and Lady St. Hyde, and kept all of them entertained with light-hearted stories of his brother's younger days and the scrapes they'd got into, some of which even the countess had been unaware of.

And always, he looked to Regana, his eyes softening as they rested on her face, his glance somehow regretful, Regana was inclined to think. She looked up many times to find those dark eyes watching her and was shaken by the intensity of emotion she saw there.

Before the dessert was served, Peter called for everyone's attention. "I'd just like to say a few words, if you can bear with me," he announced sheepishly. "And I promise I shan't become maudlin," he added, glancing at Richard, who rolled his eyes expressively. "But I see gathered round me at this table my friends, and my family, and it makes me proud to know that some of these friends will soon become my family," he said, smiling at Regana and Aunt Mary. He hesitated, as if trying to find the right words. "I feel very fortunate that Clarisse has consented to be my wife. Not so long ago, I never thought I would see the day when I'd be asking anyone to marry me. But I was moved by a greater force to wake up and resume my life again. I'm sure all of you know the greater force I refer to is, of course, my brother Richard—" he laughed as a round of applause went up "—without whose encouragement and constant belief, not to mention an occasional brotherly shove, I know I wouldn't be standing here tonight making this frightfully eloquent speech. So, in honour of everything he's done for me, I'd like to ask him, in front of everyone, so that he can't possibly refuse, to do me the great honour of standing beside me as my grooms man."

Amidst more hearty applause, all eyes turned towards the earl. It was clear from the look on Wesmorlen's face that he was surprised, and touched. He looked up at his brother, for once at a loss for words, and merely nodded his consent.

Watching him covertly, Regana felt the prickle of tears behind her eyes. He was so good to the ones he loved, she sighed, so solicitous of their welfare; one had only to look at the faces of his family and close friends to see that. But at the same time, there was a ruthlessness about him that boded ill for those who did not command his respect and affection.

Botheringham had suffered that ruthlessness, Regana knew now, as had perhaps the spurned Lady Chadwick. Was that why they had conspired to get their own back on Wesmorlen? Was it possible that she didn't know the whole story, and that she had misjudged Wesmorlen, as she had the very first time they had met?

The idea continued to plague her, like a hungry dog worrying a bone. Perhaps she had acted too hastily in breaking off the engagement, without giving Wesmorlen a fair chance to justify his actions. What if there were mitigating circumstances which even she could not fail to understand?

Regana sighed, torn by her indecision. Pride goeth before a fall, Regana reminded herself sadly. Had her pride brought her to the brink of just such a fall? Belatedly, Regana returned her attention to Peter, aware that he was now speaking about Clarisse.

"... and, as my fiancée is reluctant to stand and talk in front of everyone assembled here," Peter was saying, "she has requested that I speak for her, by asking Regana if she would do her the similar honour of standing up with her as her bridesmaid."

Again a round of applause went up, but this time, it was Regana who had cause to glance at her sister in dismay, as a multitude of conflicting emotions began to swirl through her mind. How could Clarisse possibly expect her to stand up with the earl, their estrangement on display for all Society to see? She would be required to stand next to him and listen to the vows of marriage being repeated by her sister, trying not to remember that it should have been her own vows she was taking.

No, she couldn't do it! It was more than she could bear. It was more than anyone could be expected to bear, Regana thought frantically. Wasn't it enough that she was here now, being tortured by his presence, drawn against her will to look upon that face, a face she loved more than life itself?

Feeling the scalding tears which she'd been trying so hard to hold back spring to her eyes, Regana pushed back her chair and, muttering a muffled "excuse me," fled from the room.

"Oh, dear, Regana," Clarisse called, starting to rise. "Regana, wait!"

"No, stay here, Clarisse. I'll go to her," Wesmorlen said, throwing down his napkin.

Emily glanced at him in concern. "Richard, are you sure?"

The earl nodded tensely. "I think it's time we cleared the air, Emily. I must make her listen."

He found Regana outside on the balcony, her slim body pressed against one of the marble balustrades.

"Regana!" he whispered, stopping a few feet from her.

"Go away, Richard!" she cried, her words muffled against her hands. "Can't you just leave me alone?"

"No, I can't," he said, clenching his fists at his sides. It tore him apart to see her like this, to know that he was the cause of her pain. He took a few steps closer to her, until he could almost feel the warmth emanating from her body. Her nearness was like wine to his senses.

"Regana," he repeated. Still there was no response. "Damn it, Regana, look at me!"

He put his hands on her arms and forcibly turned her round. Her head was thrown back, and her eyes, red-rimmed and wet, were closed, as if to shut out the sight of him. "Richard, go away! Go away and leave me alone."

With a stifled groan that came from the bottom of his soul, Wesmorlen pulled her into his arms, holding her as though his very life depended upon it.

"Forgive me, Regana," he whispered against her hair. "Forgive me, for as God is my witness, I can't live without you. These past weeks since you left me, I've been a man without a heart. Without a soul. Without a life. I thought I was satisfied with my life before you came into it, but that was only because I didn't know what life with you could be. Now I do."

He pressed a gentle kiss against her shining hair. "I love you, Regana, more than I knew it was possible to love a woman. Can you not find it in your heart to forgive me? I never meant to hurt you."

Regana stiffened in his arms, and immediately he released her.

"You lied to me, Richard," she said, her voice tired and defeated, her body drained by the power of her emotions. "Why didn't you tell me what had happened between you and Lord Botheringham? I fell in love with you. And I thought you were in love with me, too, until I realized you were only courting me to get revenge on Botheringham. That's why you went to see him the morning we became engaged, wasn't it?" she asked, her voice flat. "You went to tell him that you'd seduced me away from him and to gloat over your victory."

"No!" The word shot from his lips like a bullet. "It was never like that. I did not gloat about anything."

"Then why, Richard?" she repeated, her eyes beseeching him for the truth. "What did I do to deserve this treatment from you?"

The words tore at his insides, the pain on her face ripping at his heart until he couldn't look at her. His hands reached out, then fell uselessly back to his sides. "I did not mean to fall in love with you, Regana," he said finally. "I didn't think there was room in my heart for love. But then when I met you, from that first morning when we rode, I couldn't stop myself. Goodness knows, I tried."

The earl dropped his head, his words coming so quietly that Regana had to lean forward to hear them. "I wonder if you will ever be able to understand," he said, his eyes briefly closing on memories which still had the power to wound. "My heart was filled with anger, Regana. A destructive, gnawing anger that consumed my every waking moment. My brother's life had almost been ended by a man who sought to destroy him for no better reason than to conceal a folly of his own youth."

"Lord Botheringham?" Regana said, struggling to understand. "What are you talking about, Richard? What folly?"

The earl shook his head. "It matters little now. Suffice it to say that he committed an injustice which my brother inadvertently stumbled upon. And, not knowing whether Peter was likely to spread the story all over London, Lord Botheringham thought to silence him. Or at the very least, to frighten him into silence."

"So there *was* a duel," Regana said, her eyes widening.

"Oh, yes." He nodded heavily. "There was a duel. I was there the night challenge was given, and I was there the night Peter was shot, badly wounded in the leg."

Regana drew a startled breath. "In the leg? But why didn't Botheringham—" Regana stopped, aghast that she had almost put into words what she'd only wondered at before. She blushed uncomfortably, and lowered her eyes. But Wesmorlen, knowing all too well the question which trembled on his beloved's lips, held nothing back.

"Why didn't Botheringham kill him? A reasonable question, and one I asked myself at the time. I knew he could have." Wesmorlen smiled faintly. "There are few men deadlier with a pistol than Botheringham. But, as time went on, I began to think about it. Why, I asked myself, would Botheringham go to the trouble of provoking a duel if he had no intention of killing Peter? That's when it began to dawn on me that Botheringham never intended to kill my brother at all, but only to scare him. That Peter might have been crippled for the rest of his life as a result, however, seemed to be of little consequence.''

The earl's mouth twisted bitterly as he recalled an image Regana was unable to see. ''I carried Peter home in my arms that night and over the next few weeks, watched him deteriorate in front of my eyes. I had the best doctors in London to see to his leg in the hope that he wouldn't lose it altogether. But none of them could assure me that he wouldn't. None of them could tell me for certain if my brother, barely twenty-five years of age, would be crippled for the rest of his life.'' He paused, as if the memory cost him too much pain. ''I was angry, Regana, so angry that I began to look for ways to settle the score. I wanted revenge, but I didn't know how to get it. So I lived with my anger, and with the bitterness which grew day by day. Then, when I was nearly ready to give up all hope, Peter's leg began to heal. He started to come back to us, and when the doctors finally told me that he wasn't going to lose the leg, I got down on my knees and thanked God for His mercy. But I still swore I'd get revenge on Botheringham for what he did.''

''Then we met,'' Regana said, her heart going out to him in spite of what he'd told her.

Wesmorlen smiled at her crookedly. ''Yes, but I was already in love with you even before I learned who you were, or what Botheringham was to you.''

Wesmorlen turned away from her, rubbing his fingers wearily over his eyes and across the bridge of his nose. ''Regana, I admit to you here and now that the idea of taking you away from Botheringham and thereby obtaining my revenge did cross my mind. That night when I met you at the Dalmenys' ball, and saw you with Botheringham, it seemed the answer I'd been looking for. But you must believe me when I tell you it was not my reason for falling in love with you, or for asking you to marry me. As time went on, and I came to know you, I found that I couldn't imagine my life without you in it. I still can't. I suppose it became clear to me the morning I went to see Lord Botheringham after visiting your aunt. You don't know how I'd longed for that moment, Regana—to repay Botheringham in some measure for what he'd done to my brother. But," Wesmorlen admitted with a rueful laugh, "when I actually stood facing the man, armed with the information that you were to marry me, I was aware of nothing more than a desire to tell him and have done with it. I received no gratification in informing him of it. I suppose in that regard, my revenge was never achieved. However," he said, drawing a breath, "I suppose that's of no consequence now. I can't force you to love me, or to marry me. When you accused me of lying to you, I was wounded. Deeply so. And disillusioned. Until I reminded myself that I had no right to be. For hadn't you told me, in your own words just a few days before, that honesty was the most important ingredient of love. And hadn't I violated the very trust you held most dear?"

Wesmorlen glanced down into her face, his eyes so full of love that Regana felt her breath catch. "I can't change the circumstances, Regana. God knows I wish I could. Nor can I be any more honest with you than I've been. But I wanted one more chance to talk with you, to try to make you understand why I did what I did. When I received Emily's invitation, it seemed too important an opportunity to miss."

Wesmorlen drew himself up, and smiled at her wistfully. "And, having said what I wanted to say, I won't bother you any more. I give you my word as a gentleman that I will not stand in your way should you wish to choose another. Only know, Regana, that I love you, and that if you can ever find it in your heart to forgive me, you have only to find me. For I will love you. Always."

Wesmorlen looked down into that perfect face for a few moments longer, as if to commit it to memory, and then turned away. He hadn't gone more than a few steps, however, when Regana said quietly, "My lord. A moment."

Wesmorlen hesitated and looked back at her. She hadn't moved. Her hands were still by her side. Yet for a moment, for the very briefest of moments, Wesmorlen thought her eyes reached out to him. Her voice, when she spoke, was soft, yet clear. "Why didn't you tell me all this the day I broke off our engagement?"

Wesmorlen shook his head helplessly. "Because I didn't know how to. I was so...staggered to hear you say you were ending our betrothal that I...didn't know what to say. To be honest, I never expected you to call me to book."

Regana allowed herself the tiniest of smiles. "Yes, so I recall hearing you say."

The earl looked at her askance. "What do you mean? When did you hear me say that?"

"At our engagement party."

He glanced at her sharply, his face still registering confusion. "At the engagement party! But when...?"

"When I overheard you and Peter talking in the conservatory," Regana said, averting her gaze. "That's when I heard about the duel, and the...part I played in your life. Oh Richard, don't you understand?" she said softly, gazing up into his dark face. "That's why I was so devastated that night. Not because I learned the truth from Lord Botheringham, or Lady Chadwick, or anyone else, but because I learned it from you. And that wounded me a hundred times more, because I knew if you said it, it had to be the truth."

Wesmorlen gazed at her in surprise, and then swore softly under his breath. "My God, I never dreamed you should hear it from my lips, Regana," he admitted, feeling more foolish by the minute. He permitted himself a rueful laugh. "I thought perhaps Amanda had found out and had taken it upon herself to inform you." He permitted himself a rueful laugh.

"Such was her intent," Regana admitted, calmly meeting his gaze. "I'm afraid she was quite disappointed to learn that I already knew about the duel. And what I didn't know, I let her assume I did." Regana chuckled softly, able to look back on it now with a certain satisfaction. "I fancy it quite trimmed her sails."

"I think I should have liked to be the one to do that!" Wesmorlen muttered, his face darkening ominously.

Regana looked at the strong, handsome face before her, and wondered how she had ever contemplated going through life without him. She knew what it had cost him to tell her what he had. Richard was a proud man, and one not used to explaining his actions to anyone. And although she could not consider his behaviour utterly above reproach, she could at least admit to understanding his reasons for it. She knew how strong the bonds of affection were between sisters and brothers. Would she, placed in the same situation, have acted any differently?

"I wonder," she said, almost to herself, "if Clarisse and Peter would mind if we stole a little of their thunder, my lord?"

"Stole a little of . . . ? Regana, do you mean what I think you mean?" the earl asked, as if unable to believe what he was hearing. Regana, feeling that her heart had been set free again, nodded and laughed. "Well, it is, after all, an engagement party, my lord. Would it matter so greatly, I wonder, if there were two betrothals celebrated instead of one?"

Judging by the ferocity of his reply, Regana was left in little doubt as to his feelings on the matter. Wesmorlen answered her with his lips, his kiss blotting out every thought but that she was back in the arms of the man she loved, and would always love. It was as though in that single kiss he strove to drive away any lingering doubts she might have had regarding the veracity of his love.

Sometime later, Regana opened her eyes and rested her head against the hard strength of his chest. "Does this mean you still wish to marry me, my lord?" she teased, her eyes twinkling mischievously.

"Impertinent baggage!" he murmured against her hair. "Only try to stop me. Speaking of which," he said, putting her away from him slightly as he reached into his pocket. "I have something here which belongs to you."

Regana watched in amazement as Wesmorlen drew forth her engagement ring and slipped it back onto her finger. "You take a great deal for granted, my lord!" Regana admonished, struggling to maintain a solemn face. "Were you so confident in your ability to turn my head that you came prepared?"

"Not at all," he said, pulling her back into his arms. "You may not believe this, my dear beloved girl, but it was Mama who thought to bring it along. She gave it to me in the carriage."

"Her ladyship?" exclaimed Regana. "What on earth would make her think to do such a thing?"

"Call it a mother's intuition, if you like," the earl said with a laugh. "Or call it anything you like. All I know is that it's back where it should be. And this time, I don't intend it to come off again! Although I do intend to see what the vault holds in the way of rubies," he murmured huskily as he lowered his lips towards hers again. "Have I told you, Miss Kently, how utterly devastating you look in red?"

HARLEQUIN®

R E G E N C Y R O M A N C E™

IF YOU THOUGHT ROMANCE NOVELS WERE ALL THE SAME...LOOK AGAIN!

Our new look begins this September

Framed by its classic new look, Harlequin Regency Romance captures all the romance, charm and splendor of the Regency period.
Romantic and flirtatious, lively and fun, these love stories will transport you into the entertaining world of Regency Romance.

Watch for a sneak preview of our new covers next month!

HARLEQUIN REGENCY ROMANCE—
Elegant entanglements!

WELCOME TO TYLER

The quintessential small town where everyone knows everybody else!

Finally, books that capture the pleasure of tuning in to your favorite TV show!

GREAT READING...GREAT SAVINGS...AND A FABULOUS FREE GIFT!

Each book set in Tyler is a self-contained love story; together, the twelve novels stitch the fabric of the community. The covers honor the old American tradition of quilting; each cover depicts a patch of the large Tyler quilt.

With Tyler you can receive a fabulous gift ABSOLUTELY FREE by collecting proofs-of-purchase found in each Tyler book. And use our special Tyler coupons to save on your next TYLER book purchase.

Join your friends at Tyler for the sixth book, SUNSHINE by Pat Warren, available in August.

When Janice Eber becomes a widow, does her husband's friend David provide more than just friendship?

BIG SUMMER READ

Summer Reading At Its Best

In July, Harlequin and Silhouette bring readers the Big Summer Read Program. Heat up your summer with these four exciting new novels by top Harlequin and Silhouette authors.

SOMEWHERE IN TIME by Barbara Bretton
YESTERDAY COMES TOMORROW by Rebecca Flanders
A DAY IN APRIL by Mary Lynn Baxter
LOVE CHILD by Patricia Coughlin

From time travel to fame and fortune, this program offers something for everyone.

Available at your favorite retail outlet.

BSR

JAYNE ANN KRENTZ